ADVANCE PRAISE FOR *OFF TRAIL*

"Debut author Polito writes excellent dialogue, nailing his wiseass teenagers' snarky observations: "The road to hell is paved with good wintentions." Also on target are the camp's maddeningly earnest lingo and maxims, like "sarcasm…is simply the scar tissue of the soul." Beneath the jokes, though, is a compelling story of growth; as Vera puts it, "Quest Trail is the epicenter of suckitude, but real shit happens here, real friends happen here." That Daniel wrests an authentic experience from the camp's "jackass solemnity" speaks well of him and his growing maturity. An entertaining, comic, but also thoughtful coming-of-age tale."

— Kirkus Reviews

Rick Polito's "Off Trail" is a spit-out-your-drink, laugh-out-loud riot while also being a heartwarming coming of age journey and a perfect snapshot of the early 1980s. You'll want to go off the beaten path for this one!"

— Lee Matthew Goldberg, author of
THE ANCESTOR, THE MENTOR and
THE RUNAWAY TRAIN series

"It was refreshing to see a YA book written with two of the most common features of teenager language: swearing and sarcasm!"

— Damon Hesford (educator/reviewer)

OFF TRAIL

OFF TRAIL

OFF TRAIL

RICK POLITO

 WISE WOLF BOOKS LAS VEGAS

WISE WOLF BOOKS
An Imprint of Wolfpack Publishing
wisewolfbooks.com

Cover design by Wise Wolf Books

ISBN 978-1-953944-52-8 (paperback)
ISBN 978-1-953944-02-3 (ebook)
LCCN 2021931924

First Edition: June 2021

Printed in the United States of America

To my lovely "Chief Operating Muse" Angela Innes and to my brother Sam Polito, who didn't inspire anything in this book (as far as Mom knows)

1

I saw Dad's car and I stopped so fast I felt the gravel scrape the sidewalk under my feet. For most kids, seeing both of your parents' cars in the driveway would be a big *who cares?* It might even be good news. I'd seen it on TV, Brady Bunch, crap like that. But when your parents are split, especially when they're split like my parents are split, it's different.

Very different.

So when I saw Dad's car in Mom's driveway, I felt that fight-or-flight rush that I think everybody gets when they know something's going to suck, but they're not sure whether it's about them or something else. They just put their head down and shrug their way into the situation. That's where I found myself walking up the driveway, ready to console mom if Aunt C had croaked, or ready to make excuses about something I was not sure I'd done but I was sure, or almost sure, I could lie my way out of.

Really bad stuff usually happened in the living room, which was always right off the front door in every 70's faux pueblo stucco 3-bedroom in every cul-de-sac on the east side of Tucson. Coming in through the side door, I might hear whatever was going on before they knew I was home. I'd either bug out if I was the target of today's parental concern, or I'd be a good attentive son if something bad had happened to somebody else, like Aunt C on her 17th cancer scare. I opened the door as carefully and quietly as I could.

And Mom and Dad were standing right there, in the kitchen, both of them.

Dad leaned against the Formica counter and Mom stood in front of the harvest-gold Kenmore fridge, as grim as pallbearers in contrasting shades of polyester. Mom wasn't crying. That was bad news. It meant Aunt C was still kicking and being sensitive wasn't going to get me shit. Dad was stiff-chinning it like he'd been practicing a speech he was about to give in front of the real estate association or whatever ties-and-slacks group he was networking in at the moment. Dad gives fatherly speeches like he's in a contest, convinced that his nod and raised eyebrow combo were the charm-the-cobra kung fu of family encounters.

I was screwed, nailed to the linoleum.

Fight or flight works a lot better when one or the other is possible. At 15, flight didn't seem like much of an option and fight wasn't going to go well either. Dad still had a height advantage, though I was look-ing to catch up, and a weight advantage I still hope I can avoid. In enough words to suck, I was trapped. Mom spoke first, and she used what I'd heard (from Dad!) are the worst four words any woman ever spoke to any man. She said, "We need to talk."

What I said was, "I don't want to talk," which was really stupid because it's hard to sell innocence when you're being defensive. What I thought was *Oh shit, what did I do?* I ran through a mental list of possible offenses and nothing seemed worthy of a two-parent stare down.

School was OK. My grades had slipped a bit since middle school, but it's not like I'd been slotted for after-school study club. My sister practically had her name brass-plaqued on one of the study-club chairs. She'd burned through three study-buddies from Kino Community College. I guess no amount of extra-credit was worth dealing with Jackie.

OK, so my room could've used some cleaning. The average 15-year-old boy's room is only a cave painting or two away from the stone-age. Mine wasn't even that bad. Mom didn't like the way I'd masking taped the Boston "Don't Look Back" poster to the wall (She says masking tape peels off the paint, which is bullshit because masking tape is made for not peeling off paint) but there's nothing growing in my sock drawer. And no kid ever got the two-divorced-parents-in-one-room assault for having a dirty room anyway.

That left trouble of the vague-and-could-be-any-thing kind. To be honest, I wasn't all that worried. There are a few cool things about being the second kid, the main one being that the first kid kicks down all the hurdles and you can step over them like nobody cares. When the first kid "sets the standard," the second kid is screwed, because that means mom, dad and every teacher from geometry to P.E. is going to expect the kind of brilliance that Kid No. 2 never got a chance to develop because he was too lost in the glow and glare of Kid No. 1. But if the first kid is a "lowered the bar" kid, the second kid has it easy. Just show up and don't burn the school down and the sigh of relief will echo out of the parent-teacher conference and down the hall.

Jackie didn't lower the bar. She called in napalm strikes on the bar. The bar was in ashes, smudged into the carpet in the back of her closet, next to the diaphragm she'd borrowed from our cousin (I know, gross! Right?). Don't forget the bong water spill. Not like I could forget it when I could smell it from my room.

This whole list of things I hadn't done raced through my head before Dad echoed Mom's "We need to talk" with his classic narrowed-brows-with-tightened-jaw move.

"Maybe we should go into the living room," my Dad said.

"Your dad's right, Daniel," Mom followed.

Crap, I thought. And I didn't know the half of it.

I could never decide which was worse about the living room, the Mediterranean furniture or the Southwestern art. It was like Mom took a class in art aesthetics that was taught by a blind guy and held the same day as the Sears President's Day Sale, like mixing clashing plaids if the plaids hated each other. Mom sat down on the couch; an eight-footer printed with Spartan warriors carrying shields. I sometimes wondered if they were marching off to battle with the guy in the sombrero on the painting over the couch. That guy probably had no idea he was about to get his ass kicked by Spartans.

Dad leaned back in a leather recliner that had been "Dad's chair" before he moved out to live in a generic stucco apartment complex, which had a pool to offset the sadness but still looked like a ghetto for single dads. From the way he was sitting, he looked like he missed the chair, but Mom, not so much.

He opened with a raised eyebrow and the exaggerated inhale. "Son," he said. I never heard "son" unless it was really bad and I was about to receive some sage fatherly advice. "Son" was immediately followed by "Your mom and I" which came right before "need to talk with you," which almost always meant "talk *to* you." I always thought there should be a Mad Libs for concerned parental chats. "We've noticed that *your NOUN* has been *VERB* lately and we need you to **oh crap, here it comes**.

"Your mother and I are concerned," he said. "We know we weren't the best parents, but I don't think you know how hard we tried." *Oh, shit,* I thought. They were laying on the guilt to make what comes later sound reasonable. Mom was leaning forward, like she wanted dad to do the talking but accepted that a lot of this was her idea. Mom ran the house when they were married to the degree that I'm not sure dad even knew how to match his socks without her ok.

Mom pursed her lips. "Daniel, we've made mistakes," she said, "that we don't want to make again."

She gave herself away in those 11 words. The biggest mistake they made was now living with her boyfriend in Phoenix and considering community college while shopping for shirts that hid her lame dragon tattoo when applying for jobs, or seeing her parents. I've yet to see a tattoo that wouldn't look better airbrushed on the side of some dirtbag's "Love Wagon" van, but I think most dirtbags would spray paint over Jackie's tattoo out of embarrassment.

It was getting more and more clear that I hadn't done anything wrong, or at least not wrong enough to merit the two-parent tag team. This was trickle-down parenting and it wasn't the first time I'd seen it. Trickle-down parenting is when the younger sibling gets to pay for the sins of the older sibling. It's the "so you don't turn out like…" strategy. Lots of kids I know have gone through it. I'd already accepted that I wasn't going to get my driver's license until I was 25 after Jackie's Pinto vs. mailbox experiment.

When we were both little, or kinda' little, Mom and Dad would say, "Well, you know Jackie." And over time it became more like, "Jackie, you know how she is," which sounds like a subtle shift until you've heard it a hundred times and you know what they really mean is, "For GOD's sake, Jackie!"

But later it became not talking about Jackie at all unless shit was really going down or there was some learning moment. Dad loved learning moments. Then there were the times when Jackie hung about the room like the Ghost of Criminal Offenses Yet to Be. Nobody talked about her, but we all knew she was there. I imagined her sitting on the mantel like a raven or a gargoyle statue ready to come to life and explain how nobody understood what it was like to be a gargoyle, especially not my parents.

"Son," my dad said. Again, that word. "We don't want to see you go down the wrong path and your mom and I have been thinking about a different path, like a side path, just for a while." I didn't really know how to react, mainly because I was super confused. "Your Mom and I have been researching some options," Dad continued. *Researching?* "And we think we've found something really exciting." *Exciting?*

Mom stepped in. "I know this is going to sound scary when you first hear it."

Scary?

It was my turn now. "Hey, guys. I don't know how scary it really is but you sure are making it scary, like cancer or alien invasion scary. Do I have some sibling I don't know about? Are you,"—and I visibly cringed as I said it—"getting back together?" My parents exchanged a look that packed in about 80 emotions, all of which fell into the quadrant of "horror."

"Oh no, son," my Dad said. That's three "sons" if you're counting. "There are no aliens." Then he smiled, in that chuckle-pop dad way. "That we know of." The chuckle evaporated almost instantaneously. "We've found a program for you," he said.

Mom came in again. "It's called Quest Trail. You get to know yourself and you do it in the desert with kids your age." I didn't need to speak. I imagine I looked like I would if I was 5 and I simultaneously learned that "Santa" was my uncle and that we were moving to Malaysia to raise penguins. *They're send-*

ing me into the desert? Anybody who grows up in Arizona knows that nature wants you dead. I couldn't imagine *living* in the desert when I knew all the ways you could *die* there. In a moment of grand eloquence, I replied, "Whoa," followed quickly by, "What?"

Dad looked at Mom like he knew it was his turn to take the talking stick, only he thought the talking stick was radioactive. Mom gave him one of her "You're up, buster!" glares. He took another breath, deeper but more tentative. "Daniel," he said. "Your mother found drugs in your closet."

Drugs? I thought. I assumed he meant weed, but "drugs?" Drugs were cocaine or something like speed, which we heard a lot about but almost never saw. *All this about a little weed?* Smoking weed in Tucson was like smoking cigarettes except weed was easier to get. Whoever was styling themselves as a "dealer" never ID'd you when you were slipping him $20 for a half lid of Columbian. Unless you were a jock or a brainiac, you were smoking marijuana, maybe not every day, but enough that you didn't cough on every bong hit. There wasn't much chance I was going to be a jock. My mom said I was "fine-boned," which was a nice way of saying "a bit of a runt, we should have fed him more," I wasn't a true brainiac either, but school was easy for me. Studying was for people who *needed* to study.

But it's not like I was ducking into some alley on lunch period and crouching between trash cans like a hardcore stoner.

And here's the thing: I knew it wasn't my weed. A $20 bag of weed was five lawns mowed, or five hours of pulling actual weeds out of somebody's gravel driveway, in the sun. I wasn't casually misplacing $20 of anything. That left one conceivable answer for how my Mom could find weed in my closet: Jackie.

At this point, I was tempted to go with "It wasn't mine," which is the universal and universally laughed-at excuse for drug possession. There'd be eye-rolling and it'd probably make whatever was coming next even worse, although, let's face it, it's hard to imagine a whole lot worse than getting packed into the desert against my will. Even though it wasn't mine, there was no point in attempting "it wasn't mine."

But I did it anyway.

"I don't know where that came from," I said, working up what I thought was a convincing shock-and-outrage expression. "You've got to believe me." It was a rare moment of justified and genuine righteous indignation. And I could tell it was going nowhere.

It may have been true. They may have wanted to believe me. This Quest Trail thing was undoubtedly expensive as hell. But there was also a game of chicken being played here. I'm sure both of them blamed each other for the disaster that was my sister. Anybody who let their finger off the trigger now was going to retroactively be responsible for Jackie. I was already starting to picture myself in the desert, standing in a trust circle and choosing a spirit animal.

Mom prefaced her response with a heavy sigh, followed by biting her lip and a second heavy sigh, for good measure. "Daniel, we're not playing games this time. Did somebody sneak into your room and hide marijuana in your closet? Is there a pot genie prowling the bedrooms of Tucson teens?" she asked.

I didn't know how to react. My first thought was Pot Genie would be an awesome comic book. My second thought was whether a tearful, though false, confession would do any good. Mom was not letting up. "Your father and I had a long talk and we both decided Quest Trail is the right decision."

I sagged into the upholstery and the Spartan warriors sagged with me. I was beaten. I knew it and they knew it. If it had been Jackie, both sides would be in for several more hours of back-and-forth threats, tears and accusations. But our dynamic was different. It's not that I lacked the will, I just knew that "fuck you" and running away was not going to go well for me.

"So," I said, "when does all this happen? When school's out?" It was only three weeks until summer vacation, three weeks which had seemed like half of forever when I was watching the clock stutter toward 3 in geometry and thinking of all the stuff I was going to do this summer. Suddenly, three weeks seemed like an incredibly brief period of time. I tried not to look like I was panicking, but I was full-on panicking. *Am I losing a whole summer?*

"We've talked to your school," Mom said.

I didn't know what that meant, and the doorbell gave me an answer before she could.

2

You could pin down the construction dates on Tucson houses by the doorbells. The older houses, pre-1950s, had actual bells. They made a good racket. My grandparents had one of those. In the 1960s, all the houses had a little white box in a hallway near the front and it gave a generic ring that was exactly like the one on the "Avon calling" commercials on daytime TV. But the newer doorbells were supposed to sound like mission bells—because we were in the Southwest and everything had to feel like the inside of a Mexican food chain.

It was the mission bells that interrupted my Mom. And my life.

Dad popped up to answer the door, which was weird because Dad didn't even live there anymore. I figured out later that Dad answering the door was kind of a giveaway. He opened the door, and two large shadows blocked the glare bouncing off the gravel in the front yard. The shadows stepped in.

"Good afternoon, sir, good afternoon, ma'am," the larger of the two shadows announced. "I'm Bob, from Cedar Transport Services." He wore those polyester shorts that are issued only to high school coaches and he had a clipboard under his left arm, completing the coach look. Except, I could tell right away that this guy had never made it through coach school or wherever it is that PE teachers go. He didn't look smart enough, and that's saying a lot because PE teachers are not the cream of academia. His companion, who later introduced himself as Chuck, had a similarly generous brow and an even duller look in his eyes. Chuck wore a plain white Tee-shirt and white painters' pants, without any paint on them, because in 1980 painters' pants seem to be mainly worn by people who didn't paint. The coach pants and Bob's rugby shirt were white too. I could only guess that there was a white van parked out front too. This wasn't an abduction. This was a goddamn cliché.

I threw Mom the coldest glare of my young life. "Do I get a phone call? A last meal?"

I actually felt a little guilty in that moment. Mom's lip was quivering while everybody found spots on the couches and chairs as though Bob and Chuck were there to sell us insurance, or aluminum siding. Dad started fussing with the hem of his slacks, which were cuffed and long enough out of style that it confirmed my suspicion he hadn't shopped since the divorce. My flash of guilt evaporated instantly, though. They were sending me off with two oafish goons who aspired to be thugs but looked a bit flabby for full-on thug status.

"Do I get to take anything with me?" I asked.

Bob spoke. Chuck was in training, apparently. "Danny," he began, and I stopped him short. *"Daniel,"* I said. Danny had been my kid name and I'd decided to switch it back to Daniel in 7th grade because I thought girls would think I was sophisticated, British maybe. "Daniel," Bob continued. It felt like he was reading from a script hovering somewhere about ten feet behind me. "We know this is a difficult moment for you and your family and our job is to make the transition as easy as possible for everybody, especially for you."

"OK," I said. "Then come back in three years when I'm 18 and I can say no."

"Daniel!" my mom said. Dad was disturbingly quiet. He'd never been in charge, and he was even less in charge now. I looked up at Bob, who was doing the talking.

"We find it best if the student, that's you, arrives at the program, that's Quest Trail for you, with the clothes on his back," he said. "The point of a healing program is to leave the baggage at home." I could see him straining to get the whole spiel right.

"Baggage?" I said. "You mean like suitcases? I just want to bring my Walkman." I paused for a second. "Or maybe I could bring my giant drug-making lab and the vats of LSD that you guys," I pointed to Mom and Dad, "think I've got hidden under my bed."

Mom's quivering lip was gone. "Listen, Daniel," she said. Mom didn't crave wisdom-sharing moments like Dad did. She was fluent in drill-sergeant speak. But sometimes, she also went soft. "We know this is hard for you," she said. "It's hard for all of us." Was she reading off Bob's cue cards? "Think of it as a little vacation, a chance to get your head together and see who you really are, take stock and all. Can you dig that?" She sounded like she'd read some *How To Talk To Your Teen Before You Ruin Their Summer* pamphlet.

"Where you are going is a place of wilderness respite," Bob began. I gritted my back teeth as I seethed through Bob's straight-from-the-handout drone and my fingernails dug into an otherwise innocent Spartan warrior. I was freaking out, but I wasn't going to give them the pleasure of seeing me freak out. "It is a place where we let the wilderness guide you," Bob kept going, "and you will not feel the need for music when the wilderness is your guide." Four pairs of grown-up eyes were staring at me. I'd say I wasn't getting anywhere with them, but the truth was I was getting in a van. I could have screamed and slammed some doors, but the person I wanted to scream at wasn't even in the room.

She was in Phoenix, living with her dirtbag boyfriend.

I have to say I was a little disappointed that it wasn't a white van. It was kind of green and kind of brown. Car colors have names, stuff like Skylark Blue or Champagne Gray. If I were in the van color naming business, I would have called this one Turd Brown, but it was probably Safari or something equally adventure-y.

Walking down the driveway, I wasn't exactly in

a safari mood. I had on a pair of jeans and a UFO Tee-shirt, UFO as in the stoner band, not UFO as in alien abduction, though it was feeling not far off from that. The Bingham kids were watching this whole thing from their driveway half across the street. The Binghams were Mormons and when they saw two guys in white, they probably thought I was headed off to learn how to be a missionary. I didn't see any parents out. Most of them were still at work, where mine should have been if they weren't busily plotting my internment. Otherwise, I'm sure they'd all be over hugging Mom and high-fiving Dad and asking to see the brochures for Quest Trail. I was passing from *oh, shit* to *fuck them!* halfway down the driveway when I saw something that made the color of the van the least interesting thing about it.

There was a commercial in Tucson about not leaving your dog in your car when it was hot, and it started with an egg frying on pavement. The next shot was a dog in a car looking really sad—I mean, that dog could act—and this really serious voice comes on and says "Hot enough to fry an egg? Hot enough to fry a dog's brain." So, if you hear anybody say, "It's hot enough to fry a dog's brain," I guarantee you they are from Tucson.

A lot of people would say Greg Pittz's brain was fried before he ever stepped in the van. So, it didn't really matter that it was blowtorch hot in there. Bob couldn't exactly leave the engine and AC running with somebody in the back when that somebody had maybe ten thousand other places he'd rather be, learning permit or not.

But there he was, Greg Pittz, in the hot sweaty flesh. I made the immediate and correct assumption that he was not there for moral support. There was no "abduction buddy" program. Whatever parental brain fever was rattling through East Tucson, it had already claimed two victims. I began to imagine us picking up other unfortunate teens along the way, a sweaty little carpool to hell.

Greg Pittz was in the van, and he was smiling. Seriously, he was smiling.

Greg was a little more committed to the stoner lifestyle than I was. I'd known him for a long time, and I used to say weed was maybe an improvement for Greg. He came off as none too brilliant the rest of the time—not one of those stoner savants who could deliver complex dissertations about Pink Floyd (*The Wall* was an emotional exploration of our innate disconnection!). But he was pretty funny after the sixth or seventh bong hit.

He was not stoned, or funny, when the van door opened. "So," he announced. "I guess our parents have been talking."

We both shook our heads. "Indeed," I replied. "So much love they have to share. What got you here?"

"What do you think?" he asked.

"They found your Master Assassins Academy application and your medieval catapult collection?"

"Nope. Guess again."

"They finally figured out that you're one of the Lizard People."

"Shhhh," Greg said. "That's our little secret."

We both smiled, a sort of surreal stress-response

reflex to a shared and shitty situation. I think they call that gallows humor, which is a funny term if you think about it, but probably not as funny if you're anywhere near the gallows. We weren't near the gallows but in the teenager universe where not getting invited to a party is at least a little bit like getting cancer, we might as well have been naked and swan diving into lava in front of every girl we'd ever thought about when we jacked off.

"Sucks, huh?" I shrugged.

"It's not so bad," Greg said, looking really thought-ful, for Greg. "I mean, being a lizard person."

We both smiled again.

I saw Bob and Chuck with Mom outside the van. Mom was signing something on Bob's clipboard. Dad was looking at anything that wasn't mom. Chuck didn't look at much of anything.

Bob and Chuck got back in the van. I refused to spare my parents a parting glance. Bob waited for Chuck to say something, like he was teaching him the ropes, but he gave up with a quick sideways glance. "Everybody buckled in?" he said. That was probably on a cue card too. "Yes sir," I said. I was mockingly cheerful. Greg picked up on it. "Aye aye, Captain," he called out.

"Shit," Chuck said. I think that was his first word, and it seemed fitting to the moment. "It's hot as shit in here."

"Hot enough to fry a dog's brain," Greg answered.

3

The van ride would have been boring but for the *what's next?* monologue in my head, which grew increasingly outlandish as the miles ticked, but did not fly by. We'd tried to quiz Bob about where we were headed, but Bob had his cue cards ready.

"It's natural to be curious," he said. "But we've found it's better if we let you discover it on your own." He said "discover" like we were going on a field trip with Magellan.

"Will there be weapons training?" Greg asked. "I think some weapons training would be appropriate."

Bob gave no answer. Chuck looked out the window.

"Fur trapping? Rodeo clown arts? Plain-old clown art? Maybe some crazy Freemason wisdom of the ancients stuff?"

I could say that Bob had heard it all, but there was no way he heard what Greg was throwing at him. Bob and Chuck were mostly stone-faced. Bob didn't have a cue card for this.

I settled back into that monologue. All I knew, so far, was "in the desert." That could mean a lot of things. The desert around Tucson was almost "lush" as far as deserts go. Up around Phoenix, where the temperature was on broil, rather than the mere "high" that fried eggs and dog's brains, it was more post-nuclear—tumbleweeds, and the rotted remains of last year's tumbleweeds. I was relieved when we turned south at I-10. Don't get me wrong, I-10 south is going to look bleak to anybody who is not a connoisseur of desert hardship like myself. The desert is a place where people get rescued, and they were *sending us* there. But did that mean we'd be sleeping on the ground and subsisting on gophers and cactus fruit? Maybe we were going to be in cabins, I thought, or some kind of Indian village with stick houses. But really, the big mystery was *will there be girls?*

I am guessing Greg was thinking about girls too, but not possibly as much as I'd been. I did not have a girlfriend. I'd never asked a girl on a date. I danced with Becky Swenson in seventh grade, but mainly on a dare and I didn't even get to the second part of the dare which was to grab a little bit of her breast through her shirt. So, I was pretty much terrified to talk to any girl who might conceivably have been anywhere near my league, that league being the acne league. I've said questionable complexion before, but the only real question was how soon would some drug come out that would turn me into a rock star like Eddie Van Halen, who I imagined wasn't stuck thinking about a missed tit grab back in seventh grade.

The thing about girls was a decent dream at that point. Since kindergarten, I'd been on the march from one school to the next through the bottleneck of "feeder schools" (feeder always made me think of livestock, which in many ways we were). That meant every girl at my school either saw that day when I tasted the finger paint and threw up all over the art room or had heard accounts. If there were girls at Quest Trail, none of them would know me. I could be a spy for all they knew, an heir to billions, or a French actor researching American teens for a movie *that's still casting the leading lady!* And I was having a reasonably good pimple week, so I was close to clean slate on that too.

I was desperate for something positive and to get there I needed to make sure Greg stayed out of the way. We used to be friends. But were we allies? Was he going to help me assemble this harem of troubled teen girls? I was some number of miles away from girls who did not know me, who did not have a mental picture of me covered in fingerpaint and vomit *and* might have loose morals, or at least poor impulse control. I could not allow Greg to sabotage my impending romantic triumphs with "Daniel the Spaniel."

The problem was that I'd been a shit to Greg. We were friends starting in third grade and then halfway through eighth grade, I started thinking I needed new friends to get ready for high school. I had illusions of maturity and sophistication that look pretty bogus in retrospect. I ditched him, hard, and even said some crappy things behind his back.

Most of my new friends turned out to be losers who jumped cliques as soon as we got to high school. I wasn't cut out for preppy or drama nerd and stoner looked convenient. I always suspected Greg had followed me into the fold. I even imagined he'd let go of resenting me ditching him and wanted to be friends again. He joined the freak league a few steps behind me, but man, he was a natural. Genuine laid-back cool like Greg's was practically soothing.

Or it should have been, if I hadn't screwed up what suddenly seemed to be a really important friendship.

I leaned over and tapped on the armrest between us. Girls were not my only concern. I had already assumed that Greg and I would not be the sole male travelers on this journey of self-discovery and outdoor toiletry. Not being the biggest boy in the kickball lineup had earned me no shortage of elbow jabs from the meatier specimens in my academic cohort. I might need backup if there was a dominant desert ape thing when we got there. Greg was of the proper size, if not demeanor, to be that backup.

"Dude," I whispered. I could tell that Bob and Chuck were trying to listen. "We need a plan."

"I can hear you," Bob announced. He let himself go off script for a moment. "But please proceed. I doubt it's anything we haven't heard before." And then he went back to the cue cards. "It's natural for young people to be anxious about where they are going but let me assure you that your health and safety are our primary concerns."

I was beginning to think I could write this shit

for him.

I turned back to Greg. "We know each other, right?"

Greg nodded, almost eagerly.

"So that means we know stuff *about* each other, right?"

He nodded again. It looked like he was getting it.

"We could be anybody to anybody we meet on this shitty expedition."

"You must always show up as yourself," Bob called back.

"Got that, Bob," I replied and immediately turned back to Greg. "What I am saying is that I won't tell anybody about the time you were a Bambi for Halloween if you don't tell anybody that I was in fifth-grade chorus, got it?"

"But you had the voice of an angel," Greg said.

"And you were the cutest darn Bambi I ever did see," I replied.

I was beginning to move through the grief stages from shock to anger. I saved denial for later. I'd already seen how well "bargaining" had gone. I thought of "depression" as more or less the umbrella stage. Acceptance? No goddamn way.

So I employed my anger and righteous indignation to best effect. I pouted.

I looked over at Greg. He was asleep. That fucker was asleep. Greg had a gift for that. There wasn't a desk at Desert Willow High that he had not drooled on. There was not a field trip on record that hadn't included him tumbling down the stairs on the bus after somebody tied his shoes together when he nodded off.

He was the sleepy giant, not giant really, but tall, the kind of stoner that the P.E. teachers looked at and shook their heads. Most of us were on the scrawny or pudgy side and Greg was this athletic-looking guy lacking all athletic skill, or most athletic skill. He'd had a remarkable streak of Capture the Flag victories in sixth grade.

Sleepy and quiet went together well in Greg. He talked in a low tone that you almost had to lean in to hear. His family was completely the opposite. The Pittzes would yell if they wanted you to pass the salt. I hadn't gone over there since before I ditched Greg, but the volume was set on high all the time. His dad sold TVs and there was a TV in every room, all of them turned on and all of them turned up. They had more TVs than there were channels. You'd hear the *Six Million Dollar Man* in one room and walk down the hall right onto *The Love Boat* before you'd get to Greg's room where he had the volume down but the TV still on, in case his dad popped in, I guess.

And, get this, his mom was a librarian. I'd say the quiet side came from her, but Mrs. Pittz could call Greg home for dinner from three blocks away.

And Greg, the sleepy giant.

Even so, I was surprised how long he clung to slumber when we turned off the interstate onto a dirt road two hours into our new life. He stirred only slightly on the washboard section. When we started to hit real ruts and the Turdmobile's suspension complained in big lurches and creaks, he sat up to look around. "Where are we?" he asked.

"The desert," I replied.

"That's real helpful," Greg said.

Part of being an easy sleeper is apparently snapping back into focus really quick. Greg pointed forward and off to the left. "That's Mount Greer," he said. Greg frequently surprised me, but arcane geography seemed both out-of-nowhere and also pointless in the moment.

"Unless there's a getaway car there, I don't care," I sighed.

"We studied it in eighth-grade history," he said.

"I wasn't in eighth-grade history with you."

"Oh yeah," Greg answered, dropping into his customary, near whisper, which was kind of annoying on a loud road. "It's a registered wildlife sanctuary. Grayson's fleck-winged hummingbird is found nowhere else on earth."

He sounded almost solemn. I heard it as surreal. This day was already weird enough, without Greg Pittz turning into the host of Wild Kingdom. Again, most of what I cared about in the desert was avoiding stuff that would sting or bite me. The first 10 minutes of every ranger tour I'd been on was filled with talk of poisonous snakes, poisonous spiders and barbed cactus prongs that require surgery to remove. All that before the really fun stuff like heat stroke and death by dehydration.

We turned off the dirt road on to one that was more rocks than dirt. The creaks and bounces got louder. Greg's nature lecture came to a close.

Up front, Bob's shoulders rolled with every lurch and bounce. Chuck let each shock reverberate up his surprisingly long neck to a chin entirely lost to a severe overbite. It was fascinating, for some reason, like a bobblehead with a stretched-out spring.

"We almost there?" I asked.

"How'd you guess?" Bob answered.

I looked back. We'd climbed more than I'd expected out of Bob's methodical pick-a-bump driving. The desert changes quickly by altitude. Every few hundred feet of elevation gain introduced a different set of plants and animals waiting to poke, jab or otherwise hurt you.

And then the road ended. There wasn't a turnout or anything. I wasn't sure how Bob was going to get the Turdmobile out. I looked around. Greg looked around too. I don't know what I was expecting, and thinking back, whatever was waiting for us was going to be anticlimactic unless it had a pool or, I don't know, dinosaurs. But it was just so *nothing*.

Some cactus, mostly low to the ground stuff like the barrel-shaped kind and thankfully not the particularly aggressive and deceptively named Teddy bear cholla, a razor-fuzz cactus that basically tosses whole clumps of itself at you when you walk anywhere near it. The rest of it was spiky clumps of grass and manzanita, a scrubby almost-tree thing that looked harmless but probably hid snakes.

"We're here," Bob announced.

"Where's here?" Greg asked.

"Your future," Bob replied.

I saw a water tank the size of a refrigerator shoved between two boulders and beyond that a banged-up camper trailer sat on tires that had more or less disintegrated into the ground. A couple of battered trash bins completed the scavenger hermit effect.

The trailer door was open and a guy with a clipboard and a ponytail looked out. He wore a green vest like photographers wear covering volcano eruptions and tropical coups. I guessed he'd have an annoying smile he was just dying to share. I wasn't wrong.

"Welcome, friends," he announced.

4

The way this guy bounded out of the door of that trailer reminded me of somebody from a commercial for an off-brand soda drink, like his enthusiasm was going to make up for the second-rate experience we were about to have. Apparently, Dr. Pepper was not available so Mr. Pibb was going to set our broken ankle and we should be excited about that. I think they call that overcompensating, but we couldn't know what he'd be overcompensating for 20 seconds into our learningship (Learningship is a relationship in which you learn and probably the stupidest word of a ton of stupid words that were coming our way). Without knowing what he was making up for, it was just forced cheeriness, which under the circumstances, was even more annoying than thinking you're getting Oreos and mom shows up with a bag of "sandwich cremes."

He was trying to put us at ease, I guess. I can't imagine he was going to get us excited about our prospects at Quest Trail. I had no intention of smiling my way through this entrance exam. I was working on my too-cool-and-can't-be-bothered look when Greg jumped in. "Howdy partner," he exclaimed, and he put on this smile that I remember him using in 6th grade when we were selling candy to raise money for the Boy Scouts before Jackie sat me down and explained that Boy Scouts essentially NEVER get laid, usually for at least five years after they decide to quit being Boy Scouts. Greg's "show smile," as I thought of it, might be the perfect tool to disarm ponytail guy, who was revving up for some stirring motivational speech but was now stalled before he could even begin. Greg wasn't stopping. "Is there a cookout tonight?" he asked. "Will there be songs by the campfire? S'mores? Ghost stories? Indian chants? Stargazing? UFO spotting? Will I get a poncho? Can I tame a bobcat as my wilderness companion?"

Even I was smiling at that point. Ponytail guy looked stuck, off balance, but cognizant that he was being confronted in a way for which he had no packaged answer.

The learningship had been turned on its head.

"Well," said the Ponytail Guy. "It's not common that I hear such enthusiasm from the new clients."

There was that word again.

I should say here that Pony Tail Guy had a name. It was Dean something, and it's not like we didn't use it. But by universal agreement among the campers we were soon to meet, he became the PTG as soon as he was out of earshot.

I could see PTG breathing in composure. He had

this look on his face like he was either writing poetry or deciding whether he needed to fart and, if so, whether behind the trailer would be far enough to hide the audio. He started his act. He was different from Bob. For Bob, the cue cards were a job. PTG believed this shit.

"I realize the two of you might be very disoriented right now, a lot of thoughts racing around about why you might be here and how soon you might get to leave. Well, I can tell you, the answers to both of those questions are really up to you."

"That's great," I said. "Because I think right now might be the perfect time for leaving." I turned to Bob. "Can we get a ride back to Tucson?" Bob barely acknowledged my sarcasm. I turned back to PTG. "Sorry to have put you through so much trouble," I said, borrowing the church-mixer smile from Greg's comic insincerity pamphlet.

Ok, so the initial shock had worn off. The PTG had seen this act before after all. He reached into his little knapsack of self-help wisdom and smacked me with what he would later, and continually, refer to as "a truth wrench." A "truth wrench," according to the PTG and his ilk, is a piece of truth that unbolts locked down feelings. It's near the top, but behind "learningship" on that hierarchy of stupid terms we'd be learning. "Humor is a wonderful device to share between friends, but when it becomes a shield against real feelings, it stops being witty and starts being needy," he said. He was looking at me with this earnest missionary holy gaze, like he was going to peel back the layers of one-liners and general smartassery and get to the "real Daniel." He wasn't letting up on it. "Sarcasm," he said, "is simply the scar tissue of the soul."

Suddenly, I was the one who didn't have a come-back, not because I accepted this new wisdom, but because *what do you say to that?* I looked at Greg. He had nothing. Bob and Chuck started back to the van in this weird slinking-away-quietly stroll. The PTG went on:

"Boys, I know it doesn't feel like it, but you are already beginning to shed the false identity you built for yourself out in what people call the real world but isn't real at all! And you were the least real part of it!" He was smiling, as though it not only made sense but we should be happy to hear it. "At Quest Trail, we think it's important to take off all the masks we've constructed for ourselves and leave them at the trailhead."

Greg stared at his feet, as though this was an awkward moment that would pass if he were quiet long enough. "The first thing I'm going to need is your shoes," PTG announced. It wasn't like there'd been a long pause, but it was such a weird thing to say that it still felt like it came out of nowhere.

"I thought you wanted our masks?" I asked.

"Masks are a metaphor," PTG said. He dropped the act, for roughly two seconds. "I need your shoes to keep you from making a run for it while I explain why you shouldn't make a run for it."

What followed, for 5 minutes while we sat cross-legged on the ground without shoes, was basically a summary of every one of those things-that-could-kill-you ranger tours but with added elements of "and this is exactly how screwed you are."

We were, the PTG informed us, 30 miles from water. "The average man can make it 11 miles in the desert without water, and only if he travels at night," PTG said.

In addition to losing our shoes, we'd be trading our "dungarees" and Tee-shirts for a Quest Trail yellow jumpsuit and all local law enforcement was familiar with the program. This was a corridor for drug smugglers coming across the border and "not someplace boys like you would want to be wandering around without protection."

The local ranchers were, according to the PTG, more or less an armed posse from some Old West movie and not particularly fond of delinquent teens.

Now, I think it's important to point out two things here.

One: we grew up in the desert. He didn't need to put the fear of cactus in us. Not only had we been on all those ranger danger tours and field trips, we knew you had to take water with you just to walk out to the mailbox.

Two: He actually used the word "dungarees," which, I learned a few minutes later, when I was surrendering mine in the heat box trailer, were basically jeans.

But with Bob, Chuck and the turdmobile gone, PTG had us right where he wanted us: barefoot, surrounded by miles of desert, with no water and nothing to carry it in. He'd lied to us. Sure, he'd say it was "metaphor" and he'd be wrong about it, but when he said that when we'd leave was really up to us, he failed to mention that we'd die if we tried to exercise the free will implied in that.

It's not like the weight of the situation hadn't hit me yet, but every once in a while it slammed into me like a TV thrown through a picture window.

"Did you catch all that?" PTG asked. The "I'm here to help you" tone was gone.

I had little more than a nod of the head left in my dazed "this is some real shit you've stepped in now" state. Greg looked at me, before turning back to the PTG. "So what you're saying is." I loved how Greg would sometimes go for a dramatic pause. "That we're completely screwed."

In the 1970s, everybody grew up on detective shows. After stuff like *The Sonny and Cher Show* or *Three's Company*, every other show was *McCloud* or *Columbo* or *Ironside*, a show about a guy in a wheelchair who was really good at solving mysteries that, I presumed, happened on the first floor. When we stepped into the trailer, I was more *Mannix* than Sherlock, but I was definitely keeping my eyes open for clues that would let me in on what was going on below the PTG's psycho-shtick.

The trailer was maybe 25 feet long and locked with a padlock the size of my fist. It looked like government surplus – olive green on the outside and toothpaste green on the inside, the kind of green that gets hosed down with bleach between deployments. It was lined with shelves, except for a space at one end that was blocked by a canvas shower curtain. On one side, I saw the jumpsuits and racks of what we used to call "desert boots," suede leather and ankle-high. On the other side, the shelves were stacked with folded jeans and Tee-shirts and such, the street clothes we wore back in the real world that wasn't real. It basically looked like the closet of every teen I knew, except for the girl's clothes, which included a lot of low-cut jeans what for some reason were called "peasant shirts," because knowing what a teenage girl's closet looked like would mean having been in a teenage girl's room, which, at that point, I had never entered. Even Jackie had a lock on her door before she left. She could have had a bomb-making lab and taxidermy supplies in there for all I knew.

Of course, the girls' clothes meant there'd be girls there, the first evidence of that I'd seen. And unless they were actual peasants, they were from somewhere near my point on the social spectrum. I wasn't expecting preppy plaids, but I didn't have to be Columbo to know that these girls knew their way around a bong. The rest of the shelves were filled with canteens, packs, shit like that.

I was still thinking like a detective, sorting through clues, but also noting what I'd grab from the inventory if I decided to step off the Quest Trail unannounced.

"Now, this part might feel a little awkward," the PTG announced. *This part?* "I need you two to re-move your clothes one at a time and stand behind that curtain." Here we go, I thought. I was suddenly thinking of the places on my body where it wasn't worth it to hide drugs and wondering about how the PTG was planning to search them.

Thankfully, it wasn't as bad as I thought. We basically got undressed and he had us squat down like we were taking a dump. No Vaseline. No latex gloves. Greg was quiet, even for Greg, but there wasn't really much to say. It was like the locker room at school and pretty much every men's room in the western world. A code of silence prevailed. Five minutes later we were standing outside the trailer adjusting the straps on our backpacks.

I had zero experience backpacking. My parents took us car camping when we were little, maybe a half dozen times before Jackie began to turn anything more arduous than a walk through the mall into an expedition. But what I did know about backpacking was that the gear was supposed to be light, modern, efficient and sleek, like you were camping on Mars. I imagined Civil War soldiers busting their way up Bull Run and complaining about how heavy this shit was. I looked at Greg. He looked awfully casual for a guy carrying half a refrigerator on his back, but he was also three inches taller. Greg had a way of accepting stuff in an "I guess this is how it's going to be" kind of way and there were times when I admired that. I was standing there wondering how many pounds I was carrying while Greg was gazing across the desert like he might see one of those hummingbirds he'd been talking about. He plucked at the fabric of his yellow jumpsuit. "So much more comfortable than those dungarees," he said.

And then I smiled too.

I saw the PTG locking the trailer with a chrome padlock and tucking the key under his yellow Quest Trail Staff T-shirt. He didn't have a backpack on. Apparently, his mule skin bedroll and brass-buckled cannon sling were already up at camp. But he was carrying a 3-gallon jug of water in each hand. He looked pretty tough, I have to admit. My backpack seemed more reasonable all of a sudden.

"You boys ready?"

"Depends," I said. Greg's happy act was not fully rubbing off on me. "For what?"

"For the first steps on a journey into the rest of your life," the PTG answered. It was almost like a skit, but he was dead serious. "Every mile we travel away from this trailhead is a mile into your future. You get to define what that future is. Everything ahead of you is a growth opp, that means opportunity for growth."

"I find I grow best in air conditioning," I said.

Greg was smiling at both of us. I felt a little bit betrayed.

"The trail awaits, companions," the PTG announced and settled his shoulders into the weight of the water jugs. He stepped onto the trail, which was mainly broken rocks barely threading the way between ankle-attack cactus and the occasional scrubby bush. The PTG looked perfectly at home. It wasn't just the cartoon-sized waffle stompers and that stupid vest with 15 pockets, none of which had anything in them, as far as I could tell. He looked like an ad for some new granola or one of those beer commercials where the people are hiking and kayaking and doing all kinds of shit that people are too lazy to do when they drink beer.

I had no such enthusiasm. It's not that I hate nature or anything. Nature's great when you have a rough idea about when you'll be returning to civilization. But there was a lot to be unhappy about and the 300 pounds biting into my shoulders wasn't giving me that mountain-goat-prancing-down-the-trail exuberance.

Greg wasn't straining at all. He had adopted this weird gait that wasn't exactly skipping down the trail but wasn't Bataan Death March either. We'd just learned about the Bataan Death March at school. It was this World War II thing where the Japanese made these American soldiers march across half of China and it was hot and full-on jungle and guys were basically dying because it sucked so much. We were merely walking into the desert and trading our freedom for some learningship and growments, which are, of course, moments when you grow. They never actually said "growments." I made that up. But it's the kind of stupid-ass thing they would say. So, we weren't on an actual death march and nobody was saying "growments." How's that for the crappiest bright side ever?

The PTG led the way and I was behind Greg, whose legs were probably 8 inches longer than mine. That meant I was falling behind and appreciating the fact that it was bugging the PTG who kept looking back over his shoulder, which made his ponytail flip over his other shoulder. Greg noticed it too. Soon, Greg was asking questions just to see the ponytail flip. He didn't ask the obvious question, which was "How much further?" because

I was asking it every three or four minutes. Instead, he was asking ridiculous stuff like, "Is it true that the water in the barrel cactus isn't really water but more like liquid chewing gum?" And then he'd ask "Can we expect to see any javelina and shouldn't we make spears in case one of them charges us?"

I should probably explain that javelina are basically hairy pigs and the males have tusks that are wicked long. It turns out they only fight each other and it's basically to see who gets the female javelina, but everybody who sees a javelina in a picture or in a zoo thinks they are fierce. People like us who grew up in Arizona mostly knew that you don't need to be afraid of a javelina unless you're a garbage can. But Greg was playing it up like we'd grown up in a New York high-rise.

"I heard that they can run 45 mph when they're really amped up," he said, as though he hadn't even heard the PTG's explanation that they are "quite docile" and not really related to pigs, which was stupid because they are obviously pigs.

After a while, the PTG said "there will be plenty of time for questions about nature when we get to camp. Let's enjoy the silence," which was basically Quest Trail code for "shut the fuck up, already."

We still got the ponytail flip but only when he was looking back to see how far back I was and by then I'd figured out that it was more fun to walk right behind Greg so that the PTG would have to look over both shoulders to see me and we'd see the ponytail go back and forth like it was a ping pong ball.

It went on like that for maybe an hour and it was

getting almost dark when I saw what looked like a tent maybe 300 yards down the hill next to a really tall saguaro, which is one of those telephone pole-sized cactus that looks like a dick with arms. We got a little closer and I got a bit excited for the first time since I'd been thrown into the Turdmobile by the would-be goons.

There were girls.

Or at least one girl. For the first time since we'd left the road, I made a point of keeping up.

5

The other campers, "clients," I guess, heard us coming and seemed to appear out of the desert as we got closer. All seven of them were out by this fire pit thing when we got to camp. They were mostly guys, all of them right around our age, but there were two girls. I was barely listening to the PTG who was calling out something like "Hello friends," because I was watching one of the girls, who had hair past her shoulders—blonde but not completely blonde, which was my favorite—and was actually able to make the yellow jumpsuit look almost good. I mean, it was the last bit of the sunset light so everybody was going to look at least a little better, but she didn't need flattering lighting. She was that kind of fox. She stepped out from the group like she was the welcoming committee all on her own and also like she didn't give a crap what the PTG or the two guys in the yellow "staff" Tee-shirts thought.

"Welcome to Quest Fail," she said, sweeping her arm like she was Carol Merrell on the Price is Right.

"We're the quest failures."

The PTG let a little annoyance sneak into his dandelions-and-rainbows bullshit. "Vera, I think that's enough," he said. She returned his comments with a smirk and an exaggerated sigh.

The PTG made this twirly motion in the air with his hand and everybody started to form a circle before he even said, "Circle up." Greg and I stuck close together, like we were greeting a rival tribe and we had not brought beaver pelts or wampum. Greg even looked a little tense. The PTG was smiling again.

"Friends," he said. I guess we'd grown past the client stage. "We have two newcomers to our family."

"Greetings, new friends," the whole group said, almost in unison, like they'd done this before and it had been done for them.

Vera had a leather cord wrapped around her fist with a green glass bead on the end. She did not join in the greeting. She let the bead swing back and forth like a pendulum. She looked up at me. I wanted to think it was a smile. She kept eye contact long enough for me to half-ass fall in love. She made it obvious she was ignoring the PTG, who, I have to admit, I was barely listening to. Her eyes flickered up at me and she made an exaggerated glance to the PTG, as though she were suggesting I listen up.

"Daniel, Greg, at Quest Trail one of our practices is something we call Circle Up. At Circle Up, we declare our daily wintention." Yep, he said "wintention." He didn't even bother to explain what it meant. It was almost like even the PTG was too embarrassed by it. "On a special night like tonight, we will also introduce ourselves. Quest Trail is about creating a community that exists outside the expectations and frustrations of the peer society you left behind. Quest Trail is about leaving your judgements at the trailhead."

He was nodding in a way that suggested we were supposed to nod back. I wouldn't give him the pleasure and not only because I knew Vera was watching us. Everybody was watching us. We were like the new rats in the maze and they were waiting to show us where the cheese was just to screw up the PTG's experiment.

He gave up on the nodding. Vera smiled again. I wanted to think she was looking at me, but it was getting dark. The guys in the yellow shirts had hauled out a pair of lanterns and the weird light was making everybody's face look like they were telling ghost stories, which made the whole wintentions thing pretty hilarious. The PTG turned held his open palm out to the guy on my right, which I guessed meant we'd hear multiple variations on the "My name is Joe Anybody and my wintention is to survive this bullshit and take revenge on my parents" thing before it'd come around to us. "Ivan, let's start with you," the PTG announced. "Tell us your name, your place on the Quest Trail journey and your wintention."

So, this kid is curly headed and kinda short and I'm already guessing he blew his bar mitzvah cash on dope. He didn't look comfortable in a way that made it obvious he didn't feel comfortable anywhere. He stood up really straight, as though he were giving a project update to the Junior Achievement Club. "My name is Ivan," he said. He looked around the circle before turning his shoulders to face Greg and me but stared past us into the desert. "I am 34 days on the Trail." I winced a little bit, 34 days was a big reality slap. I'd been hoping to be back on the couch for some Match Game and bong hits by maybe day 9. "My wintention tonight is to refrain from negative self-talk and realize my capacity for positive momentum."

The PTG stopped him. "Ivan, let's real-size that wintention. Just look at tonight. What do you want for tonight?"

Ivan shrugged. "Ok, then my wintention is to keep scorpions out of my tent."

The PTG looked a little unhappy with Ivan, but he did the open palm thing to the guy on Ivan's right. "Joey," he said, and he added this really dumb solemn nod.

Joey was rocking back and forth a little bit. He was taller than Ivan, which isn't saying a lot, but not as tall as Greg. "My name is Joey. I've been on the trail for 51 days." I was glad it was dark because I probably couldn't have hidden my horror that point—51 days! "My wintention is to count a dozen shooting stars and get up in time to see the sunrise."

It was damn obvious that he was sucking up to the PTG and it was even more obvious that the PTG was eating this crap right up. "Thank you, Joey," the PTG said. He sounded almost giddy in that "Darn it, these kids are so amazing when they let their light shine" kind of way. He did the palm thing again to the guy right of Joey, who cocked his head to the side before he spoke, telegraphing that he was about to unleash some attitude to counter Joey's straight-from-the-brochure suck-up.

"My name is Tony," he said. "And I am on day 19 of my trail journey, but in my heart I am on day 96 because I've grown so much." He used this obviously bullshit earnest tone as though he'd studied at the Greg Pittz School of Faked Sincerity. He didn't give the PTG or the two yellow Tee-shirt guys any time to object before continuing. "And my wintention is to put scorpions in Ivan's tent."

Everybody fought the laugh. Some were more successful than others. Vera was swinging the leather cord and bead like it was a noisemaker, silent applause. The bigger of the two staffer guys—I later learned his name was Ron—stepped into the circle and picked the lantern up, holding it over Tony's head.

I got my first good look at Ron. The lantern above his head threw this weird glow effect on his buzz cut and I could see the sleeves of the yellow Tee tight on his biceps. At least in appearance, Ron was the anti-PTG. One of us, I was sure, was going to have to drop and give him 20 before we found our way off the trail. I got the sense, later confirmed, that he was tamping down his inner bad-cop-with-a-billy-club routine for the PTG, but bits of it were leaking out, primarily in the form of spit, a spray of which caught the lantern light with every hard consonant.

"Tony," Ron announced, hitting the "T" extra hard. "We're here to lift each other up and that can't happen when somebody like you is dragging us down." He leaned in for a hard stare down. Tony gulped, the bravado evaporating into the dark. "Do you understand?" Ron went on, dropping into authoritarian staccato. "Perhaps you want to rephrase your wintention."

Tony spoke quickly, in a low almost-mumble. "My wintention is to share and earn the respect of my fellow campers."

"That's better," Ron snapped, lowering the lantern and stepping back to his spot in the circle.

The guy next to Tony spoke up quickly to pierce the silence that followed Ron's statement. Even the PTG looked rattled. "I'm Michael," he said. He spoke softly and everybody went quiet. "I am on my 38th night on the Trail. My wintention is to listen to myself and others."

Ron was quiet. The PTG nodded. Vera was up next.

"Ok, so I'm Vera," she said. Her eyes darted around the circle in the lantern light. "My camper comrades call me Very, or Vera." She paused. "It varies, according to the situation, and my mood." It was fairly tiresome wordplay even on the first rendition and this was way past first rendition for most of the camp. But she was hot and being hot comes with privileges, one of which is an indulgence for the theatrical. I was waiting for Ron, the PTG or the other yellow Tee-shirt to stop her, but Vera had a rhythm to the way she inhabited situations that silenced people really quick, especially when everybody was still coming down from the Ron vs Tony Dust-up in the Desert. "I'm a two-time loser on the Trail. I'm on what, Deano, day 27?" She looked at the PTG. Nobody called him the PTG to his face. But nobody called him Deano either. "My overarching wintention is to help the new recruits attain their highest state of being. My wintention tonight is to not complain about how goddamn awful beany linguini is." Both Ron and the PTG looked a little stunned. I got the idea in that moment that Vera was basically the Quest Trail commandant, and the grown-ups hadn't been let in on that fact. "Because, really, who can get tired of beany linguini even if we have it five nights out of six around here?"

She turned a stare on the PTG that I imagined would make a prison gang boss wince, as if she were daring him to stop her. The lantern light caught her eyes. By day, I would see that they were blue, but in that light, they flared like one of those old wire-filament bulbs I'd seen in museums. He looked away.

This time it was Ron, who filled the silence. "I'm Ron," he announced. He avoided looking at Vera. This is my second year with Quest Trail and my fourth year in wilderness resourcing." He looked around the circle. "My wintention tonight is to have our newest friends settled into camp life without unnecessary interruption." He glared at Vera, but it was brief, tentative even. She looked like she couldn't be bothered.

Yellow Tee-shirt Guy 2 stepped into the circle, even though the rest of us were content on the periphery. "I'm Pete," he said. "My wintention is to help Ron, and Dean."

That might sound quick, but it's close to as many consecutive syllables I would ever see out of Pete when Ron or the PTG were around. He stepped back to his spot in the circle and looked down at his feet with his hands folded at his waist.

"I'm Sarah," the girl on the other side of Pete

announced. "I've been on the trail for 40 days. I am also looking forward to beany linguini." She spared a glancing smile at Vera who acknowledged the tribute with a theatrical curtsey. "And my wintention is to make tonight special for our new guests."

I wasn't sure if this was a PTG-pleasing ploy or if she was being genuine. I would learn that with Sarah such things were often difficult to discern. Sarah was one of those middle run girls who would be a dream date for most guys but knew that girls like Vera occupied a different reality of desirability. Sarah wasn't sure whether to resent that or cozy up to the closest Vera to see if any of it rubbed off on her.

There was one last guy. He'd been quiet but make-no-mistake present. He had this smile that was almost, but not quite a smirk, as though he were thinking *Should I blow up this whole thing up or play along until the right moment?* He was not large, but he carried himself as though he were. It was subtle. I had no idea which movie tough guy he'd been studying, but I was instantly jealous I had not discovered said tough guy's film catalog. "I'm Troy," he said, and he paused for a half beat too long before continuing. "I've been on what we're supposed to call the trail for 62 days. My secret wintention is to make friends with the two new guys and build an elite fighting force for all that is righteous and good. My declared wintention is to celebrate the temple of nature and all its wisdom."

Troy didn't carry the charismatic oomph that Vera could deliver in three syllables or less, but the PTG and the yellow Tees said nothing. I'd seen teachers let some kids get away with things and I always wondered if certain situations took people back in time and plopped them down into their assigned spot in the schoolyard nerd/bully/predator/prey food chain, as though they knew their spot and wouldn't question it, or at least they accepted it. This was one of those times.

That left Greg and me. I'd started mentally constructing my Quest Trail debut, but I was still glad to give Greg the first go.

"I'm Greg," he said, not waiting for the PTG's open-palm approval. "I've strayed from the path of the righteous and find myself on the Quest Trail for what?" he looked at me as though I was supposed to have rehearsed an answer. "I don't know. Do we count the drive? Because that's really Quest Road, but if we're just talking trail then I don't know, two hours?" He was speaking in what would seem a casual tone, but I knew was carefully calculated to put people at ease. "I guess my wintention is to get to know all of you and figure out what we are supposed to figure out and also to find out what beanie linguini is."

He smiled and then bowed as though bowing was an expected part of the program that everybody else in the circle had somehow forgotten. The lantern light was making Greg seem even taller than he really was, which could have been intimidating but his whole sleepy giant thing was already working. Everybody seemed suddenly comfortable by association.

I hadn't figured on that and my whole plan wasn't exactly built around following Greg's genuinely good-natured act that wasn't even an act because

Greg was really like that almost all the time. So I was a little caught off guard.

And everybody was looking at me.

"I'm Daniel," I said. This was not what I'd spent the last five minutes rehearsing in my head.

"I came with him."

If you ever have to come up with a gangster name, you could do worse than Beanie Linguini. Beanie could be the gangster understudy to the boss gangster, like the little cartoon dog who prances around the big cartoon dog and makes the big cartoon dog seem both important and also kind of a nice guy for letting the pipsqueak dog hang around. If you ever have to come up with a dish to cook in the desert and make kids homesick for stuff like dry bread crust and freezer-burn sausage patties, you could do worse than beany linguini.

But you'd have to try really hard.

Beans and noodles wouldn't necessarily have to be a bad thing. I can imagine it not sucking. But beans and noodles without salt or pepper or, really, spice of any kind, that is cooked either too long or not long enough is arguably a human rights violation. I should also say that it wasn't even linguini. It was spaghetti and the kind that clumps up. But, of course, spaghetti doesn't rhyme with "beany."

It was Tony's turn on "Chef Duty" that night, we were told, and he was apologizing as we broke up from the circle. "Don't blame me," Tony called out to the desert sky, "blame society! It was society that allowed beans and noodles to come together in this unholy way." Nobody laughed. I saw Ron give the PTG this impatient look as he bent down to scoop up the lantern in one hand. Two steps later the lantern, and Ron, were inches from Tony's face. "Do you want to rephrase that? Perhaps in a way that is more helpful for our new friends here?" The tone hovered around sharp. Tony didn't hesitate. "Bean linguini is proper nutrition for growing bodies and growing spirits," he said, looking to the side as if somewhere out in the desert he had an ally because he certainly wasn't drawing anybody else into the line of fire.

The other kids were plopping down on foam pads that were covered in black duct tape and, as far as I could tell, were "furniture." Pete bent down by the packs that Greg and I had dropped outside the wintention circle and reached into the side pockets. He stood up with an aluminum mug in each hand. Attached to each mug by a lanyard was something like a spork but closer to the spoon end of the dining utensil spectrum. Our names were magic-markered on the sides of the mugs. He handed them to us almost solemnly, very aware that the PTG was listening. "These are your food mugs," he said. "You are responsible for keeping them clean. Every meal you eat is going to be served in this mug."

I held the mug in my hand. It felt flimsy. Greg tapped his with the spork thing and looked at Pete, before holding it up with his pinky raised. "And what of high tea?" he asked, in this really exaggerated British accent, that was more Ringo than anything. "Will there be China, like me mum uses at home?" I flinched a little, worried that Ron would take issue with Greg's thespian skills, but Ron was across the campsite. Pete looked relieved. He dropped into whisper territory. "Tea, my dear sirs," he replied, a notch above a whisper and this time more Monty Python than Ringo, "will be served on the veranda." He smiled.

It was, I'll admit, an unexpected bright spot. From Bob's by-the-script act in the van to the PTG prancing down the trail like an enlightened rainbow of love and then Ron's thinly veiled authoritarian streak, I'd accepted that every adult in this experience was more or less an adversary. We'd met Pete 15 minutes ago and he was already sharing whispered asides. I wasn't ready to call him an ally yet, but he was not fully signed on to the other team either.

I saw the other kids lining up with their mugs. Tony looked subdued as he ladled out the bean and noodle gruel. His "customers" echoed his enthusiasm. If it had been an afterschool special it'd be the moment when the kids would realize they were all in it together and had no choice but to work together. But this was reality, and everybody shuffled toward their gloom.

I looked over at Greg and mimicked his pinky raised salute. "After you, sir," I said.

We were about to join the line of doomed diners when Troy stepped in front of us. It was about as obvious an attempt at pack dominance as you are likely to see outside a National Geographic special on mountain gorillas. He slumped into a can't-be-bothered-with-this-shit pose, but he obviously could be bothered. If he'd been as cool or as tough or as he was attempting to be, he wouldn't have looked over his shoulder at us, but he couldn't help himself.

If you're like me and you are on the small and receiving end of the tough-guy posing, you recognize insecurity when you see it. Sure, everybody's mom tells you that the bullies are insecure and anybody who picks on you is "just jealous," but it doesn't feel that way most of the time. Once in a while, however, you can see the "did it work?" stage fright leaking out. This was one of those moments.

Vera stepped in behind me.

She tapped me on the shoulder and used her other elbow to point toward Troy. "Don't worry," she whispered. "The Oompah Loompahs are working up a song for him. What are you in for?"

"I don't know," I said. I'd seen Troy try the too-cool act and did not have one of my own prepared. So I went with smartass, my default setting. "A rollicking good time? A life-changing experience that teaches me the true value of friendship."

She gave me a look that said "It's not working, but keep trying, kid. I admire your pluck."

What she actually said was, "You stole that from the brochure. I mean, what did you do that got you this all-expenses-paid vacation?"

"A little bit of weed," I said. "And it wasn't even mine."

"It wasn't mine? Did you really try 'It wasn't mine? Silly Rabbit, that trick never works!" Her smile was creeping in now. "I'm not your mom anyway. Be honest, was it Colombian? Kona? Acapulco Gold?" she asked. "What do the kids smoke where you come from?"

"I come from about 100 miles from here," I said. I saw something shift in her eyes, as though such relative proximity had triggered a sequence of mental calculations. "Colombian, when we can afford it," I continued. "Mexican buttweed when we can't."

"But wait!" she said, and she brought her hand to her mouth in feigned shock. "I thought it wasn't yours! I thought somebody snuck it into your stash of Famous Scientists collectors' cards!"

She'd dropped out of whisper mode and I could see the PTG eyeing us from the across the fire pit. There was so much going on that I almost forgot I was talking to a beautiful girl. I might have even been flirting, which would mean that Vera was flirting with me because I'm sure both parties must be engaged in flirting for flirting to have occurred. "Well, you know," I said, slightly under her volume but loud enough that Greg, and definitely Troy, could hear. "Sir Isaac Newton was a total stoner."

She smiled. I expected to see her look around the group to make sure that the group witnessed her seal of approval on my attempt at banter. Girls that look like Vera usually want to make sure their audience is following the action.

But she didn't. She smiled at me. At least for that moment, I was the audience.

I've always wondered if teepees came with instructions. Except for caves, tents have to be the oldest form of human housing, which means they are way up there on the oldest sources of human frustration. I can imagine Fred Flintstone and Barney Rubble coming to blows over how to set up the Masto-dome while Wilma and Betty sipped wine spritzers out of turtle shell mugs. Luckily, it was dark while I flailed with canvas and poles. Ivan had offered to help, but the last thing I wanted was Vera seeing me getting schooled in the manly arts by some guy who, like every other Y-chromosome-packing biped in the area, was also in love with her.

I had tried three different positions for what I assumed to be the main pole and was sure that I at least knew the top of the tent from the bottom when I looked over at Greg already unrolling his sleeping bag. His tent looked like tents in catalogs look, every stake at the perfect angle, every crease and fold pulled taught. He might as well have been putting in a lawn and hanging Christmas lights.

"Hey, junior ranger nerd," I said. "Can you give me a hand here?"

"What?" Greg asked. "May I be of assistance?" He wasn't going to rub it in too much, but he sure as hell was going to rub it in some. Greg had the poles lined up and was straightening the tent without waiting to see if I cared to observe his handiwork. I didn't even feign participation. He knew me that well.

Greg was the kind of kid I always assumed dreamed in Legos. Every model car kit I ever got ended up as a tangle of glue and plastic. Greg didn't even look at the directions. He knew that Tab A goes into Tab B by instinct alone. If I'm ever trapped on a desert island and that island happens to be covered in build-your-own-boat kits, I want Greg there.

I take that back. I want Vera there.

I'll take my time with the boats.

"You know," Greg said, snaking the main pole (which I'd guessed right!) into a set of loops that I hadn't even noticed. He reached for another pole, making a show of keeping me in suspense. "I'm thinking of asking Vera to the prom."

"Oh, shut up," I said. "I was just making conversation. It seems like she's got this place figured out. We could use a friend."

"Just makin' conversation," he replied, in a bit of sing-song voice. He gave a quick jerk on two cords and the tent bloomed into shape as though it were waiting for the right moment to appear. "What would Becky Swenson say?"

"She'd say 'Daniel? Isn't he the one who almost grabbed half of my left tit in seventh grade? Such a worldly man!'" We were both laughing.

"No, really," Greg said. "Vera looked, well, interested."

I was, of course, thinking the same thing, or at least hoping the same thing, but there was no way I was letting Greg know that. "Dude," I said, "Vera's 14 levels of babe out of my league. And we're out here where she's the *only* babe."

"So?" Greg said.

"She's just paying attention to the new kids because she's bored with the old kids," I told him.

"So you're saying she won't go to prom with me?" Greg was smiling again.

"Oh, I'm not saying that," I said, dropping into an exaggerated dad voice. "I just want to know if your wintentions are honorable."

6

If I were a morning person, I wouldn't admit it. Morning people are not, as a rule, considered cool, ever. You're not going to read a biography of Debbie Harry and find out that she was "chipper" in the a.m. Nobody talks about David Bowie's passion for scones and tea.

As a teenager, morning can be considered the kryptonite hours. According to science and some Reader's Digest article that everybody's mom is assigned to read as soon as she gets pregnant, teenagers need something like 8 hours of sleep, but what science doesn't tell you is that it's ideal if those hours are packaged somewhere between 3 a.m. and noon, roughly.

That's one of the reasons high schools look like drug rehab clinics until at least 10.

Out in the desert, things are different. There were no electric lights. No lame-ass movies on post-midnight TV. No parties to sneak out to. I don't know if

I expected a campfire sing-a-long or ghost stories. I certainly didn't expect everybody to crawl into their tents as soon as they'd choked down their beany linguini, but that's where I found myself at what must have been 8 p.m.

And camping sleep is not "sleep." We didn't evolve to sleep outside and not hear every little noise. That's basic caveman shit.

That's camping sleep.

And so, the sun was barely up, and I was peeking out of my tent, maybe not chipper but awake, not the groggy wreck that finally responded to my mom's 10th "get the hell up" intrusion. I didn't ask anybody for "five more minutes."

I was up. And so was everybody else.

Even Greg. The sleepy giant was zipping his tent closed and straightening the tent spikes, which he was likely surprised to see the morning light revealing were as much as 3 degrees out of alignment.

Troy, Vera and Tony were over smashing peanut butter over apple slices in the "kitchen" which was really just a big wooden box, and a crate where they piled the pans (javelinas be damned!). Sarah and Ivan were sitting on the foam pads, working in their journals.

These aren't teenagers, I told myself, no way. These are *morning* people.

I dragged myself out of the tent and looked around. The others acknowledged my activity with a glance, but nobody offered a hearty "good morning!" The PTG was 20 yards past the kitchen with Pete and Ron. I half expected him to come trotting over with some sunny affirmation along the lines of "let us all praise the glory of the day and its wonder," which, even if I were a morning person would have had me recruiting my fellow clients for an impromptu stoning. I'd left my socks stuffed in my boots and when I grabbed the closest one something came out with it, something jiggly and spidery. A scorpion two inches long plopped onto the sand. I scooted back hard and got caught in the tent flaps.

The scorpion did not follow me. Plastic bugs don't do that.

Troy was pointing and laughing. "Dude, you should have seen your face!" I saw smiles from Tony and some others. Sarah looked annoyed. Ivan acknowledged it with a slight glance and turned back to his journal. Greg tensed up his shoulders, looked from me to Troy and kept his eyes locked there.

Vera followed Greg's stare and then brought her eyes back to me. "Welcome to Quest Trail," she said. "You survived your first night." She nodded toward Troy. "Lizards and bugs aren't the only creepy creatures you will encounter."

She was looking right at me. My first thought was of Troy and can be summarized as "what an asshole." We'd all met our share of Troy's, not really large enough to be full-on bullies but obviously keeping score of their triumphs. My second thought was "she's looking right at me." My third thought was "how do I look?"

I reached up to draw my hand back through my hair. The elaborately feathered terraces that I was sure would look good on an album cover if I knew how to play guitar and owned a leather jacket were not particularly well suited to camping. But at least there was nothing stuck in it, no twigs or grass, or plastic scorpions.

Everybody was staring at me. This was the point in the taunt-and-response cycle when I was supposed to say something incredibly funny, a comeback that would earn me accolades and respect to counter the spectacle of me jumping three feet to get away from a plastic bug. I reached over to said scorpion and picked it up by the tail, holding it up a few inches above eye level as though I were examining it for science class.

"Breakfast in bed," I said. I deadpanned it, looking up at Troy the whole time. "So kind of you." I wanted to see Vera's reaction, but I couldn't break the stare.

Ron broke it for me and snatched the plastic scorpion out of my hands.

"Enough with the welcoming committee," he announced. I saw him offer Troy a half smile as he shoved the scorpion in his back pocket. Troy nodded back. If I couldn't bring a Walkman, I doubt Troy had been allowed a plastic scorpion on his packing list.

Through all this, I was still sitting in the dirt in front of my tent. It wasn't exactly the triumphant pose from which to cast down my rivals, but I wasn't really sure if Troy was my rival or just some guy pulling a prank. I'd been the guy pulling the prank more than once and more than once it'd been at the expense of a friend. So I sat there, in the dirt, trying to diagram the implications, and the rest of the camp basically went back to what they were doing.

By the time I was watching Ron walk away with a scorpion-shaped bulge in his back pocket, Vera had already turned back to her peanut butter and apple creation. Greg stood by his tent, maybe 8 feet away, and looked over at me. "Maybe that's a tradition, like hazing," he said. "Or maybe it's an honor and you've been chosen as the leader of our tribe."

"Or maybe Troy's an asshole," I replied.

"Indeed, though that will require additional field-work. What do you think they have in store for us on this fine day?"

"Not sure," I said. "But I bet it involves a circle up. Got your wintentions ready?"

"I was up half the night making a list," Greg replied, feigning giddy.

So apples and peanut butter were the obvious and only breakfast option and when I'd strolled the 30 feet or so to the kitchen I could see why Vera and the others had looked to be laboring at their culinary creations. "Troubled" kids don't get real knives because they might slit their wrists, or somebody else's wrists, or stage an elaborately choreographed West Side Story-styled knife fight. But we were granted plastic knives, which are good for cutting things like butter or jello and not good for anything with more structural integrity than whipped cream. People were leaning into the cuts on the apple and then being careful not to snap the knife in the gooey resistance of the peanut butter, which was super gooey because it was generic peanut butter.

Generic was a big concept that year, plain white labels and blocky black type, because somehow there was honor in letting everybody in the grocery store know you were a warrior for frugality by filling your cart with plain, white-labeled stuff, as though that made you Supermarket Gandhi, when really you were just a cheapskate. Toilet paper was the worst of the generic genre—simultaneously too thin and too hard, which is impressive, if you think about it—but peanut butter was no treat. I found myself with the others, maneuvering my plastic knife through the too-gooey and too-lumpy mess and slopping it onto my dismembered apple.

The PTG came out from behind a palo verde tree (palo verde means "green stick," which should give you an idea of the lush nature of our wilderness home) and clapped his hands. I was surprised that he didn't have a whistle, but then I guessed a whistle would be too authoritarian for his nature worshipper sensibilities. And a wooden flute would be cumbersome to carry around.

"Morning friends," he shouted into the brightness of the desert morning. "Circle Up! We're going to play a game."

When I saw the others slump, I got ready for something either corny or embarrassing and probably both. Every time an adult asks kids to learn from a game, the main thing we learn is that adults have completely forgotten what it's like to be a kid.

I was in after school care once and the guy who ran it had this one game called Find Your Partner where you were supposed to write five things about yourself on a piece of paper and then each person would pick a different slip of paper out of a box and try to find the person it described. So, of course, one round in and we're all looking for the hunchback with a fake eye and a criminal history or whoever wrote: "I am a collection of insects masquerading as a human." Try to turn me into a better person and you're going to turn me into a better smartass.

I could see the PTG attempting something similarly prone to satire. And I could see him attempting it morning after morning.

I was not disappointed.

"I hope everybody's ready to do their self-work today, but I thought we'd start with something a little fun," he announced. I looked around the circle. Vera had her swinging bead out again, metronome set to "slow." She wasn't making eye contact. Troy was rocking from foot to foot in a way that was supposed to be cool or tough but seemed a little twitchy to me. Tony had his head cocked to one side like he'd been to an acting class and was working on "forlorn poet." The rest of the group was in similar don't-give-a-shit repose. Ron and Pete were off doing staff stuff, probably digging shallow graves.

"This is how the game works," the PTG announced. "We're all out here to learn from the nature, the silent teacher. Every creature and plant out here has been learning from nature for eons. Adapting, evolving, like we're doing!"

Greg actually perked up a bit. He was probably thinking of that hummingbird.

"I have the names of ten desert animals in this hat. Each of us is going to pick an animal and then talk about how that animal is resilient and what we can learn from it. Ready?"

"Ready?" was purely rhetorical.

"I'll go first," the PTG said, as though there were any chance in the world that he wasn't going to go first. It didn't matter to him that none of us were buying into the possibilities for growth. He reached into the basket, pulled out a slip of paper and announced "tortoise!"

If you'd grown up in the desert, you'd know that a tortoise is basically a turtle that doesn't have enough smarts to go where the water is. Turtles can swim, which is pretty much the only thing you'd want to do if you have short legs and you're carrying an RV on your back. Tortoises are all descended from some turtle that got kicked out of the pond by cooler turtles.

Then the PTG did this really weird thing, which I was hoping he didn't expect the rest of us to do. He started pantomiming a tortoise poking its head out of its shell to gaze in wonder at the beauty of nature before starting in on his tortoise soliloquy. "The tortoise is a creature of patience," he intoned in a solemn voice. "It accepts the harsh nature of the desert and can go weeks without water because it conserves its movement." He looked around as though we were all going to share in his enthusiastic respect for slow-moving reptiles. "When threatened, it does not engage, it merely retreats to its shell and waits it out. The tortoise is patient."

I was silently praying for this to end. It did not. "But the tortoise also knows that it cannot stay in its shell forever. When the conflict is past, it stretches out of his shell and relates with the world in exploration, accepting what is right in front of it and not looking too far ahead to what may come. The tortoise does not dread the future. It lives in peace with the now. The tortoise is patient."

I don't think he was expecting applause and maybe he thought his enthusiasm made up for our total lack thereof.

He turned to Ivan with the basket and did that annoying open palm thing again. Ivan pulled out a slip of paper and stared at it for a second. I couldn't tell if it was a smirk or a grimace, but it was definitely a reaction I wouldn't call neutral. "Roadrunner," he proclaimed, as though the name of the animal was profound all on its own.

It was the first time I'd suspected the words "drama nerd," later confirmed, were part of the biography. "I guess the roadrunner is resilient because it's agile. Roadrunners run. I mean they're not road walkers or road strollers. They have direction. They have a goal in mind." He was starting to meander, like he was leading up to something and not sure how to get there. "But when they need to, they can stand up for themselves. They can kill snakes," he said.

And then he looked around the circle, obviously drawing on whatever theater summer camp training he'd racked up to calculate the dramatic timing. "And they're good at avoiding falling anvils dropped by coyotes."

We all laughed, not a guffaw laugh, but a chuckle laugh, like we were all in on the joke with him. It was an obvious joke, but that didn't make it less funny for anybody.

Anybody but the PTG.

It'd taken exactly one kid to turn his little "game" into a joke, a joke on him.

"There was so much intuition and intelligence in how you described the road runner's emotional agility," the PTG said, in this solemn wistful way that told us he was trying to turn it into a teachable moment, but also like he was saying "you just earned yourself another 20 days on the trail, kid." And then he added: "But I think your attempt at humor was your way of denying your self-truth."

I could see Ivan's jaws twitching. He realized he'd found some thin ice in the middle of the desert and inched back from the spreading cracks. The PTG swept his gaze across the whole group like he wanted us to know he'd won the encounter.

He turned to Troy, skipping the open palm and holding out the hat. Troy picked up his piece of paper, folded it and threw it back in, closing his eyes before he spoke. When he did, he looked the PTG right in the eyes, like it was after school and they were meeting at the flagpole for a rumble.

"The coyote," he said. The PTG shrank into little half flinch/half wince. If he'd been smart, he never would have put the coyote and the roadrunner in the same pile, but the PTG had a way of not seeing shit coming, even when it was coming right at him. "He hunts, he scavenges, he runs with the pack when that's what works, and he goes out on his own when he needs to. He can hide. He can fight." Troy stood taller for a moment and then pulled one shoulder back, eyes still right on the PTG. "He can get away with anything, anywhere, any time."

He used the dramatic pause from Ivan's workbook. "And he has an unlimited explosives budget."

The PTG didn't offer a review, not a word. He pulled the self-help jujitsu on Ivan, but Troy occupied a different playground niche on the bully-toady-victim spectrum. He turned quickly to Tony who took long enough picking his slip of paper to make the PTG look uncomfortable. He didn't attempt the open palm thing. The hat quivered slightly in his outstretched hand.

Tony looked around the circle hoping for some nod of approval, as though he'd taken the baton from Troy and was about to crack the PTG in the head with it. And then he looked at the PTG, as though he were running through doing emotional algebra calculations. I imagined it as a "story problem" like this: "If a boy leaves home in a van and is sleeping outside for three weeks with a bucket for a crapper and there are only two girls to impress, how soon will get to go home if he sucks up a little bit?" He took a breath and stared at the ground for a few seconds.

"The cactus wren picks the biggest guy in the neighborhood, the saguaro cactus, and builds his house right there. The cactus wren knows how to ask for help."

The PTG looked visibly relieved. He turned to Vera, holding out the hat. She stepped forward and took a slip of paper with an exaggerated feminine delicateness. "Ah," she said, "the javelina, just my luck."

She looked down at her desert boots and nodded to herself while she constructed an answer, weighing her options.

"The javelina is a badass," she said. She made a point of not looking at the PTG for reaction. "The javelina wakes up and says 'Oh, yeah, I look like a pig, but I ain't no Wilbur barnyard pig. Don't need Charlotte to tell me I'm *some* pig. I'm my own god-damn pig! I don't wallow in somebody else's mud. I make my own mud." She got louder, grander. She looked at the PTG for the first time and then swept her eyes around the circle. "They can't build a barn that would hold me."

I wasn't sure if we were supposed to applaud or not. So, I didn't. But I felt like it.

The PTG looked into the distance for about 20 seconds, which doesn't sound very long but is way long if a bunch of people are standing around awkwardly, waiting for you to step up and get control of a situation that you never really had control of. He was wearing his too-many-pockets vest again and a tie-dye Tee-shirt. I'm still surprised whoever ran the operation would let him wear because tie-dye is full-on stoner wear, the devil's fashion statement. He could have been selling joints outside a Rush concert, but he was devoting his life to being annoyingly hopeful.

He didn't look hopeful in that moment, but I had to admire him. He could have admitted defeat and sent us all off to write in our journals about why we'd hurt his feelings. He could have smacked us in the head with a truth wrench. But he didn't. He kept going.

"Ok," he said. "Thank you, Vera. I accept that for you the javelina's resilience comes from his independence. That's beautiful, in a way." He slowed. "But maybe that resilience isn't as deep as the javelina thinks it is. Maybe the javelina needs some javelina buddies to help it feel safe."

Vera looked dumbfounded. That's not a word I use very often, because, you know, I don't live in the 1800s, but she looked dumbfounded. She'd tossed the PTG's bullshit game back in his face, the third volley of bullshit tossing, and he'd caught it gracefully and offered it back to her in a way that knocked her back, because, she had to be thinking, maybe the PTG was right, maybe the javelina's independence made it less resilient and maybe Vera needed other people more than Vera was willing to admit.

I don't remember her stepping back from the center of the circle. I just remember her back in her spot, as though she'd evaporated from one point and then re-condensed as a smaller Vera.

The PTG seemed unaware that the whole enterprise was teetering on the rails before he even put the paper slips in the hat, but he also seemed convinced that he could turn it into a golden moment we'd all remember when we had shithead kids of our own to deal with.

His expression changed when he got to Greg. He probably had some idea that Greg was new enough that he'd play it safe. He didn't know what I'd begun to appreciate more in the last 24 hours: that Greg was never really playing it safe. He only looked like he was. Greg was like a cobra hypnotizing its prey if cobras could smile while they were doing it and speak really softly so you had to lean in to hear, close enough for striking distance. And then, the cobra would give you a big hug, just so you'd know he could have killed you if he'd felt like it.

The PTG held out the hat with his left hand and did the open palm thing with the other. Greg nodded like he was a Shaolin monk who'd achieved enlightenment as a warm-up to kicking your ass. He came up from the nod with a slip of paper in his hands. He didn't even look at it.

"I am Grayson's fleck-winged hummingbird," he announced, keeping the whole solemn monk thing going. Now, there was no way that "Grayson's fleck-winged hummingbird" was on any slip of paper in that hat. I knew that for certain and so did the PTG, obviously. But the PTG was in a weird spot. If Greg had said something like "narwhal" or "Sir Thomas's rhinoceros," he could have waved his hands and brought Greg's improv exercise to a close. But hummingbird was at least conceivable and there was a chance Greg was going to deliver something safe and the game could keep going without another coyote/roadrunner moment. He let it go, but I could see him rolling forward onto the balls of his feet as though he were going to spring into the air if the moment required and unleash some heavy duty "enbrightenment" on us.

"I can flutter. I can float," Greg began, he had a slight lilt to his voice as though he were beckoning us on a storybook journey. None of the other kids had figured out that he had this silent confrontation going with the PTG. But I could see Vera and Troy were beginning to pick up on it.

"If you can float," Greg continued, "you can get to the nectar that the other birds can't get close to. And I am found only here, in the shadow of Mount Geer. To me, it's a big, sweet, syrupy nectar bar and it's all mine because I can float. I can flutter."

The PTG looked relieved. He thought Greg was wrapping up. But Greg was just getting started.

"Did you know that my heart can beat 1200 beats per minute? And that I can mate with up to 16 female hummingbirds in a single afternoon and that I protect my hummingbird harem with a form of aerial combat that is studied by both NINJAs and Pentagon scientists? Did you know that the Native Americans worshipped the Grayson's fleck-winged hummingbird as a sex god?"

The PTG stepped forward and held his hand out like he was a crossing guard. "Greg!" he said. He sounded almost assertive and I had this vision of his ponytail coiling like a scorpion stinger. But he didn't have it in him. Greg was barely acknowledging the PTG's presence. "Greg," he said, trying again.

Greg stopped. "But I haven't gotten to the resilient part?"

"Ok," the PTG said. "Tell us, but quickly, how is the Grayson's fleck-billed hummingbird resilient?"

"Fleck winged," Greg said in his best "I'm so goddamn helpful" tone.

"Yes," the PTG said. "Fleck winged." The PTG was sweating. It wasn't like with Troy or Vera where he'd seen it coming and did his best to deal with it when it arrived. Those had been more direct confrontations. Greg took a more circular path that the PTG wasn't ready for and kept the whole exchange going as though he were playing by the rules, but in a way that had him completely in charge.

This was the part where the cobra strikes. I think everyone in the circle knew that. Everybody but the PTG.

"Well," Greg said. He looked around the circle, all eyes were on him. "If you can have sex 16 times in one afternoon, I think that makes you pretty fucking resilient."

7

The thing about falling into a pattern is that it implies that whatever you are going through is "routine," as though that makes it OK. Quest Trail had a routine, but so did Genghis Khan and the Mongol hordes. I suppose ol' Genghis woke up most mornings with "pillage" on his to-do list and he didn't even underline it. It was part of the "routine."

But if you were a villager, a visit from Genghis and company would be a notable exception to your routine. I mean, being out in the field and toiling with a wooden garden hoe and wearing a wool tunic sounds like a crappy routine, but it beats getting pillaged. You wouldn't look out the door of your hovel and say "Oh, look, it's Genghis again." You'd be more like "Who's that dude and why do they have so many spears?"

A lot of time at Quest Trail, I felt like that villager. And I was not ready to accept anything at Quest trail as "routine."

There was a schedule of sorts. There was always some group circle thing and we almost always had to list our wintentions. Then we spent time "journaling," which was supposed to be a time for us to reflect on our feelings but since we knew we'd have to share them with the PTG or even in a circle thing, it was really us reflecting on what we thought the PTG wanted to hear or what we thought we could survive saying in a group of screwed-up teens like ourselves without waking up with 30 plastic scorpions in our desert boots.

And you couldn't be really obvious. You couldn't write "Today I reflected that everything was my fault, and I should honor my parents with love and straight A's." You could tell when somebody was thinking *this journal entry is my ticket outta here* when they used the words "gratitude" or talked about how much they'd "grown." But you couldn't be 100 percent honest either. Otherwise, every entry would more or less consist of "This is so unfair, and I'll make them pay."

Usually, sometime after lunch, we'd hike somewhere. For me, hiking is a break from normal life, which includes school and TV and homework and fighting with your parents about all of the above. Walking in the desert, when you've been living in the desert, is just walking for the sake of walking.

Most days, very few of us felt like "hiking."

But there we were on a trail and not the conceptual Quest Trail that was going to turn us into responsible adults at some point and have us looking back in gratitude at how much we'd grown. A week or so into it for me and Greg. I wouldn't say we were getting "used to it," but the "what the hell's going on" quotient had notched down by half a point on a scale of one to 10 with one being "yeah, mom, whatever" and ten being standing naked in front of the whole school and explaining that your boner is for that girl who's been your friend since 4th grade but you've secretly been imagining naked in your parent's bedroom.

Greg and I were much sticking together, and I was in front of him on the trail, right behind —oh lucky day!—Vera. It says something about a girl if she can look good after sleeping in a tent for most of a month, but it says just as much about the boy behind her being 15 and thinking he could somehow pull off the yellow jumpsuit-and-one-shower-a-week look in some suave and debonair way that would have her falling in love with him at any moment.

I was marching along, a breakfast of cold beanie linguini feeling heavy in my gut, and wondering how to start up a conversation that didn't start with "Hey, Vera," when she looked over my shoulder and said, "Hey, Daniel."

She spun around on her heels mid-stride in this way that looked a bit like she'd studied dance—I had not expected anything so perky—and said to me, "What are you missing about home? You know, right now, first thing that pops into your head."

Obviously, I wasn't going to say the first thing that popped into my head, which I'd be embarrassed to admit was my mom. As tough as I was trying to put on, I missed something solid like a mom to take care of me. I suspected the same of pretty much everybody on the trail but admitting that would be up there on the embarrassment trauma scale with the boner explanation. So I said, "Music."

"Really?" she said. Her backwards prance had slowed Greg and I down and I was sure Pete, who was bringing up the rear to make sure none of us bolted into the cactus to die of thirst, was going to bark at us to step it up. "I miss the tunes too, but not as much as I miss beds and showers. I'm a dainty little thing, you know. So, what are you into?"

This was a test. Which bands you listen to is the college application essay of the teen-to-teen cool calculus. One wrong move and you might as well confess that you still watched Saturday morning cartoons and were upset that Jabberjaw got cancelled. Or that your dad still tied your shoes for you, or you couldn't sleep without your blankie.

If confessed to even a passing interest in the Eagles, she'd be asking if I preferred my denim suede or brushed. A couple of years ago, I might have gotten away with Lynyrd Skynyrd, but the whole southern rock thing ran out of gas about the same time their plane did, and everybody collectively agreed that cowboy hats and weed didn't go together after all. I had every Judas Priest cassette the band had ever whipped up in their dark cauldron of dread, but if I told her that she'd be wondering if I worshipped Satan or guys in tight leather pants, or both.

So I did what most teenage boys do when a teenage girl presents them with an opportunity to show them how cool they were. I showed her how cool I wasn't.

I decided that I needed to throw out something that would make me seem sophisticated, worldly, smart but cool. I put two words together that should never be uttered again in that particular order. I said, "Jazz fusion." Then I made it worse.

"I've really been getting into Jean Luc Ponty lately," I announced. I had this idea while I was saying this that she would picture me at some cocktail lounge, sipping something out of a brandy snifter and not exactly wearing a tuxedo but wearing the sheen of sophistication and maybe worldly sex appeal that a tuxedo would imply, sort of a James Bond but less stuffy.

I don't think that's the image that popped into her head.

Jean Luc Ponty had a violin that he plugged into an amplifier. A neon blue violin. That right there should tell you enough, but he also called his band The Jean Luc Ponty Experience. And he feathered his hair. I mean, everybody feathered their hair in 1980, but you can't call yourself a jazz musician and feather your hair, no way. The album I was sure Vera would hear about and suddenly think I was a worldly man worthy of her lust? A Taste for Passion. Seriously, somebody named an album "A Taste for Passion." I might as well have said something like "My poetry is inspired by the Hardy Boys" or "My mom and I have similar musical tastes."

Until this moment, Vera looked surprisingly graceful and collected walking backward down a rocky trail. She didn't stumble when I said "Jean

Luc Ponty," but there was a momentary stiffness in her step, as though she'd forgotten whatever she'd learned in those dance classes.

Her chin dipped. She wasn't wearing sunglasses. Quest Trail did not allow such obviously necessary desert accouterments. But if she had been, they would have been aviators, dark, not mirrored like cops wear. And they would have slipped down her nose as her eyes, super blue in that moment, drilled into mine like I was being interrogated and I'd accidentally confessed to stealing a blind kid's lunch money.

"Seriously?" she said. I could see her pause, as though she were weighing the value in bringing the rest of the group in on whatever cooler-than-thou screed she was about to unload on me. I'd already figured out she was from California, L.A. probably, without her even saying it. Sometimes you could just tell. And California kids could be mean. Arizona was only 400 something very dry and very boring miles of highway east of L.A., but in the eyes of the California kids, we'd only learned to walk upright and use tools maybe five or six years ago. For them, we were the Ingalls family and as likely to throw a hoedown at the barn raising as we were to know about the coolest new music.

But somewhere in her pause, I saw something else: a softness in her eyes that hinted of mercy. She'd had a whole social takedown scripted and thought better of it. I knew in that instant, the way she turned her head, the way she brought her eyes around, that I would walk away intact, maybe limping, maybe bleeding, but largely intact. She dropped her voice. Whatever takedown I was to endure would be more or less private. We were walking through what qualifies as a "dense" stretch of desert, the path winding between mesquite trees and spiky sprouts of yucca plants. It was almost like we were alone. I'd already figured out that I was destined for a pummeling, but I was also excited because I was having a moment with this beautiful girl, my infatuation with who was crippling.

"So," she said, and she wrinkled her brow in this way that, like everything about her, made me want to spend the rest of that day and every day with her, "you're a jazz man. Are you sipping martinis in the clubs while you listen to Jean Luc riffing some tasty licks? Did they make you take off your beret and shave your goatee when they scooped you off to Quest Trail?"

I wanted to get mad, but she had that smile. I wanted to have an answer. But I didn't.

"Do girls in your school fall for this jazz-fusion-lo-vin'-sophisticated-man-of-the-world bullshit?" I was suddenly a little more ready to get mad. "I mean, nobody actually likes jazz fusion. It's like listening to a bunch of band geeks masturbating. People pretend to like it because they think it makes them look cool."

"That's rough," I said, feeling proud of myself for keeping eye contact and also very impressed that she was walking backward on a winding trail without even looking over her shoulder. It would have been easy for me to look to the side, to crawl out of the laser beam eye lock. But she was practically daring me to flinch. "Who made you the expert on music? Jazz in particular?"

The corners of her mouth twitched with the suggestion of mischief. She added a dance-like hop to her step.

"My dad," she said. "That's who."

8

Growing up on the east side of Tucson didn't leave a lot of room for envy. I'm not saying we were inner city kids or wearing pants we stole off the clothesline from the one-notch-up trailer park next door. It's just that everybody was pretty much in the same economic boat. Three-bedroom house and a Dodge in the carport was standard from all I could see. Some kids had pools in the backyard, which granted you movie-star status in the everybody-wants-to-be-your-friend social stratum, but nobody had mansions. The world was laid out as a flat plain of modest ambition and more-modest accomplishment punctuated by the occasional RV. It wasn't haves and have nots. It was have-somes and have-sames.

And every bit as dull as that sounds.

Then I met Vera and I suddenly knew what envy meant.

On that trail, with Vera walking backward as though she were a forest sprite gliding over the rocks with preternatural nature goddess abilities, I got to hear about growing up two blocks off Venice Beach with a dad who worked with rock stars and a Triumph TR7 waiting in storage for when your desert exile adventure was over. They had a maid. They had a gardener. She had a French tutor who was actually from France.

She went to a private school with movie stars' kids and a few actual movie stars (she'd been invited to Jodie Foster's birthday party in 5th grade). She'd been to Europe three times.

And she was more bored, lost and lonely than any kid I'd ever known.

If she'd been a boy, or even a little less attractive, I could have hated her, but she wasn't a boy, or unattractive. She was Vera. And as miserable as she struggled to be, she was the most intriguing, glamorous, and flat-out most incredible human being I had ever met.

I knew the "most incredible" part from the first seconds of our first encounter and her "Welcome to Quest Fail" greeting. The full depth of her coolness was revealed over maybe two miles of trail before Pete, who was on stragglers-and-escapees watch at the back our march got impatient. Greg stayed politely out of eavesdropping range but I'm sure he heard parts of it.

Because he quizzed me about it later.

"So," he said, back at the camp during "free time," which meant the almost too-many hours when the PTG wasn't trying out new growthtivities on us and we were supposed to entertain ourselves in the middle of the desert. "Was she dropped off at school in a gilded chariot pulled by Muppets? Was David Cassidy her prom date? Is she, in any way, bionic?"

I looked at him with that "Ok, enough" look that I probably learned from my mom. "She's not a spoiled bitch, if that's what you're getting at," I said. "She's, you know, California."

"California," in some instances was the kind of insult the insulter hands out and everybody knows they'd trade places with the insultee in an instant.

"I think her life is generally unavailable outside of a few specific zip codes," I said. I knew Greg could tell I was straining for the sarcasm. Admitting I was smitten/crushing/fascinated/infatuated/hopelessly in love would have been redundant. Every guy in the program had signed up for the Vera Adoration Society, but I think Greg knew I was gunning for president, treasurer and chief obsession officer. "She's the most interesting girl I've ever met," I told him. I'd surrendered sarcasm for sincerity, a rare dish to be served between teenage boys.

"'Interesting' is not the word I was expecting," Greg said, quickly pushing sincerity off the plate. "When will you be running off together to start over in some small desert town where the glow of your love will bring the community together?"

It was the first time "running off" had been spoken aloud since the PTG had run through the "top 50 ways you're screwed out here" routine. I had to figure we were all thinking it but when Greg said it, I suddenly remembered Vera's "two-time loser" introduction in our first Circle Up and put it together that Ron staked his tent out practically on top of hers. I had to wonder how she'd left the first time. Greg didn't know what I was thinking, but he saw me lost in thought.

"Daniel?" he said. "Are you having a moment of profound insight? Should I go get the PTG?"

He was standing over me and I swatted at the cuff of his coveralls. "Dude," I said. "Why are you riding me like this? She's just a girl and I was just talking to her."

I thought I'd signaled that our conversation was either done or overdue for a change of subject, but I didn't have to wait for his acquiescence. It was somebody else's conversation that ended ours.

"That fucking fucker" were the words that stood out. That the words came out of Sarah's mouth was no surprise. Sarah used "fuck" the way other people use commas.

She sounded closer than she was, standing about 50 feet from us, but words like "fuck" have a way of catching the ear and cutting the distance in that "Oh, something interesting is happening!" way.

Greg and I exchanged a look that was equal parts "what now?" and "this is going to be cool" and I got up to walk over. Sarah was standing with Ivan, their volume had dropped and she was leaning toward him in a way that looked kind of like she was concerned and kind of like she was interrogating him.

"So, what did he say then?" she asked.

Ivan looked down and to the side in an obvious "Shit! What have I done?" slump. "He said it'd be a 'great winnergy' if I dug the latrine and he watched," Ivan said. "He said he needed to 'master the art of sharing the burden.' It was full-on PTG bullshit."

"And what did you do?" Sarah said, slipping into full interrogation mode. Ivan practically bowed his head. "I dug the goddamn hole," he said.

"Christ," she said, "like the Three Stooges weren't enough. We needed a mid-level management asshole." I knew who the Three Stooges were. That's what we called Ron, Pete and the PTG. "Mid-level management asshole" was an easy guess.

Ivan's body language bordered on cowering at this point. Sarah looked about 11 inches taller than she normally stood. I wouldn't say righteous indignation looked good on her, but it did wonders for her posture.

"You're going to let Troy bully you out here?" she said. "Dude, you've never been in a better place to call out a bully. Troy doesn't have a gang. Troy has Troy. And for all you know, the PTG would give you a smiley face on your diploma and a helicopter ride home for standing up for yourself."

They were both quiet for a moment. I wasn't sure if Greg and I were supposed to participate in the discussion or act as referees. We didn't have time to figure it out because Vera appeared almost out of nowhere—her ear was as tuned for "fuck" as anybody's—and, like she usually did, she took charge.

"So, catch me up here," she began. She'd stepped, basically, into the center of the group. If there'd been a talking stick—which the PTG must have left at home because I was downright shocked I hadn't seen one yet—she would have been holding it up like a torch. "You and Troy get sent on shovel duty and Troy decides he's management and you're labor? And you accepted that contract?"

If Ivan was wilting in front of Sarah, he was full-on evaporating in front of Vera. I'd gotten the picture, in the first 5 seconds of meeting him, that Ivan was not a guy who spent a lot of time talking to attractive girls. One out of every three guys I knew had put the Farrah Fawcett poster up in their room at some point, the one with the "NIPPLES! I can see her nipples!" swimsuit. I imagined Ivan was too shy to make eye contact with the poster. He certainly wasn't the kind of guy who was ready to explain himself to an attractive girl, or even start to defend himself.

"I don't know," he said. "He said I should do it and so I did it. It just seemed easier."

"Yeah," Vera said. "Easier for Troy maybe. How did you end up out here, Ivan? Did you forget to write a thank you note to the kid who stole your lunch money? Did you see an old lady crossing the street and not help her? I'm not getting a big rule breaker vibe out of you."

We all knew why Ivan was there. Greg and I had already heard his wintention to stay off drugs 70 or 80 times, but I never got a real idea what kind of drug problem he had. I never imagined him stealing TVs to support his smack habit, but I had to hope that it was something a little more severe than his mom finding his sister's weed in his closet. I didn't even know what drugs kids in the DC suburbs did. I assumed it was weed, but he was East Coast, and they could have a whole different set of drugs back there. Arizona had peyote and they had, I don't know, psychedelic ivy, something colonial, and full-on stoney.

The fact that Ivan had repeatedly shared his win-tention didn't stop him from unwrapping it again. "I have a drug problem," he said, like it was a big confession, and we were supposed to admire his honesty. "I stole money from my college fund and spent it on drugs."

"And did you *do* any of these drugs?" Vera asked. "Or did you share them with friends, friends who showed you how to get the money out of your bank account."

Ivan didn't answer, finding a sudden interest in the rocks at his feet. All of us slumped a little, all of us but Vera.

"Look," she said, "that doesn't matter out here. The PTG is more full of shit than any latrine Troy can get you to dig, but like he says." She dropped into a dopey earnest. "Every step on the Quest Trail is a step in a new direction. I think the direction we need to take runs right over Troy's ass."

Vera had an edge. Some kids are the playground police, doling out justice by ratting out the offend-ers. Other kids preside over the sandbox scuffles as the benevolent judiciary, defusing the discord with wisecrack from their "Do you want to spend the rest of your life at the loser table?" quiver. Vera was of the latter. She wielded charisma like a billy-club.

She swept her eyes across the four of us as a little "you know I'm in charge, right?" check-in. We didn't even need to nod.

But Greg spoke up. "Do we need to give this little mission a name? Operation Condor? I like the idea of a name." Greg was taller than the rest of us by a few inches, even with Sarah's righteous indignation stature. If you'd looked at us from the other side of the camp, you might have thought he was in charge. But he was perfectly happy in the role of comic relief and like always, he was dead-on right. He'd diverted this off the bitter-revenge track and onto a circuit that could involve hilarious hijinks and certainly nothing violent, less Death Wish and more The Parent Trap. "What about Operation Space Force X?"

Most people took a while to figure Greg out. I got the picture that Vera's first assessment had been straight-up correct, and she was merely marveling at the manifestation of that. "Greg's right," she said, adding a dash of deviousness to the growing grin. "Welcome to Operation Troy's A Dick," she said, not waiting for our approval. "TAD for short."

Sarah had stepped back. Ivan looked like he wanted to say something, but he often looked like he wanted to say something, as though he were forever paralyzed in a hesitation loop. Some people are quiet because they have nothing to say. Ivan, I'd already surmised, was quiet because he was afraid to say it. I knew that because I'd spent my own share of time perched on that same uneasy precipice, mentally revising speeches I'd never give and watching snappy comebacks doomed by hesitancy. In the eye of the Jackie storm, there was not a lot of room for my voice. If there was a break in the action, it came after somebody slammed a door and stormed out.

But in that a moment of silence with the five of us standing between the tents and a pair of mesquite trees, I skipped the hesitation part. "Before we go into full caper mode on this," I began, "we need to decide how public TAD needs to go. Is this a more private, 'Hey Troy, we're on to you, watch your back' thing or is this pants down during circle work?" I scanned their faces for a reaction.

Ivan finally spoke. "I don't know, guys," he said. "I don't want to make a big deal of this. I've got enough problems."

Vera would have none of it.

"Look," she said. "You go to PTG and Ron and you do the resolution dance with Troy and he apologizes and shuffles his feet during circle up and then you wake up with real scorpions in your boots every morning. You may get a golden ticket home and the PTG will call it courage, but you'll know, for the rest of your life, that Troy got it over on you."

She'd been twirling the bead on the end of the leather cord with her right hand. She looped it wide and brought it to a stop in her left palm to punctuate a dramatic silence. "Or you can take him down in front of everybody and know what really standing up for yourself feels like. It may be the desert, but the law of the jungle is in effect."

I didn't let myself get too excited by the promise of jungle justice. I'd seen any number of revenge vows that seldom became more elaborate than "DORK!" scrawled in magic marker on somebody's locker. The real law of the jungle told us that Ivan would be supplying Troy with lunch money well into his 20s. High-school Darwinism dictated that everybody would evolve into their own niche. Guys like Troy made sure that kids like Ivan got shoved into the chess club niche and stayed there.

Still, with Vera at the wheel, this little vehicle of vengeance had possibilities.

There was a sequence of nods around the circle and we broke up for lunch and PTG time.

9

Troy had seen us talking and eyed us semi-warily as we approached the kitchen for lunch, which would likely begin with a circle up and end with more peanut butter and apples. If we were lucky, it'd be peanut butter and crackers, with the crackers supplying a break from the routine, but it was a reasonable assumption that there'd be peanut butter. I imagined a peanut butter tanker backing up to Quest Trail HQ and pouring a whole mess of into some vat that Ron would stir with a backhoe. My guess is the average Quest Fail grad takes three or more years to even think about eating peanut butter again.

If it had been just Ivan and maybe me and Greg, and it had been some other bully of more substantial physical stature, there might be some chest-puffing and posturing at this point, but Troy saw Vera and turned his body half away from us, not facing us but not exactly looking away either, as though he knew something was up and he wanted to know more without looking like he wanted to know more. For a guy like Troy, too small to pull off inherently tough, the comings and goings of people like Ivan, or me, couldn't register on the barometer of badass he was desperately looking to cultivate. An ill-timed glance could crack the entire cool/tough façade.

Of course, I am speaking pure behind-his-back bullshit. In the moment, there was no way I was going to strut up to him and announce, "You're just trying to look tough." In real life, that would be followed immediately by "But please don't hit me." My record with playground bouts ends with shoving Roger Tills off the monkey bars in third grade. He kicked me in the balls, and I spent the rest of the afternoon in the nurse's office moaning and clutching my stomach like I'd taken shrapnel. That's my core level of toughness.

And something that there was no way I'd let Vera see.

She was giving Troy the "your number's up, buddy" glare-down. Girls can get away with stuff like that and girls who look like Vera can really get away with it. Ron and the PTG only thought they were in charge. She added a little nostril flare to her stare that had Troy fighting a full-on flinch.

"Ok, friends," the PTG announced. I could see his ponytail lift slightly like a half erection every time he said "friends." "Let's circle up!"

We shuffled into something less than a circle and more like a drooping oval. Vera had her feet at shoulder width and her chin up. Troy was alternating between kicking at a tangle of small sticks and grass and looking past all of us as though he were scouting for game, or a rescue party. The PTG found a rock big enough to stand on but not wide enough to give him a solid perch, forcing him to constantly adjust his stance to stay balanced. It didn't give him the air of authority he was very visibly looking for.

"Today we are going to do something a little different," he told us. We sighed in unison. "Something different" was PTG speak for "Something really stupid and possibly embarrassing." "I want to talk about what we expect to find in ourselves when we leave the trail. It can be a confusing time for a lot of us. We learn so much out here that it's hard to pack it all into our rucksack and take with us."

The first thing I focused on in that was the word "rucksack." I had this thought that it would go well with my "dungarees" and I wondered if the PTG had a secret cowboy fantasy and was dreaming up a self-empowering exercise in which we'd learn to rope tree stumps as a way of "forging connections." He'd probably already ordered cowboy hats.

The sack at his feet did have a bit of a pioneer chic look to it, all canvas with some leather straps. I could imagine, the PTG hanging it on a wooden peg in the bunkhouse before getting gussied up for the hoe-down down at the Self-Empowerment Saloon. "Today," he announced, in that classic upbeat PTG tone that made me want to strangle kittens, "we are going to draw treasure maps. That's what we're all looking for out here, treasure, the treasure of strength and self-knowledge."

Ok, so it was even stupider than I'd anticipated and that's no small accomplishment coming from the PTG, the guy who'd once decided it was a good idea to blindfold us so we could "open our senses to the natural world" and then spent 20 minutes pulling cactus out of Tony's butt after he'd wandered into a cholla-choked ditch opening his senses to "Ow! Oh fuck! Ow!"

Nobody said anything. We didn't need to roll our eyes or exchange "really?" glances. There was a communal acceptance that this was a new low that didn't require acknowledgment, verbal or otherwise.

"We know life is a journey," the PTG went on. "And journeys have destinations. I want to see yours on the maps you will create." He held out a handful of charcoal pencils. It wasn't just going to be stupid, it was going to be messy. I could instantly imagine all of us smudge-faced like we'd been auditioning for the part of the somber raccoon in a woodland creatures' production of Our Town.

"I've taken the liberty," the PTG went on, "of drawing a map of my own journey." He rolled out a piece of paper on a flat patch of sand and beckoned us over. We all recognized the genre. There used to be a comic strip called Family Circus that was about some especially middle-class family in some especially middle-class suburb that had especially middle-class suburban problems like melted ice cream and missing socks—the sort of comic strip that other comic strips were embarrassed to share a page with.

The PTG's treasure map looked like one of the strips where baby PJ wanders through the neighborhood swinging from clotheslines and playing jacks with the neighbor kids as though he'd embarked on some Homerian epic and there was a chuckle-warming adventure behind every hedge. The PTG's artistry lacked the clean lines and gleaming colors of Family Circus. It was charcoal, after all. But we could see his journey dash-marked from a Wisconsin childhood with stick-figure parents and five siblings, through a few summers as church camp counselor and then on to an unnamed liberal arts college where he apparently majored in figuring out that a ponytail and a guitar could distract chicks from the fact that he was just some upper Midwest guy raised on canned green beans. At some point, he had an epiphany. At first, it looked like his moment of clarity came to him at a McDonald's, but it turned out they were mountains and not the golden arches.

Like I said, charcoal.

The whole time the PTG was taking us on this tour of his personal hero's journey, he was smiling like we were going to want to postpone college to retrace his steps and pointing with pride at his artistry which was half-assed to begin with and then got smudged. And I was thinking what the hell I could draw that wasn't school and huddling around the TV to escape the broilerscape that is Tucson when Vera used a stick to poke at the PTG's scrawl and said, "I thought you said these would be treasure maps. Where's the treasure? All I see is a white boy getting whiter."

It was rare that we saw the PTG knocked off his love-and-warmth groove, but Vera had obviously picked at something that, if I were inclined to mock the PTG parlance—and I am!—I would label a "soul scab," something deep and hard to look at that you know is there but you don't want to talk about, not even with yourself. Everybody picks at their scabs We think by picking at them, they'll go away, which in the case of actual scabs eventually works but if the scabs are more emotional, soul scabs, picking at them keeps them all gooey and gross. The PTG was trying to pretend that he was somehow more than just the second smallest stick figure in the stick-figure troop, He had a boring safe childhood and was trying to convince himself that a boring safe childhood had somehow prepared him to help kids whose childhoods were not so squeaky suburban clean.

And Vera had rolled up his treasure map and swatted him across the face with it.

"When you say treasure map," Vera said, still holding onto the saguaro rib, "it means there's something to find, something to dig through. I don't think you had to dig any deeper than some book your psych professor handed you."

The PTG had been crouched down over the sheet of paper and he stood up quickly with his shoulders jutted back. He dropped the stick he'd been using to point out his smudged "journey" without looking to see where it landed. I saw his eyes trace a pattern around the group, avoiding Vera until his gaze finally settled on hers. "Vera," he said, "every journey begins with a single step. Sometimes that step takes you forward. Sometimes that step takes you back. Both of us have followed a succession of steps that brought us together on this patch of sand, in this desert."

It sounded like another PTG-line or some happy-ass self-esteem talk on a motivational poster in your high school counselor's office, but the group was quiet as the PTG explained this, because, well, it made us think. Sure, the PTG had a Family Circle childhood but the decisions he made and the decisions we made brought us to the same place. Except, he's not wearing a yellow jumpsuit and he's getting paid, which is a pretty major difference. With a couple of lines that weren't rehearsed, sort of forced out of him by Vera's confrontation, he managed to make the whole stupid exercise make sense.

I was a little surprised, maybe more than a little, when Vera went quiet and she took the paper and charcoal stick from the PTG without offering even a shrug. We followed her resignation to the inevitable and illegible and a few minutes later, I was sitting on a flat rock with a piece of paper rolled out and charcoal all over my yellow jumpsuit.

Some days in the desert, there are just enough clouds to tame the worst of the glare. It was still bright, really bright, but I could at least look at the paper without squinting. I leaned over my cartoon cartography, starting the map at the hospital where I was born and trying to make it look like a hospital without writing "HOSPITAL" in big letters when a shadow fell across the glare.

I looked up and Vera was standing over me. It was one of those dramatic silhouette shots with the sun lighting up her golden hair like she was some radiant Middle Earth elf goddess, and her eyes were even bluer than normal. If I sound like a sappy smitten teenage boy, it's because in that moment I'd never been more sappy or smitten. I wanted to abandon my map and sketch out this vision of foxiness except I knew that my charcoal rendition would look like a stick figure with tits.

"Hey, mapmaker," she said, "got any ideas to make this not suck? I'm thinking of going with 'Here there be dragons' and sailing a galleon to an island full of unicorns. This is some seriously stupid."

In that moment, for a few seconds, I was able to shrug off sappy, smitten and, let's face it, horny teenage self and approach half-ass clever. "Indeed, fair princess, I feel a tale of yore coming on," I said. "Yore is somewhere near Fresno, right?"

She smiled—at me!—in all her elfen gloriousness. "Ah," she said, and she sat down next to me. I almost had to scoot over. She was that close. "Fresno, I have heard tell of this magical realm." She smiled, again! "But I'm thinking my map starts in Venice and kind of stays in Venice until I'm pulled into the underworld by the PTG and his dark horde."

"No enchanted forest?" I asked.

"Nope," she said, "unless you count Pacific Plaza mall, and some of my friends would totally count that, drawn as they were to the mysterious kingdom of Contempo Casuals."

Ok, so every girl in my school was all about Contempo Casuals—our yearbook was like a catalog for high-waisted denim and crop tops—and Vera was mocking it like it was somewhere my mom would shop. I knew that California kids were ahead of the curve, but she was ahead of the California curve. She was so cool it hurt.

I tried to speak as though I were not in awe. "Yes,"

I said. "The legend is known far and wide. But now I must draw my own tale of woe."

She spread out her sheet of paper. I decided that saguaro cactus were easy to draw in charcoal. So I probably made too many of them and I was too intimidated by her California-ness to draw in my 5th grade trip to Disneyland so I decided to attempt the Grand Canyon, which looked embarrassingly vaginal by the time it was done.

Glancing over at her sheet, I was instantly mortified by my own scrawlings. She'd probably been to summer art camp or maybe her babysitter was an art major because I could actually tell what she was drawing, even in smudgy charcoal. The law office where her dad worked with rock musicians looked like a law office, desks and shelves of books and everything. The Eiffel tower looked like the Eiffel Tower and I could even tell that the Coliseum was the Coliseum.

"Europe, huh?" I asked, instantly aware of how not-European that sounded. Europe seemed a land of castles and sophistication to me, like you should gain IQ points just getting your passport stamped.

"Yeah," she said. "A couple of times. Dad gets to follow pop stars over there." I noticed she said pop stars and not rock stars and I detected some dismissiveness in her tone, as though she were stumbling over music legends on her way to the bathroom every morning and was completely over it.

"My dad took me to Yuma once," I said. "It was divine."

"Europe is cool," she said. "It's also kind of normal, you know? It's people going to work and coming home. They're not sitting in cafes writing literature or painting masterpieces all day. They've got boring people in Europe too."

"It's hard to imagine you hanging with the boring crowd," I said. I'd dropped the feigned indifference and let my smitten self out. I attempted a recovery. "Aren't all your friends celebrities?"

"Even my dad doesn't like his fabulous life all the time. My dad doesn't even like pop music. He'd rather be representing jazz legends instead of rock legends."

"What? I thought jazz was, how did you put it? Band geeks masturbating?"

"Jazz fusion is the jerk-off fest," she said, and she squinted her eyes at me with something I should probably call sarcasm, but I wanted to call flirting. "My dad loves to talk about real jazz. I'm named after a real jazz singer, you know."

"Really? Who?"

"Vera Lee. Don't I look like a golden-throated black woman? Don't you think Vera Lee Buffington is a great jazz name?"

I wasn't sure what I was supposed to say. So I just smiled for a second. She looked right at me. "Get it out," she said. "I know what you're thinking."

She did know what I was thinking, but I wasn't saying it, no way.

"Boff-ington as in 'I'd boff Boffington,' yep, heard that one," she said. The smile was playful but there was a don't-fuck-with-me glint in her eyes. "'Buffy', check. 'I'd like to see Buffington in the Buff', check."

"I bet you have," I said, "but I like your name *Vera*' much."

I was sure she'd heard it before, but she pretended she hadn't. "That one's ok," she said.

I took her reserved approval as an opening. "Now about those non-boring friends," I began.

"Shut up," she said. "If I'd had more boring friends, maybe I'd still be there, and missing all the excitement out here."

"Really?" I said. "Excitement? They don't allow that in Arizona." She looked at me and offered a playful "I noticed" before turning back to her map in progress.

"So, these non-boring friends that got you ditched in the desert with us," I said, even though I was beginning to realize it was time to take "shut up" seriously. "Gang members? Bank robbers? International assassins?"

"Nothing so glamorous," she said. "How about super crappy boyfriend with drug dealer aspirations?"

"Oh," I said. It wasn't like I didn't think there was a boyfriend or boyfriends in her history—not a lot of girls on the convent-to-wilderness therapy track—but boyfriend still was not a word I'd been looking forward to hearing. I attempted a recovery with, "Is there a Quest Trail program for that?"

"I don't know," she said. "I was thinking of something involving a sequence of increasingly ugly and mean girlfriends ending in a trailer park."

"A trailer park in Fresno?"

I got another smile. "Now, about that treasure," she said.

I picked up the charcoal stick and turned back to my map. "I'm still looking for it," I said. "But I think I might be getting closer."

The maps, it turned out, were even more ridiculous than I thought they'd be. And way more ridiculous than the PTG thought they'd be. But I could tell he was searching for nuggets of insight and interpreting our less-than-subtle scoffing as self-discovery. Sarah said her treasure was getting her own room when her dad took half custody of her older brother. Greg found his treasure hidden in the Lost Dutchman's Mine ride at Legend City, an amusement park in Phoenix where decommissioned rides from better amusement parks stop on their way to the junkyard. "I could see my parent's love in how my father gave her the front seat in the ore cart," he said. Troy said his treasure was understanding his need for acceptance and he found it "through motocross," which made about as much sense as Ivan claiming that his cat showed him "the treasure of solitude."

It was sort of like we were standing behind the PTG, making devil horns in the class photo, but he completely didn't get it.

"I thank you for your openness," he told us in his jackass solemnity. "The treasure I found today is in each of you."

Our collective groan was implied. Vera swung the bead on its leather strap over her map as though she was a prospector dowsing for gold. She let the bead rest on a craggy set of mountains, next to a cluster of saguaro cactus drawn so much more artfully than what I'd scrawled on my map, which was mostly a smudgy tour of Arizona at this point.

She looked up from the map, at me.

10

It's not like we were excited about beanie weenies. Nobody, in the whole of history, has ever been excited about beanie weenies. We were excited because the word "linguini" was not on the menu that night. Maybe not "excited," but not prison-chow-line dreary for a change, just the meal-in-a-mug routine. Until Vera's turn, that is.

She waited at the back of the line before walking up to where I was standing over the big aluminum pot filled with beans and dismembered hot dogs. She leaned in close, closer than she really needed to and whispered, "You seen Tad?"

I'm sure I looked puzzled. I didn't have much going on in my head beyond getting the beanie-to-weenie ratio right.

"You know, Tad, project TAD."

I didn't have time to reconfigure my expression so I guess I still looked puzzled because she whispered again, even closer this time, "The Troy's A

Dick thing, you know?"

"What about it?" I said. It's hard to look anything approaching cool with a ladle full of beanie weenies in your hand, but I tried anyway. "Is something going down?"

"Yeah," she said. "Something's *going down*. Wander over past the tents after circle up, tell Greg and Ivan. I'll bring Sarah. Look casual, though, really casual."

"Got it."

I got lucky and Ivan and Greg were sitting together on a tarp that we sometimes called "the veranda." It was only a tarp, but sometimes you get tired of sitting on rocks or right on the ground and a tarp starts to look like a veranda, maybe a patio, but veranda is a lot more fun to say, especially when you say it with your best snob voice.

I plopped down with my steaming mug of beans and meat by-products and looked at both of them. "We've got a meeting for the project," I said.

"Project TAD," Greg immediately chirped up. He did not need to have the intrigue explained. In contrast, Ivan looked like he was pre-regretting whatever it was we were going to do.

Luckily, Greg had enough enthusiasm to cover for Ivan and anybody else who wanted to join our little revenge club. "Do we get to wear that black commando-camo makeup?" he asked. "Can we get some Mission Impossible music and stuff?"

I stopped him before he could offer his humming rendition. "I don't know," I said. "She told me we are supposed to meet after circle up on the other side of the tent. She said act casual."

Greg swept his eyes between Ivan and me. "Casual," he said. "That's my game."

Circle up wasn't particularly lame. Wintentions were not requested, but we did have to share the best thing that happened to us that day. The PTG called those moments "great-itudes." The term did not catch on. Even Ron and Pete couldn't bring themselves to say "great-itudes."

Most of the day's high points involved the culinary duality of beanies and weenies, though Sarah said something about "seeing all of you with charcoal all over your faces."

Right after circle up was always a bit of a slow-motion scramble. We were supposed to brush our teeth and most of us did. There was a rotation through the "latrine," which the rules said was a hole somebody had to dig but was really anything past a big rock that pinched off the ravine to the west. And then we were supposed to be in our tents and according to the PTG "exploring what great-itudes and wintentions there are in your life right now."

So it was a great time for a short conference on Project TAD. We floated past the tents and away from the well-trodden path to the latrine quadrant. We kept it casual. Greg made one little Mission Impossible crouch and that was it.

Vera, as if it would have been anyone else, brought the meeting to order.

"I've got it figured out," she said.

We all leaned in. But Greg wasn't giving up on his caper fantasy.

"Are we going to tunnel our way out?" he asked. "I copped a spoon from the kitchen."

"No, dumbass," Vera replied. I'd never heard "dumbass" used as an affirmation of friendship, and I should admit I still haven't, but she came close. "I've got the Troy take-down figured out. You two know cactus," she said, pointing at me and Greg. "Troy is from Ohio. He knows not to step on pointy things, but he's heard of peyote, right? I heard him talking about some Carlos Costa Mesa dude who was a psychedelic witch doctor or something. He wrote some book about connecting to the ancient wisdom of the desert by getting really high."

She couldn't see it in the darkness, but we were all nodding along.

"Let's say we take a little trip together. We find some cactus that looks like it could be peyote, which is probably any cactus as far as Troy knows."

I thought I could see where she was going, but I needed to know a little more. "And then what?" I asked. "We smoke it or eat it? Or we just get Troy to eat it?"

"We eat it," she said. The "duh!" was silent. "We get Troy to eat it too, and then we all act like it's the most awesome high we ever experienced. He's going to be out-tripping us like he's that Carlos dude and saying stupid bullshit about nature magic and ancient aliens."

I liked what I was hearing.

"Then we tell him it was plain-old cactus and that

he's a fucking wannabe loser."

There was a pause. Sarah was the first to speak. "So let me get this straight. Troy's going to pretend to be tripping? What if he just says 'Hey, it's not working for me?'"

I couldn't see Vera's expression, but I imagined it to be impatient. "I know guys like Troy. I grew up with guys like Troy, tons of 'em," she said. "Troy needs to be the coolest and I'd bet anything being the coolest means being the highest."

Ivan had been quiet this whole time. "Then what?" he asked. "Does he get called out during school assembly? Do we write something nasty in his yearbook?"

This was a less timid Ivan than I'd seen before. Maybe it was the darkness talking.

"Don't worry about that," Vera said. "Like I said, I know guys like Troy. They crumble without their cool and we're taking every last bit of cool he ever had."

The rest of the meeting of Team TAD, which Greg wanted to rename TAD Force One, was generally where/ when, but the duty that got assigned to me and Greg as the "cactus experts" was to find something that could be passed off as peyote. Troy was from Ohio and we doubted he was poring over botanical literature. We could assume the depth of his scientific knowledge was that peyote was "trippy."

The first problem was that we'd have to chow down some of it too. The second problem was that we'd be doing this whole thing with one of those plastic knives. The third problem was obvious: stickers.

The desert, as previously discussed, is trying to kill you, or at least hurt you, and stickers are its first line of attack. There are the big stickers that are pretty obvious and easy to avoid, and then there are these little fuzzy stickers that require laser-guided micro-tweezers to get out.

I looked at Greg the next morning. "You're probably going to tell me there's some perfect cactus like that stupid hummingbird you were talking about that grows only here and this miracle plant tastes like strawberry licorice? Right?"

He looked thoughtful for a moment, like he was working up some nature ranger schtick, and then he said, "Succulents."

Succulents are these gummy little plants and as a desert boy, it's sort of embarrassing to admit, but I'm not really sure that they even count as "cactus." I'm also not sure how they survive in the desert. Every other plant is bristling with stickers like some demonic pincushion and the succulents are sitting there all velvety soft and vulnerable. My assumption has always been that they taste like shit, shit rolled in cough syrup and salt maybe.

Greg came back a few minutes later with a few lumps of green wrapped in a sock.

So, we had that extra layer of gross to deal with.

11

When I heard "nature moments," it sounded to me like going off to take a piss somewhere, but for the PTG, nature moments were a growth-ortunity to "Drop out of your rabbit brain and embrace the teachings of nature's stillness." Yeah, he really said that. We ended up out there for 15 minutes that felt like three hours and then we had to come back together for a circle up with our eyes closed and talk about what we'd experienced sitting on a rock. I wanted to say "my butt was sore and I missed the concept of a couch" but I came up with some "concept of self-love," which I didn't know sounded like jacking off until I'd already said it. I was glad everybody had their eyes closed or they would have seen me blushing and there would have been pointing and laughing.

But it got stupider from there, which distracted everybody from making the masturbation jokes that would have pushed "laughing at Daniel" to the top of everybody's great-itudes lists that night.

Ivan said he watched a trail of ants and appreciated how they all work together. Sarah said it was "the way the wind spoke to the trees." Greg had something about "the echoes of ancient people."

The whole thing was ridiculous and made incredibly so by the expression I imagined on the PTG's face. The asshole was probably having one of those "I've really reached these kids!" rhapsodies when we were all mentally making that jack-off gesture behind our backs.

I know that's a lot of jack-off references in one hike but camping in tents all close to each other does not offer a lot of opportunities for relief. I'm not saying that deprivation of that sort made Vera more attractive—she was already a stone-cold fox—but it didn't make her *less* attractive.

Then she took herself to a Charlie's Angels level of gorgeous by distilling something that was actually profound from the PTG's bullshit profundity. "I got out there on that rock and I sat with myself, not with nature. Nature was only a backdrop. I let my thoughts go," she said. "I looked for my silence there, not with a bunch of cactus. I can have that silence anywhere I want. I don't need a temple of nature to find that."

I kept my eyes closed. I didn't want to find out that the PTG was watching us the whole time. So, I couldn't see the expression on his face, but I can't imagine he was smiling, even though that fucker smiled way too much. What she'd said more or less meshed with what the PTG wanted us to go find, but if you don't need nature, his whole nature-temple

Quest Trail sales pitch starts to sound like some expensive and uncomfortable bullshit. We could have done this back on the couch.

She'd never been more beautiful.

And I had my eyes closed the whole time.

12

One of those sunsets where it looks like the world, or maybe just Phoenix, is ending in a fiery cataclysm did little to distract us from the culinary insult du jour and it was starting to stay hot, so none of us wanted to crawl into sleeping bags. Ron, trying to take over chief love-vibe officer for the PTG, tried to draw us into a "storytelling circle," but got exactly zero of us inspired with his story of how he didn't make the high school football team but still managed to get a girl to go to prom with him as though that were a triumph of the human spirit—conquering adversity with a bitchin' El Camino. The PTG had gone back to the real world for the night, presumably to restock his supply of fake smiles, and after Ron's abbreviated attempt at a "moment of resonance," we were left to our own.

It was the perfect moment for Team TAD to put phase two into action. We'd maneuvered towards Troy's position past the kitchen box in a way that probably looked obvious to everybody but Troy. There was a little light from the lantern over the veranda, and you could see him sitting like the shadows were going to make him look cooler, or tougher. Sarah opened the conversation with a certain eloquence. "Dude," she said.

He looked up. I'm not sure Troy had ever seen a James Dean movie, but he swung his head up in a way that was basically James Dean by way of Fonzie, a sort of half-assed James Dean from a show called *Happy Days*. He didn't say anything. He was too cool to say anything. And he blew the whole James Dean thing by scrunching his eyebrows in this way that was so practiced it looked like he was trying to send a secret message.

"We found something interesting, something trippy," Sarah said. "Something you'd be into."

Here's where the James Dean thing got really stupid, because he tried to look like he was curious but in this TV detective kind of way, so he raised his left eyebrow, which was really a Spock move and you can't be Spock and James Dean at the same time, especially when you've got Fonzie there as the third wheel in the circle up.

Ok, so maybe I was the only person who was seeing it exactly like that, but we were all watching him pretty closely because we were all late-in-the-game realizing that our elaborate skit would require some acting. We had to act like it was real peyote and then we had to act like we were tripping on peyote. I was glad it was dark—there's no way I could have pulled it off by light of day.

"Trippy, you say," came Troy's reply. I couldn't tell who he was trying to be, but it almost sounded like he was talking like he was a hipster poet, but street tough, a street-tough hipster poet, I guess. "Trippy like you've discovered some mystery or enigma, or trippy like something you take at a concert?"

He bracketed "enigma" with these long pauses, sort of like a professor or the narrator on a British documentary. He was all over the affectation map. We weren't going to have to act. We could hand the whole business over to the master thespian: An Evening with Troy Colton dinner theater with your choice of beanie linguini or beanie linguini.

"Something you take," Sarah answered. She'd gone monotone, which made Troy sound even more weird or desperate or desperately weird. "You ever taken peyote?"

We were all staring at him—which is probably a stupid thing to do if you're trying to pull a prank of this magnitude—because this was a crucial moment. If he'd taken peyote before, he'd know what it looked and tasted like. If all he'd done was read a few pages out of that desert witch doctor book, we could pull this off. His tough guy revue evaporated for a moment, as though he had rehearsed a bunch of James Dean/James Dean/Spock reactions and none of them fit with peyote.

"Peyote?"

"Yeah, Troy, peyote," Sarah answered. "Greg knows all the different cactus and he found some today coming back from today's nature be-in thing."

"Right on," Troy said, but he sounded less confident than his words, as though he understood that his whole persona would implode if he showed the slightest hesitation. "I'm in."

The rest of what he had to say was full-on preposterous, made all the more ridiculous by the way Troy pronounced shaman as sham-man. He explained that peyote was a "sacred" plant and should be "honored in the way of the original desert peoples" and for a moment it was like we were in circle up and the PTG was telling us how to do drugs.

We threw in some scheming to make it sound more real. I'd tell Ron and Pete that we were going to try our "nature moments" beneath the "stellar cathedral of the night sky" and we'd meet on the other side of the hill in 15 minutes.

Ok, so my scientific speculation was correct. Succulents, at least the kind that Greg wrapped up in that sock, taste worse than shit. From the first touch of the tongue, I understood how they can survive without the razor wire thorns every other plant uses to take themselves off the javelina buffet. Imagine a shit-flavored gummy bear soaked in bleach and vinegar. For a moment, it felt like we were pulling a prank on ourselves.

Ivan wretched. Sarah presented a combination of profanity that made no sense for anything but this exact situation. Vera kept it simple with "Man, this is foul." And Greg waited till they were done to observe it as "the most delicate aperitif."

But Troy continued to be our guide to the wisdom of the ancient stoners. There were guys who tried to talk about drugs as a "gateway," as if dope made them sophisticated and intellectual, when normal freaks just wanted to get high. Drugs were a "gateway to enlightenment" to these people and Troy played that desert holy man crap hard. "The taste is part of the passage to the mystery. It is recalled in the rituals."

Then, came the awkward part. We couldn't start acting wacky right away. All the psychedelics take time to kick in. They "come on." Luckily, Shaman Troy had advised us we needed to "honor the transition" in "shared silence."

So far, the hardest part of our thespian exercise was not laughing out loud.

We'd already agreed to keep our hallucinations consistent. We'd all say that the stars were spinning across the sky and the cactus was "breathing." I came up with the cactus part. Greg wanted us to all say that we could hear the "music of the celestial beings," but we shitcanned that idea because we didn't think we could keep a straight face.

So we shared the silence and waited.

In the ultimate sign that our plan was going to work, Troy went first.

It wasn't very wisdom of the ancients, but his exclamation came in an obvious "I've been rehearsing" hush.

"Whoa," he said. He let a few seconds go by, as though he were suddenly privy to the inner workings of one of his enigmas. "Did you feel that?"

We hadn't, but Vera decided this was the moment to make her stage debut. "Yeah," she said, drawing out the word, her voice lower than normal.

I had not sought out the drama nerd lifestyle. But it turns out I didn't need to. I was born to this role. "Wow," was my opening bit of eloquence, followed quickly by "Dude," except I stretched it out to "duuuude."

We'd found one of those rare patches of sand and gravel free of anything spiky or jagged and we were all lying on our backs staring up. "Can you see the stars breathing?" I asked. Yeah, I know, the cactus were supposed to be breathing, but this was improv.

Greg joined in. "They're not breathing, man. They're singing." It sounded authentic, I think. Even though I had yet to venture into anything so druggy, Jackie had told me about tripping on mushrooms and even when she was talking about it, she had a dreamy tone.

Sarah dropped in with "everything's so beautiful and electric." I could hear Ivan fighting a giggle with "I can hear the bugs crawling through the earth underneath us," and then he went on with "the planet sings to us as it rolls through the great vacuum," which I have to say was an ambitious soliloquy for the venue.

But mainly the plan was to wait for Troy to strut his sham-man stuff.

We didn't have to wait long.

"Think of this sacred plant as a doorway," he announced. "When you pass through that doorway, you enter the landscape of the profound truth."

It felt like a good moment to stand up and tell Troy that this was all a prank, but he wasn't done yet.

"The colors and beauty and magic around you

right now are always there, but we don't let ourselves see it. We've walled it all off. The doorway of peyote let us through."

He stood and stretched his arms as if he were on some cliff-top pulpit addressing a mass of adoring followers. All he needed was a robe and a staff and he'd be having his Gandalf moment. He was ready to summon the elf kingdom.

"Come," he said. "Follow me."

We got up and trudged after him. Walking in the desert at night is tricky. The cactus and other forms of pointy menace are even more pointy, and more menacing, but I had an idea what he was thinking. Around a knobby hill from our camp, there was a canyon ended in a set of steep rock walls. In Arizona, they called that a box canyon and it was the kind of thing that would show up in old Westerns my mom would watch. Outlaws were always getting trapped in box canyons—the cul-de-sacs of the Old West.

The rock in the one near the camp was sort of hollowed out, creating an overhang that produced weird echoes. The PTG took us there once and had us "talk to ourselves" in "I statements," which quickly turned into "I think we should make a bunch of really crazy hoots and evil laughs and other weird sounds." But I had a thought when Troy started walking that way that was more or less "If I were eating real peyote, that'd be a really trippy place to go."

Along the way, Troy would say stuff like "open your senses to the web of life" and "let the stars guide your heart." If not for the part where we were supposedly taking peyote, it was the kind of nature hippie bullshit that the PTG would say.

I drifted back to Vera. We attempted to communicate with nods and eyebrow flicks but if you think that's not clear in normal circumstances, try it at night. It was already hard not to laugh as Troy guided us through the "journey of the wise man." The nudge/wink stage direction was only making it harder.

We both bit our lips not to laugh and almost stumbled. She grabbed me by the shoulders and pulled me toward her, putting her forehead against my chest. She was fighting the laugh so hard she was shaking. Ordinarily, my inner voice would scream "Dude, she's touching you! The really hot girl is touching you!" But I was fighting not to laugh too. Still, it was this moment we were having together. I swung my arms around to hold her and we both quaked for a moment before she pulled her head away with a deep recovery breath. We weren't biting our lips anymore. We just looked at each other.

But the other kids were getting ahead of us and I was starting to hear the "Dude!" voice in my head. I gave her one of those sideways nods that mean "hey, let's go" and we broke our gaze. Somehow, I wasn't fighting laughing so hard.

We got into the little box canyon and Troy was whispering, except the whispers were echoing in this way that made them louder. And he was saying some crazy shit.

"The vision is the answer," he said. And then he said it like five more times, but in different rhythms and pitches like he was trying to be five different guys.

And it was really hard not to laugh again.

Especially since Greg was joining in the performance.

"The vision is the key to the doorway, right?" he asked. Of all Greg's many false sincerity skits, this one was his Oscar moment. "We cannot open the door without the vision."

Sarah stepped up with her own bit of improv. Singing in this sort of whispered opera voice that created this pattern of sounds bouncing off the cracks and folds in the rock.

If any of this had been true, it might have been profound or magical. The fact that it was bullshit, made it fucking hilarious.

I don't think any of us could have lasted much longer. I could sense the laugh coming from the five of us like a water balloon right before it bursts.

Vera provided the relief.

She interrupted another Troy psycho ramble with clapping. It wasn't applause. It was that slow sad clapping that people do when you really screwed up. The echo off the rock made it really sharp, and kind of jarring.

Troy cut short his speech. I guess we'd never get to use the vision key after all.

"Hey, your holiness," she said, pausing while the last echo of her clapping faded. "I got news for you." She paused again. "That wasn't peyote."

Troy was quiet for several seconds, several of the most uncomfortable seconds I'd ever experienced. I've always imagined his face going white, but I couldn't tell. It was dark.

"It was just some shitty cactus that Daniel and

Greg dug up," Vera said. "You weren't tripping. You were just making a fool of yourself."

Troy didn't get any more out than "But," though he managed to say it twice before Vera cut him off again.

"You see, your holiness, the only doorway we've gone through tonight is the one that's marked 'Troy is a gigantic loser'."

"Oh, yeah?" Troy said, he was trying to pull on a snarl, but when you start and end your reprisal with "Oh, yeah?" you get ranked near the top of the "least effective comebacks of all time" list.

"Yeah," Vera said. "In fact, hell yeah."

I should note that all of this was happening in double stereo because of the echo effect. It wasn't just "hell yeah." it was "hell...hell...yeah...yeah... yeah." You've never really had your ass chewed out until you've had it chewed out in echo stereo warp. It was truly grand.

The last "yeah" echoed off into the night and there came a stretch of silence. I figured this my moment to step up. Vera was obviously in charge, but I saw her look to me for a moment. It was only a flash of a glance—but I got the idea that it was my turn at the podium.

I cleared my throat. That echoed too. Troy leaned against the wall of what became known after that night as the Grotto of Humiliation. He wasn't exactly cowering, but his body language said, "oh shit, what have I done?"

I moved over so I was standing more or less shoulder to shoulder with Vera. "Troy," I said. "We've had enough of your crap. Not only that, we've had enough of the same crap from a whole mess of guys like you and most of them were better at it."

Troy's posture stiffened some as though he were going to stand up and stare me down, but when somebody calls you out on your tough guy act, you can't jump back into it and expect it to work.

"You thought it was working but we were just ignoring it. Then you picked on Ivan and that was when we decided to cut your act short. You will not be renewed for a new season," I said. "Tough Troy has been canceled and will be replaced in the same time slot with 'Troy Does Everybody's Latrine Dig From Now On'."

Vera was smiling at me. I nodded at her.

"And with that," she said, "I turn over the floor to Ivan."

Ivan looked different, like he wasn't searching for an excuse to flinch. His voice was deeper and not in that "I'm going to try to sound like my dad" way. It was still his voice and retained all its nasal resonance. It was just stronger.

"Look, Troy," he said. "There are five of us here who heard you talk about ancient wisdom and profound truth and all five of us know your profound truth is that you're a scared little boy, otherwise you would have said the obvious, which was that it was just some really gross cactus and there was no doorway of perception or web of life or any of your sacred hippie bullpucky."

Ok, so bullpucky was not the best choice of words. It definitely robbed what had been a pretty good speech of some of its thunder. We could forgive bull-pucky in the spirit of the greater good, but if you've got your shining moment on the takedown throne, the last thing you want to do is talk like your weird uncle who sells plumbing supplies in New Jersey but wears a cowboy hat.

I'd really expected Troy to mount a defense, trot out some kind of "I was just fooling on you" line. But this was an ass kicking of historic proportions. He knew he was beaten. You could tell because he wouldn't make eye contact with Ivan. Ivan was not a guy bullies shrink away from like that in most circumstances, pretty much all circumstances, really.

But there was Troy, blinking and looking to the side.

We walked back to the camp in silence. It was like now that it was done, we were all a little embarrassed for Troy. "Landscape of profound truth?" that's cringe-worthy to think about much less talk about.

It was only maybe 300 yards back to camp. I think if Ron had cared, he would have heard the echoes and checked it out, but on the nights when the PTG was off fetching supplies or getting his ponytail tightened, he didn't really give a shit what we were doing.

We could have done real peyote and gotten away with it.

So I was surprised when we turned past the big boulder at the top of the hill and saw Pete sitting on a dishwasher-sized rock with his arms folded across his knees. He saw us before we saw him, which was to be expected when six people are walking through the desert at night. There's only so quiet you can be walking on gravel and stepping around cactus in the dark.

"Nice night for a stroll," Pete declared, and we came to a crunching stop. The awkward silence closed in and the six of us stood looking at him for a few seconds, before he mercifully pierced the awkward silence. "Getting in touch with our celestial essence, were we?"

He paused again. I'd never seen six teenagers so quiet. "Look, I don't care where you've been, but I care how careful you are when you go there. You guys were over there yelling in the bullhorn chamber and Ron would have heard every word if he weren't sacked out like the whiskey-sneaking hog bear he is."

We all nodded along. Troy suddenly wasn't the only one suffering mortal embarrassment. We felt like amateurs, our magnificent accomplishment marred by sloppy execution. But Pete was not there to rub our noses in it. "But you didn't fall off a cliff. You didn't set the desert on fire. I don't have to whip out the snakebite kit and suck the venom out of your ankle. If you go home in one piece, my job is done. I don't care if you buy the PTG's line of shit or not."

We were all quiet for a moment. Pete had been largely a lurker, shuffling a few steps behind Ron and basically being a grown-up-on-call set of adult eyeballs more than anything. But the fact that he said "PTG" told us a couple of things:

He was listening while he was lurking.

He hadn't forgotten what it was like to be a teenager, which was not surprising since he was maybe 24 and had been "between semesters" for a few years.

Vera had done that thing where she was standing

in front of us without ever having stepped in front of us, sort of appearing there, and was obviously in charge. "We're cool with that, Pete," she said. "And we're cool with you being cool with that. Ron's out cold?"

"Yep," Pete said. "He hits the flask hard when Dean's off site. Don't bang any pots and pans and you can slide right in. But I have one question."

"What's that?" Vera asked.

"Do you know where the doorway to the eternal truth is?"

Vera stopped. "Ask Troy," she said.

13

The whole early riser/morning person thing is harder to pull off when you're not crawling into the sleeping bag minutes after sunset, but the PTG wasn't there when we got up. And Ron didn't look eager to rustle us into a circle up. I saw him squinting at the camp stove and coffee pot as though he expected them to leap into action and perform the miracle of percolation without assistance.

He made one announcement—"Seems like a good mornin' for journaling"—and then crawled back into his tent.

And so the morning proceeded, creeping toward the afternoon in a state of truce.

I dusted sand off a corner of the veranda and sat down with my journal. I didn't even bring a pen. Every 40 minutes or so, Ron emerged from his tent and pivoted his gaze across the camp. It didn't matter if I was actually journaling, but it should look like I could have been journaling.

I'd been sitting like that for more than an hour, watching the shadows disappear as the sun crept higher and listening to the way the birds would change their song when a hawk flew overhead, when I had a troubling realization:

I was having a fucking "nature moment."

Through no intention of my own, I had tuned into the world around me and come perilously close to meditating. I'd closed my eyes and reached out with my senses to feel the earth beneath me and the sky above.

I opened them and Vera was sitting across from me.

"Caught you," she said.

"Please, oh, please," I said, blinking at the glare and miming distress. "Don't tell Ron!" It wasn't like your eyes could ever adjust to the desert sun, but even a short blink came with an "It burns! It burns!" reflex when you opened them again. And I'd been grooving into the nature beat with my eyes closed.

"What'ya doin?" she said, in this sing-song voice that was mocking but not mocking me. "Wanna run down to the lake and go canoeing? Maybe drop by the arts and crafts cabin and weave lanyards?"

"Lanyards!" I exclaimed in feigned shock. "What would our spirit guide say if he saw us using plastic cord? Maybe we can weave yucca fibers into yarn and sculpt Gandhi in macramé. Weave the change you want to see in the world!"

I leaned back on my butt for a second, impressed with my cleverness, given that I'd been in the desert Zen zone a moment before.

She laughed. "Oh, my," she said, and she brought her hand across her forehead in pure Southern belle. "My ignorance astounds me."

"But really," I said. "What brings you by during PTG furlough? I almost feel like defacing public property, or maybe carving my enemies list into the rock face, to floss the peace and love gunk out of my brain."

"I get it," she said. "There are moments when my spirit animal needs a break and wants to eat some other spirit animal's young. I just wanted to check in. You were great last night, by the way."

Ok, so I can't always be clever on cue. I could have gone hillbilly, "Aw shucks, ma'am, I'm just doin' my job," but instead, I was the guy who dropped out of banter mode, unable to comprehend that I was getting a compliment from a girl.

"Really?" I said, in all my suave eloquence. "Me?"

"Yes, you, loser," she said. "Sometimes I feel like I need to run the show by myself around here and last night you stepped up. It was like I had a partner."

I'd recovered some. "Don't ya' mean, pardner? That's how we talk, out west," I said, and I added "Missy" with a half note of drawl.

"Shut up. Be real for a minute here. Quest Trail is the epicenter of suckitude, but real shit happens here, real friends happen here."

I was silent for maybe 10 seconds, which felt in the moment like one of the especially long geological epochs. It seemed like that bit of forever because for the whole of it, all 10 seconds, I held her gaze. I don't imagine I'd ever looked at anybody for that long, or at least not in that dreamy locked-eye way since I'd stared up out of the crib. Time stopped.

I spoke slowly when I regained the gift of speech. "I feel that too, sometimes," I said. "A lot of times, really."

"Good," she said. "Ready for a real circle up?"

"I guess so. Is your spirit animal leashed? Muzzled?"

"At this exact moment, my spirit animal is in puppy pile mode. I want to know more about Daniel, not the Daniel navigating the PTG's dopey gratitude obstacle course, the real Daniel. How did Daniel get here? What did Daniel leave behind? Is there a Mrs. Daniel crying over her prom dress at home?"

"I wish," I said, and then I caught myself. "That's not true. I don't wish. My life is complicated."

"Complicated by you, or by somebody else?"

"Complicated by me, probably, but my parents aren't helping and my sister sure as fuck isn't helping."

"Ah, that was one of my theories," she said. "The sins of siblings past."

"Not past enough. She's why I'm here."

"Your sister? Big sister?"

"Yeah," I said. "Her name's Jackie."

I got the feeling Vera had rehearsed this part, which was weird because I'd come to think of her as so complete and self-assured that nothing for her was tentative, that gorgeous and glorious creatures such as her strode the world in utter confidence. When her words slowed, she seemed more real.

And more beautiful than ever, even in the desert glare. She held the leather cord and bead in her right hand, rolling it between her index finger and thumb.

"Sometimes, I think about what it might be like to have a sibling," she said. "When I was younger, I thought it would be all hide-and-seek and playing tag. Now, I think it'd be like having a co-conspirator."

"Clearly, you haven't met Jackie," I said.

"But listen to me," Vera said. She wasn't looking at me, she was looking at the bead. "You may blame your sister for lots of stuff, but you've got a bond with her that kids like me don't get to have. Maybe my dad and I are tighter than you are with your dad, or your mom. It's been the two of us since mom left, basically longer than I can remember. But who else have I got? Who do I get to share secrets and capers with?"

I could have or maybe should have inquired about the mom departure, but I wasn't feeling ready to pull on my PTG magic cloak. I suddenly wished I had a bead to fidget with, or a sibling like the one Vera seemed to be describing. "I don't know," I said. "I don't have any other siblings to compare her to, but she's different, harder."

"Harder for you? Or harder for her?"

"Harder for everybody."

"Let me tell you something, Daniel," Vera said. "It's not easy for any of us."

That quiet thing happened again. It wasn't easier this time, but it was more familiar. She was right. Maybe I thought things were simple for Jackie. There were plenty of times when I thought she had the whole world dialed to her frequency, like she set the standard for cool and the rest of us dog paddled in her wake. I guess I knew that she struggled, if I really thought about it. But it didn't make it easier to like her. You know your cat would probably love to learn to use the toilet, but that doesn't make it fun to clean out the litter box.

"Yeah," I said. "But I don't see her out here processing with the PTG and living the circle-up lifestyle."

"She didn't get that chance," Vera said.

I was stunned, for a moment. None of the many thoughts I'd had about Jackie since I stepped onto The Trail had anything to do with sympathy for her, much less something like "Gee, it'd be super keen if my sis' were here. She'd love this place."

I wasn't sure what to say, so I went with "What do you mean?"

Vera had stopped messing with the bead. She was holding it between her middle finger and thumb and looking through it at me.

"If her life's messed up, and it's messing everybody else's life up, she needs help, maybe not Quest Trail, but help, from somebody. Doesn't sound like she got it from your parents."

"They didn't know what to do," I said. "Nobody did."

"They knew what to do with you, or at least cared enough to try. Maybe it should be you who helps her."

"Me?" I imagined I looked like Neil Armstrong if he'd stepped onto the moon and saw somebody else's footprints all over the place. "Why is it up to me?"

"Are you her brother?"

"Yeah."

"Then it's up to you and anybody else who cares

about her: friends, teachers, random people she only met a few times."

"And how am I supposed to help her from here? Have the PTG send her a notecard inviting her to Circle Up? This is so not her speed. For Jackie, nature is something that happens to other people."

"You could go see her. It's starting to feel like time for a field trip."

I looked surprised before, I probably just looked confused when she said, "field trip."

"Were you listening during the orientation briefing?" I asked. "The part about 'you'll die if you try to hike out' and if you don't die, the drug smugglers will kill you, or the redneck army will string you up for being the godless druggies you are?'"

She looked at me. "C'mon, Daniel." She reached out and punched me in the arm. "They haven't built a jail that will hold me."

I didn't say anything, which she took as an invitation.

"Think about it Daniel," she said. "You've heard the trains, right? That tank we haul water from is filled up by trains. They go real slow at the top of that hill. Sometimes they stop. I've been listening for 'em."

I wasn't really following her logic, but I guess I was nodding because she kept going.

"Hiking," she said, "is for losers."

14

I actually wrote in my journal that day. It ended up as a few pages I immediately imagined hiding under a rock at the bottom of a pit surrounded by barbed wire and Dobermans—the kind of secret crap that you feel like you never should have allowed near paper in case somebody saw it and mailed it to everybody who had the slightest urge to get into your shit. But Vera had poked at something and pen on paper felt a bit like cleaning a wound, or at least dabbing at the wound with Kleenex and a Q-Tip. I felt like I'd gotten sucked into a space I wasn't familiar with, or at least not comfortable with. First, I had my little nature moment with the bird calls and cactus shadows. Then I had a full-on circle-up-for-two with Vera. Then I was journaling. I felt the back of my neck to make sure a ponytail wasn't sprouting.

Everybody had drawn into whatever shade they could scavenge from the mid-afternoon sun. Vera had found a spot in the shade of a rock. I'd looked over and seen her holding her cheek against the coolness of it and remembered doing that on the front porch on hot days when I was little, delighting in the contrast of the cool solid mass against the rippling heat of the air. I think she knew I was watching her but didn't acknowledge it.

I sensed the PTG before I heard him.

I imagined his aura skipping up the trail like a cartoon Billy goat. He couldn't have snuck up on us if he'd tried. You knew when he was getting close. When he walked into the camp and made his super-corny "Friends, I have rejoined the circle of us" pronouncement, we all groaned but we also almost welcomed the diversion. It was sort of like the way you'd almost be ready for school to start again at the end of the summer, something you'd only admit to your closest friends.

His backpack, which you may recall he called a "rucksack" because we were all cattle rustlers and prospectors, bulged a bit. He usually didn't bring much back with him. Food got Jeeped to the trailhead every week and we'd all get the privilege of hauling it the rest of the way. So it wasn't like he was returning from the trading post with provisions. He plopped the rucksack down in the middle of the camp and people were all naturally converging on him without him even having to whistle a circle-up.

"Friends," he announced, the second time he'd used the word in the last 30 seconds. "I return today with gifts." He knelt and unfastened the leather buckles that held the sack closed. I'd already taken a half step back. Normally "gifts" would mean something cool, but PTG's gifts were usually something like a "delightenment" or any number of cheery psycho-babble bullshitisms from his fixation on gratitude.

Basically, I was as prepared to be disappointed as I'd been by the "treasure chest" at the dentist when I was 5 and I ended up going home with a soccer ball keychain. Because, you know, what 5-year-old isn't excited about a fucking keychain?

But it was worse than a keychain. The PTG started pulling out hats. They were basically baseball caps of that cheap kind that companies put logos on, like we're all itching to wear hats advertising Uncle Wally's Roto-Rooter and Septic. Except these hats had our names printed on the front and my first thought was "If the PTG doesn't know our names yet, he must have hit his head on the hike out."

I felt instantly like I did when my parents took me and Jackie to Sea World when I was 6 and mom thought it would make it easier to keep track of us if we both wore Day-Glo green beanies with orange feathers. Jackie and I do an occasional rummage through the family albums and boxes of photos to make sure all evidence has been destroyed. It's the kind of thing that could ruin a kid's life if it fell into the wrong hands.

I looked around the group and my discomfort was shared. Troy squinted at the pile of hats. Greg stepped back suddenly when he saw his name come out of the backpack. Sarah picked up one like she would a dead lizard on a hot sidewalk.

And there was the PTG beaming as if he was ready

to accept a blue ribbon at the science fair.

"Friends," he announced. "We're going to try an experiment. You can all see that these hats have our names on them, but here's the surprise," he said. "You're not going to wear the hat with your name on it. You're going to wear somebody else's name and you won't know what name you're wearing."

We recoiled as though we'd walked in on our parents having sex with our teacher. We didn't know where the PTG wanted his experiment to go, but we were sure it wasn't someplace good. The last time I wore an embarrassing hat, I got to go to Sea World. This time, I'd be stuck in the desert wearing a yellow jumpsuit.

"Now, I want you to all turn facing away from me," the PTG announced. It was not like he was waiting for us to agree with his experiments. It was his maze, and we were his rats. "And close your eyes," he said.

In retrospect, I'm not sure there was anything more than curiosity that compelled us to go along with it. We turned around. We closed our eyes. I could hear the PTG crunching the gravel and dirt as he stepped behind me and pulled the hat onto my head, the bill blocking the sun that glowed red through my eyelids. He stepped to the side and placed a hat on his next test subject, then the next, and then we were commanded to open our eyes.

And we all knew instantly what hat we were wearing.

On Star Trek there was a chess set in Capt. Kirk's quarters that he never played. He was too busy putting the moves on some alien chick to waste time on chess, but it was pretty cool looking with three different levels of board and spaceship pieces—super-genius chess, basically. The PTG's would have been a checkerboard with four squares and two pieces of the same color. He never thought more than one move ahead.

There were seven of us. Three seconds of deduction would tell you whose name was on your hat.

I was Troy. Being Troy wasn't my first choice but it's not like anybody was giving me a first choice.

I looked around the group. Troy was Ivan. Ivan was Tony. Tony was Sarah. I had zero idea what to do with that information.

But Vera was Greg. That was interesting. Greg was Vera. That was weird. You'd think that after a few weeks on the trail, we'd be way past awkward, but we were teenagers. Awkward was a baseline. The hats turned it up to excruciating.

Vera, as always, broke the silence. "Ok, Dr. Dean," she said to the PTG. "What now? You said it was an experiment. Do you put electrodes on our head and show us flashcards?"

The PTG presented his *"no, really, this isn't weird!"* chuckle that he probably learned from his coach at bible-ball camp before announcing "No, Vera, it's simpler than that. We just go on with our day. We treat our friends the way we'd treat the person whose hat they are wearing. It helps us see how other people see us. You get it?"

If we got it, we weren't going to admit it. I mean, it was an interesting idea, but interesting and stupid can occupy the same space on the PTG's dumbed-down chessboard. It was looking that the way we treated each other was to not make eye contact or speak. Everybody was basically daring everybody else to go first and nobody was taking the dare.

The circle broke up in a shuffling silence, like headhunters who'd just heard the chief declare he had room on the mantle for a new head "and not some stranger this time!"

15

In the desert, in June, the sun is an enemy. Shade is a treasured commodity and toward middle afternoon, a bit after the PTG's triumphant return, we were all seeking that commodity in whatever small slice we could find it. There was a boulder with a touch of overhang in a dry stream bed down the hill from the camp, and I knew that if you dug away the top layer of sand, it was a little cooler. I felt like a marsupial rodent making my bed every time I did it, but it became my go-to refuge. Greg came with me. We took our journals, not because we meant to actually write in them but because they felt like an excuse not to talk.

Nobody had said a word since we'd fled the circle, but pared down to the two of us, it felt a few inches closer to "not weird." But only a few.

"So, Troy," Greg said. "Should we round up the gang for a rumble and then get tattoos and shop for switchblades? Maybe we could steal a car."

"I don't know, Vera," I said. "Maybe we could go to the beach with the Surf Tone Twins and then have the servants dress like cats and serve us tea in silver chalices."

We both smiled.

"It doesn't get much more stupid, does it?" I asked.

"Nope," Greg said. "But we could make it more fun."

"How?"

"Let's turn it into theater. Let us strut the boards as the actors of old."

I had assumed the faux peyote performance had satisfied Greg's inner thespian for the season. I was wrong. I didn't know how much acting I had in me, but I was intrigued. The PTG needed to have the hat stunt thrown back in his face and simply sneering might not get our point across.

"So we make up something that Vera and Troy would do?" I asked. "Will there be singing? Sword fights? I didn't bring my sewing kit, so I guess costumes are out of the question."

Greg was quiet for a moment. I saw his eyes move from side to side as though he were mentally rehearsing the skit he was obviously concocting.

"What if we do prom?" he said. "Or not really prom, but Troy asking Vera to prom? That could be hilarious."

"Yeah," I said. "Like Vera would go to prom with Troy, or go to prom at all, really."

"Yeah, but that's just it. He can ask her, and she can say no and then he can try to convince her."

Greg did a tough guy voice that was a little too

musical theater to sound tough. "What light through yonda' windah breaks?" he said.

I didn't attempt an accent, but I went with the idea.

"Ah, it is but the mall and they are having a sale on lip gloss!" I said, injecting a touch of squeal.

We were both quiet for a moment.

"I don't know," I said. "I thought this couldn't be stupider, but you may have actually found a way to peg the stupid meter."

Greg gave me a half smirk. "Ah, c'mon, you're in the desert, five days from a shower. You're wearing yellow coveralls and a dork hat. We might as well see how far stupid can go." He paused. "For science!"

"For science," I nodded. I let the quiet go on for a few minutes, which was something that might have happened basically *never* back home. Teenage boys don't do a lot of quiet time with each other. You could be having a conversation and if you stopped to take a breath, somebody was either interjecting something else to talk about or turning on music or TV. But we sat there for a while, maybe five minutes, without a whisper.

And then Greg took his hat off. "If you weren't Troy and I wasn't Vera, how would you ask her to prom?"

I was already missing the silence. I wanted to make a joke out of it, something like "with chloroform and a rag," or "before or after I win the lottery?" But the preceding five minutes of just sitting there together did not set the stage for verbal hijinks.

So I said what I was thinking. "She wouldn't go to the prom with me. She'd say something like 'isn't it sweet of you to ask,' which is hot-girl-speak for 'nice try, loser.'"

"Why would she think you're a loser?" Greg asked.

"Because all girls think that."

"All girls?" Greg said. Suddenly perky, he picked up his journal as though it were a clipboard and said, "Excuse me, miss, I'm doing a survey and you're the last girl on earth I haven't reached. Do you think Daniel is a loser?"

"Shut up," I said.

"I'm sorry, that's not one of the available answers. Shall I put you down for 'not a loser, maybe just insecure' then?"

"Shut up."

"Seriously, Danny."

I glared.

"Daniel," he said. "What makes you think all girls think you're a loser?"

"Because none of them ever told me I wasn't." I let the sand flow through my fingers and then repeated the process before I spoke. "Because," I said. "Because Jackie is a girl and I saw how she talks about guys, and let me tell you, we're all losers, every last single one of us."

"Well, that will save a lot of time with the survey," Greg said, putting his journal down on a rock. "Instead of asking the 2.3 billion female inhabitants of this planet, I can just talk to Jackie."

"Yeah," I said. "And then ask her why I'm out here instead of her."

"Maybe we need a Jackie hat," he said. He wasn't smiling, which made me uncomfortable.

"Who's doing to wear that one?" I said, in a tone

that I'm sure betrayed my unease.

"I think I'd try it on," Greg said. "I'd tell you to step outside your own head. You think the world is as hard on you as you are on yourself." I felt my eyebrows twitch, but he went on. "Like with us," he said. "We were friends and then we weren't friends. You were making up stuff in your head, not paying attention to what was really going on. And now we're friends again. And you know what? That's ok. That's life. That's life *outside* your head."

"Really?" I asked.

"Really."

"You're right," I said, as I brought my eyes up from their close examination of the sand. "You sound suspiciously PTG, but you're right. And I'm sorry." I let the pause linger for a few seconds. "Inside *and* outside my head."

"Thanks," he said. "I'm glad."

It wasn't really an awkward moment—maybe the "real shit" that Vera talked about could feel ok—but I was still glad when Greg granted a reprieve with his goofy grin. He put the "Vera" hat back on and started in with a girlish voice. "This Jackie girl, she sounds like she can party."

I glared at him, but it was a mock glare, as glares go.

I put on the "Troy" hat. "Yeah, Jackie, I think I remember her," I said, scratching my cheekbone and looking up from my furrowed brow in the same trying-to-look-tough expression I'd seen Troy use a hundred times. "I might have knocked her up or sold her drugs or helped her hold up a liquor store or one of the other 300 things I made up to sound cool."

We were both laughing again, which felt like a huge relief.

"See?" Greg said. "This has possibilities."

16

The sun had pivoted by late afternoon and erased our patch of shade when we returned to a camp-wide case of the silent treatment. People still had their hats on, but they had yet to take on the characters they were supposed to be playing. Two hours into the PTG's psycho-drama production, it was looking like the most boring play ever.

Leave it to Greg to liven things up.

"All the world's a stage and we are but clients of Quest Trail Inc.," Greg announced and did this weird bow while sweeping his right arm wide in this way that looked more like he was closing a performance rather than making an entrance. But it worked.

The show had begun.

"Dudes and dudettes," he announced in a sing-song voice and pitch that sounded nothing like Vera before dropping into a dismissive tone that was pretty dead-on. "What's happening with your lame selves? Somebody die around here? Or, even worse, get a bad haircut or go to school in last year's fashions?"

Greg looked at me. I wished we'd rehearsed this.

"Yeah, man," I said, nodding my head side to side in a way that was part stoner and part movie street thug. It was an exaggerated version of Troy but it was still Troy. "What gives? What's the downer? Nobody's diggin' the jive, my man."

There were a few seconds of silence, but only a few. Vera stood up from the Veranda and rubbed her eyes as if she'd been sleeping. "Yo," she said in the low monotone that had at least the cadence of Greg's Sleepy Giant. "Where are we? What's going on? I think I dozed off. Is it time for Circle Up?"

Greg managed to add a second and third syllable to his name in a voice that was clearly more Jan Brady than Vera "Gre-eh-eg," he said. "Get with it. Let's drive my dad's Porsche up to Malibu and go shopping."

The real Vera glowered a bit here, but the let's-fuck-with-the-PTG Vera came back. "Or we could listen to Pink Floyd backward and make bongs out of coke cans. Maybe we could steal a Playboy from somebody's dad and look at pictures of girls' boobies, as close as we'll get."

Greg could have reacted here, but he smiled. He was getting into this.

The PTG had a notebook like he was making careful observations that would go into his dissertation at some point. He might as well have been wearing a white lab coat. But he still couldn't see that his experiment was lurching toward catastrophe. The rest of the group gathered around the veranda tarp which was starting to feel like a stage. I cringed when Sarah approached. She had her hat swung backward, but I had memorized the names at first glance.

"Hi guys," she mumbled. "It's just me, just Daniel. I'm sorry."

There was no way I moped like that, no fucking way. She kept going. "I have an idea for something fun to do. Let's stare into space and not say anything."

I was getting super annoyed. I looked for Tony, who was already stepping forward as Sarah. "Hey Sarah," I said, remembering I was Troy at the last second. "Have you noticed how uncool these cactus are? I could kick that cactus's ass, but I won't because I'm too cool."

I wasn't looking at Troy, but I could feel him fuming somewhere behind me. I went on. "Let's tell the cactus how bogus they are and then roll our eyes at them because we're too cool."

I could see Tony struggling for a "what would Sarah say?" response. "Yeah, Troy," he said. He didn't even attempt a girl voice. "We could go intimidate them by saying sarcastic things and pretending like we don't care."

It was getting tense and I could tell that the PTG was thinking about taking off the lab coat and doing a time-out. This was going exactly the way I suspected it would go and basically 180 degrees opposite of the emotional breakthrough I'm sure he'd envisioned.

And then I saw Vera walking up to Sarah.

It felt like the world stopped. Vera was always going to be the star of A Drama in Seven Hats and now she was going to talk to "me" as if she were my best friend. I didn't think, even for a second, about being Troy. I cringed as pure Daniel.

"Hey, Daniel," Vera said, she was still using this super low voice that sounded more dopey than it did masculine. "Should we make up another bullshit story about jumping cactus spiders?" She added a clumsy stomp to her walk. "We've got these outsiders right where we want them. I can keep up my shy act until just the right minute, whenever that's going to be."

I was making roughly zero sense of her act.

Then it was Sarah's turn. I was left slack-jawed watching the exchange.

"Greg," she said, to Vera. "Do you think I'll ever get a girlfriend?" She was plugging an occasional squeak into her otherwise monotone interpretation of me. "Do you think I should ask Vera to the mall? I could buy her an Orange Julius. It would be keen!"

Troy saw the perfect moment to make his stage debut. "Yeah," he said, flipping up the visor on his Ivan hat as if we needed to be reminded of his character. He was attempting a nasal twang, I think, but it sounded more like he was a whiny kid, which wasn't far out of character for Ivan but still somehow reminded everybody that Troy could be kind of whiny too. "Or we could go to the arcade and look at girls but not talk to them."

"Or we could talk *about* them, and I could tell all my friends I'd gotten them naked," I said, pulling in a bit of Troy's slack-postured swagger, "and make it sound like I'm a stud when I'm really a poser, about as tough as a glee clubber, and just as cool."

I knew, somewhere between "naked" and "stud," that I'd taken it too far.

Greg didn't think so. "Oh Tro—o-oy," he said, notching his voice even higher and throwing in an extra dose of Vera's beach-girl tone. "Tell us about the time you faced down a street gang by looking tough. Show us how to rumble, will ya?"

So, if you're Troy at this moment, you have a choice between going after the guy who called you a poser and the guy who'd pretended to be the attractive girl calling you a poser. But if guy 2 is 3 inches taller than guy 1, the choice gets easy.

He came right at me.

I saw it coming. There was not much chance to sucker punch anybody in the rough Circle Up we'd naturally congregated into. So, I had maybe a half second to react and I still look back on that half sec-ond as a highlight of my teen existence. I stepped to the right, leaving my left leg planted, and ducked slightly to take Troy's charge on my shoulder, which forced him over my left leg and tumbling into a knot of cholla cactus that we'd all managed to maneuver around for the last few weeks.

I could say he screamed like a girl, but wounded animal would be closer. He tried to get up, but every time he moved, another sticker wedged into some painful point. I stepped back and looked down on the writhing bit of misery I'd wrought and winced along with the rest of the group as Ron and Pete came in and tried to calm him down, which didn't take as long as you might think because every time he moved he made it worse. After a minute or two, he didn't move much.

Ron didn't wait for the PTG to invite him to take

charge. "That's all!" he shouted.

We were happy to oblige.

The next two hours were punctuated with yelps and other loud exclamations of distress from Troy who was taken to Ron's tent for a meticulous and painful de-thorning. He stayed there when Ron emerged and called us together for circle up. We were well into what should have been the dinner hour, but nobody had discussed the menu, or really anything.

The PTG looked about as crestfallen as a perky little chipmunk of a man can look. It was rare to the point of "never" that he would admit defeat or and certainly not the kind of failure that the hat game had produced. If it were an "experiment," as he had proclaimed, the results were negative, to say the least, but for him, it was another "profound insight."

He actually used those words.

"Circle up, friends," he announced, with what I took to be a quiet but deliberately detectable sigh. It didn't seem to matter that we were already in the circle. "Let's talk about our learnings."

None of us wanted to participate. We certainly didn't want to "share" about it. I'd been a little inflated with my masculinity, but that had long since drained away in the echoing "ouch" from Troy's tent.

But then, of course, there was Greg. "I learned," he said, "that I have a lovely falsetto, like morning dew on gossamer strands of hope."

The PTG pulled his eyes away from Greg.

"I will tell you what I learned," he said. Somehow, he had reached into his knapsack of love and was returning to a near semblance of standard PTG. "I learned that each of you has discovered the gift of empathy. We were able to step outside the world and feel compassion for others, to walk in the footsteps and footwear of our friends."

There was a pause. I assume half of us were thinking *footwear? Who the fuck says "footwear"?*

Vera stepped forward to break the rhythm of awkward glances. She let the bead drop from her hand and whipped it in tight circles the way I'd imagine a prison guard swinging his keys as he walks the cell block. She glanced at me with a slight nod that I think only I saw. It seemed like a cue.

I took a big breath and exhaled in this very cartoonish manner and cocked my head to the left, looking dead on at the PTG in such a way that everybody could see and note and maybe gasp inwardly. Ron and Pete were on the outer edges of the circle, as though they did not want to be associated with Hat-pocalypse, but they saw it too.

"Bullshit," I said, and took a breath before continuing. "This was not an experiment. We were not your lab rats. There was no maze with cheese at the end. This was another stupid thing that you came up with so you could sit back and watch the show. It sure as fuck wasn't therapeutic."

I let my words resonate around the circle. The PTG said nothing.

"You're sick, you know?" I said. I had everyone's attention and I held onto it tight. "You're like a kid burning ants with a magnifying glass and the ants are supposed to like it because the ants' parents are paying for it."

This is a little hard to admit – it being my "moment" and all – but I took a glance to my right to see if Vera was watching. I knew she was, but still, I wanted to see it. I wasn't expecting pom poms and a cheerleader outfit, but I wasn't disappointed either. Her eyes were wide. Everybody else was probably in an equal state of "wow!" or at least "really?" But she was my target audience.

I squinted my eyes with all the subtlety of a half-drunk mime and stared the PTG down. I wouldn't say he cowered, but he didn't exactly thump his chest and snarl.

Ron had seen enough.

"Ok, Ok," he said, with the commanding huff of a police sergeant. I sort of expected him to say, "Move along here, nothing to see," but he just said, "Hat's off!" and he said it loudly. I guess he'd seen this crap going downhill because he had a canvas bag open in front of him as he stomped into the middle of Circle Up. Most of us practically rushed to comply.

I held on to the "Troy" hat and kept my glare on the PTG until Ron walked over to me with the bag open. I raised the hat up to shoulder level, held it there for a second, maybe three, and dropped it into the bag.

I took the hush as applause. I stood there for close to a minute like I was backlit on a precipice, maybe a pioneer looking out on a broad golden valley, or a factory worker in a Soviet propaganda poster.

Only I was wearing a yellow Quest Trail jumpsuit with hair that could be best described as "feral." I eventually slumped off with the rest of them.

17

I will say this for beanie linguini: it's filling. I mean that in a couple of ways. Yes, it fills your belly. First in a way that's kind of warm and comfortable and later in a way that makes it best for everybody that we were all in our own tents. But it also fills with you with that general loathing for the sequence of decisions that put you on a tarp with a mug full of beans and noodles.

Beanie linguini brought that all home.

I picked at it. Maybe "stabbed at it" is a better description. And then I looked up to see Vera and her mug settling down across from me.

"That was interesting," she said. She did this thing with the corner of her mouth that implied an eye roll without actually executing the ocular somersault. "I really think we made progress."

I thought for a moment. She was probably right if the progress meant taking the PTG's self-esteem score down 20 or 30 points. He'd made himself scarce immediately after the hats came off and Ron had nudged us through the beans and noodles process.

"Yeah," I said. "I don't know about you, but I can feel the empathy coursing through my veins."

"Nope," she replied. "That's testosterone. You were ten kinds of badass all day."

"What are you talking about?" I was genuinely curious, though I had some ideas.

"Troy, for starters. You'll notice he's not sitting down, won't be for a week. He kicked his own ass and all you had to do was step out of the way. Then there's the PTG. You pulled the macramé rug right out from under him, grabbed his ponytail and gave it a solid yank. The poor sap didn't have a comeback, or anything."

I let her words settle for a moment before replying. It was getting dark, or almost dark, but I could see the last touches of the sunset in her eyes. "Somebody had to say it."

"The only somebody I saw out there was you," she whispered.

The pink and gold disappeared from the sky, her eyes glowed all on their own, blue, electric and locked on mine.

18

The PTG must have communed with celestial beings during the night because when the morning came and we crawled out of our tents, he was eager to share his exuberance. Every morning he made tea while Ron and Pete drank coffee, and this morning he was stirring it so intently that you could hear the metal spoon dinging against his handcrafted earthenware hippie mug all the way across camp.

The rest of us were squinting our way into consciousness and he was tap-tap-tapping a greeting to the glory of the goddamned day.

Greg was 10 steps and 40 seconds ahead of me in the waking up process when I slipped my socks into my desert boots, shaking them for scorpions first, of course. Ivan and Tony were already over by the kitchen feed box. Troy quickly looked away when I glanced at him. Vera's tent was still.

I stretched my arms as I got to my feet and maybe I stood a little straighter than normal as I walked, almost swaggered, over to the kitchen.

"Morning, gentlemen," I nodded to Greg, Ivan and Tony as I reached for my mug and poured in a half scoop of Tang. I made a point of stirring it more quietly than the PTG and his "I still matter, you guys!" mug solo.

"Everybody sleep well?" I asked.

Tony and Ivan let their shoulders slump in unison, but Greg brought on this wistful look. "Like a baby wrapped in the arms of an angel," he said.

"Good," I said. "That's the perfect foundation for generous wintention sharing."

We'd been up for 20 minutes and most of us had chewed our way through apples-and-peanut butter routine when the PTG signaled it was time for the morning's sharings. He was enthusiastic as ever with his Circle Up, as though we'd mutually agreed that the hat-tastrophe had never happened.

"People," he said, which had a slightly more pleading ring to it than "friends." He looked around to see that all of us were assembled. "I think today would be a great day for journaling, but I want to start with a game."

We all shrunk back slightly. *At least he didn't say experiment* was my first thought and I'm sure everybody shared my relief. The PTG went on. "I want us to imagine it as our last day in camp, our last day on the trail."

I think we'd all imagined that and played through all the different ways we could give the whole process the finger. "How would we say goodbye to each other?" he asked. "What would we say we learned?

What would be the last wintention we'd share?"

"I'll go first," he announced, as though there were a chance that somebody else was going to hop up onto the pulpit to offer what wouldn't be much more complicated than flipping off Ron and the PTG and offering a "later, much" to the rest of the group. Vera had said "real shit happens out here" and she was right, but all of us would put that real shit in the rearview mirror in an instant if given the chance.

"My last day would begin with a smile," the PTG declared. "I would breathe the desert air and open my senses to the balance of life forces sharing the land with us."

He was about to go on when we heard Ron clear his throat.

I don't know how he'd snuck up on us—guys of Ron's dimensions don't sneak up on people—but it felt like he'd just appeared. "Campers," he announced, "we need to have a resolution circle."

I didn't know what he meant, but I got it pretty quick that he meant there was a problem, which meant somebody had done something wrong and we were all going to stand around in a circle and make that somebody feel bad about it. But we were going to call it a resolution circle because that meant we were all supposed to learn something from their mistake. I have enough trouble learning from my own mistakes, much less some other asshole's mistakes. I was starting to wonder where the whining-and-lamenting circle was going to convene because I was about ready for a little of both.

We followed Ron back to the kitchen box. The

PTG must have been still smarting from the previous evening's drubbing because he did not object.

Ron banged on the "kitchen" with a piece of saguaro rib (a saguaro rib is exactly what it sounds like) and cleared his throat again. That was his trademark. I guess Quest Trail management didn't allow him to say, "You worthless little brats," so he was left to imply that non-verbally and throat clearing was his way of saying "there's got to be better jobs than this."

"Somebody got into the reward box," he announced, "and that somebody took three packets of Swiss Miss." He looked around the circle like he was a detective about to crack the Case of the Purloined Powder. "The Quest Trail has many forks," he announced. "And I think somebody took the wrong one."

The PTG looked nervous, like he was in the line-up with us. It was almost like he knew that if he didn't stand up now, Ron would be picking on him like he was one of the "clients."

"People," the PTG announced, "is this how we treat each other? You know, they call it friendship because it's like a ship that we're all on and if we're not all rowing together, we're all going to drown."

Sometimes when you hear somebody say something like that, it takes you a few seconds to figure out that it doesn't make any sense. This was not one of those times. For starters, you don't "row" a ship and even if you did, and you stopped rowing, it's not like you're going to drown. I mean, he could have said something like "They call it friendship because even though it has nothing to do with ships, let's party like it is a ship and who cares? It's just some goddamn Swiss Miss!"

But he went on.

"Three packets of hot chocolate mix probably doesn't seem like much of a big deal," he said. For a moment, I thought *He's starting to make sense!* But then he said, "But on Quest Trail, we honor each other with respect, and we share that respect because sharing is respect." And with that, the chance for a normal morning came to an end.

Ron was looking impatient. I mean, he'd signed onto the whole Quest Trail "nature's healing temple" jive, but he was itching to go bad cop on us. I kept waiting for him to clear his throat again, perhaps with a more emphatic grunt. while the PTG was going on about how food is a metaphor for cooperation. That fucker liked "metaphor" so much he didn't care if he used it right. Then he started explaining that it was not a moment for punishment and that all of us doing without the Swiss Miss should be lesson enough. That's when Ron cleared his throat.

"I don't think that's enough," he said. "The learningship can't be complete until this is brought all the way into the open," he said. "Somebody here needs to share a confession before they can share our food." "Our" came out as menacing, like starvation was being added to the therapeutic toolbox. I'm pretty sure that wasn't in the brochure.

He and the PTG were sharing pointed glances, but the rest of us were mostly looking at our feet. Ivan had a little piece of flint he was picking at his fingernails with. Tony was tossing a rock back and forth from one hand to the other. Greg had a rock that was sorta blue, like turquoise, and that he kept saying was turquoise but was absolutely not turquoise. Everybody was doing that "I'd rather be anywhere else right now" thing, except Vera.

Vera was studying Ron and the PTG the way a primatologist would study a troop of baboons. She held the bead pinned between her thumb and the first knuckle of her index finger while she looked from Ron to the PTG and back to Ron, watching their movements and postures. Ron and the PTG were talking to us but they were really confronting each other. At some level, the most important level, it didn't matter to them who took the Swiss Miss. What mattered was who was in charge. I'm sure on the Quest Trail organizational chart, the PTG outranked Ron. But Ron was bigger. And however much temple-of-nature grooviness they'd written into the Quest Trail brochure, bigger still matters.

The moment was descending into a stand-off. I'm sure every other kid there was recognizing the feint-and-snarl dominance ritual from whatever shitty parental dysfunction had earned them a golden ticket to Quest Trail except dad couldn't stomp off to the garage to fix the lawnmower and mom couldn't sulk on the couch to express her smoldering resentment in needlepoint.

Ron was not surrendering the pulpit.

"I think we're past that," he announced. "Somebody broke the rules. And that somebody's going to pay." Pete's smart uncle distraction had cut the floodlights on the Ron vs. PTG grudge match, but Ron was still mad at us. It was sort of like he'd been keeping track of annoyances and slights in his "resentment rucksack" (PTG actually used that one, I did not make it up!) and this was his big chance to unbuckle it and spill the contents all over us. You could hear him pulling on a little bit of a southern accent. Ron was from Minnesota and he was slipping into chain gang boss. "What I see here," he said, "is the need for a good old-fashioned horse whuppin'."

I don't really think that Ron was going to whip us with cactus wrapped in barbed wire, but it was getting scary, as though he was daring one of us to confront him and give him an excuse to throw a punch. Quest Trail had been alternatingly annoying and boring, but now, after the hat debacle and with Ron's frontier justice one-man show, it was getting maybe even dangerous.

Ron had the piece of saguaro rib tucked under his arm like a riding crop as though he was ready to dress down the troops. I unconsciously straightened my jumpsuit. Even Vera looked alarmed. She hadn't stepped out of the circle, but she was near the edge with the rest of us. Whatever resistance the PTG had pretended to offer had evaporated.

Ron stopped in front of Ivan and measured him from nose-to-toes in glare. "Let me see your hands," he barked. Ivan instantly complied and Ron jerked his hands up to eye level, peering at his fingernails as though he were a medical examiner and expected to find DNA evidence that showed Ivan had had his way with the buxom Swiss maiden. He let Ivan's hands fall without comment and turned to Tony.

That's when Greg spoke up. "Hey, Sarge," he said.

Ron looked shocked that anybody would interrupt his performance. He turned and we could hear his boot heels against the gravel. "What's that?" he snapped. I could tell he wanted to add "soldier!" but caught himself.

"I did it," Greg said. I wouldn't say he used a smartass tone but wasn't groveling either. There was an unmistakable element of "check this out" to his demeanor. "I did it," he said. "I'm running a black-market operation, trading with the locals for liquor and weapons."

I saw where this was going. Greg was playing the "I'm Spartacus" card. "Spartacus" was this movie I saw at the drive-in with my parents about a gladiator who leads a gladiator revolt and at the end, he and his gladiator buddies get caught and all confess to being the guy who started it—"I'm Spartacus!"—out of camaraderie. They all get crucified at the end, but I saw little risk of crucifixion coming from Ron. I did not hesitate.

"No," I shouted. "It was me. I'm saving the proof-of-purchase stamps to buy new livers for displaced koala bears. Have mercy. My intentions were of the highest order."

Ron was in permanent nostril flair.

I didn't hand the baton to Vera, but she took it.

"Alas," she said, as though she were standing on the heath or the fjords or somewhere equally poetic and tragic. "It was I. It was I who selfishly deprived my compatriots of their cherished sustenance. Do with me what you will."

I didn't expect Sarah to get involved and then there she was. "Such shame I have brought upon my clan," she wailed. "I will be banished to the outer isles to live out my days outside the comforts of society."

It was almost like a line was forming behind the podium at that point.

Ron's eyes darted between the four of us. He was standing closest to Vera and Sarah. Greg started it and you'd think he'd be a good target, but Ron's gorilla rage wasn't calculating anything more complex than "don't hit a girl." He moved quick, for a big guy. I felt his arms on my shoulders as I simultaneously felt my feet leave the ground.

Sometimes people remember accidents and injuries in slow motion as though you could catch the glint of the fractured glass against the sun as you flew through the windshield.

That's never happened to me. It certainly didn't happen that morning. I was spitting sand out of my teeth before I even knew it was happening. I felt Ron's knee in the middle of my back press my chest into the dirt and then the weight disappeared as he was hauled off by Pete and a trio of "clients" that included Greg.

I rolled onto my back and brought my hand up to block the sun from my eyes. When I opened them, I could see several people standing over for me. One of them was Vera. I reached up with my other hand and plucked away small pebble stuck to my cheek.

I looked right at Vera. "You know," I said, "the road to hell is paved with good wintentions."

Few things are louder than silence when that silence is shared, and we were armpit-deep in it. Pete and the PTG had coaxed Ron away from camp, though we could hear the occasional sub-guttural consternation bouncing off the boulders down the hill. For most of an hour, there were no adults in the camp, and I think we were all a little too shocked for words. As much as we railed against them and talked about them like they were morons, we still looked to them as bedrocks of predictability. They were the closest thing we had to parents out there and Ron had lost his shit over three packs of powdered hot chocolate.

We polished off the whole carton of Swiss Miss, mixed cold because, you know, summer. Troy poured the last three packets out in the dirt to make the point. I thought we should all sport chocolate milk mustaches as black armbands of solidarity, but I shrugged away that idea pretty quick. Peaceful protest is one thing. Dorky protest is another. I sat with Greg and Vera on the veranda, which we'd dragged into the half-ass shade of a mesquite tree.

Vera had her bead and cord. Greg had his "turquoise" pebble. I didn't have anything. So I tugged at a tear in the leather on my desert boots. After a while, it was almost like Vera was daring me to break the quiet gloom. I rehearsed several possibilities. I rejected "So, how about them Cubs" and finally settled on, "Well, that was interesting."

Vera gave me a little bit of a "that's all you've got?" look but slipped back into her earlier scientific observation. "Indeed," she said. "The male of the species is given to sudden acts of aggression when his dominance is threatened."

It was practically a set up for Greg to follow in a scholarly tone. "Such ritual combat is common to all the great apes, even some of the not-so-great apes."

"Yeah, but now what?" I said. That brought the conversation, still in whispers, back into the teenage reality. "Does Ron come back and apologize. Do I spend the rest of my time on the trail looking over my shoulder? Or do we call Morley Safer to hike in with the 60 Minutes camera crew? Because this is bullshit."

"Yeah," Greg said. "I saw a payphone down at the convenience store. What time do you think it is it on the east coast?"

Vera echoed Greg with a shrug, saying, "If we had a phone, we could call the police too, and our parents, and Ron's parents and Quest Trail's parent fucking company." Then she brought her hands together and swung her glance across the camp, from left to right and back. "There's another option," she said.

I knew what the option was, but I asked anyway. "What?"

"We bug out," she said in the most matter-of-fact way for an idea that was not matter of fact in any way. We'd all held the same fantasy in our heads, but we'd all heard the same "peril of death" speech from the PTG. And that fantasy had an inconvenient way of bumping to the "and then, what?" question.

But now we had Morley Safer on our side. We could ride the sympathy express back into our parent's good graces and probably get a car as a gesture of deep and pervasive guilt.

I knew what Vera would say next too, though I hadn't shared her scheme with Greg yet.

"During the day, you hear the train whistle at all kinds of different times," she said. "But at night, there's always one that's maybe three hours after sunset. Everybody's asleep by then. Everybody but me, I guess."

I'd discounted the idea before, but it seemed more attractive now. I said to Greg. "There's an outhouse and a phone box at the top of the pass where we hike to get the water. They're the ones who fill the barrels. They have to stop."

"But I bet they don't all stop," Greg said, addressing a fairly major wrinkle in what I suddenly realized was reaching actually-might-happen proportions. Vera was quick to smooth it out.

"Some of them stop," she said. "But they all slow way down. It's the top of the hill. You can hear it."

I won't say I was entirely convinced. Part of being a teenager is talking about shit you're never going to do as though you're putting on your shoes to go do it, or, if you're Troy, talking about stuff you've never done as though you not only did it but did it in some extra cool way that all the cool kids are talking about and made you a legend on "the street," that street being the food court at the mall in the crappy midwestern town he grew up in.

The whole thing sounded not just crazy, but old-timey crazy. Every time I tried to picture us doing it, the picture in my head was in that yellowed tone that happens to old photographs and people who spend too much time in the sun in Arizona. "Let me get this straight," I said, trying to be both emphatic but also whisper. "We're going to jump on a train, hop a freight like a bunch of hobos and make for the city? Don't we need a banjo or a corncob pipe to do that? Maybe a dog named Bingo?"

Vera took a long look at both of us. "You know you guys are losers, right?" she said. We could do nothing but nod in the affirmative.

"When does this go down?" I said.

"Duh," she said. "Tonight."

I tugged at the tear on my boot a little harder and it started to fray. But I stopped. The last thing I wanted when I was jumping trains was a torn shoe. I didn't know a lot about hobo shoe fashion, but I was guessing traction and stability were considered pluses.

I looked up at both of them. "I'm in," I said. "But I think we need hobo names."

"What if we just call you Daniel?" Vera said.

"I'll take it."

19

Boredom and dread share an uneasy balance. There are moments when you can be so bored that you welcome whatever it is you dread because it's a break from the boredom. When you're driving to see your grandparents and you know it's going to smell like old people there and they're going to complain about "those goddamn hippies" and bring the flesh-burning magnifying glass out on all your mom's insecurities, you're still ready to get there just to get out of the car. This was not one of those moments. Ron could have stayed down the hill for the next 40 years for all I cared. He had no choice but to apologize and let the resolution circle tighten around his neck while he squirmed. From the PTG's point of view, it'd be my moment to show how much progress I'd made and from everybody else's point of view, it'd be my chance to kick dirt in Ron's face and exact a promise of perpetual servitude. I didn't want to do either of those things.

I just wanted to get to grandma's and turn on the TV.

But at some point, it had to happen, and that point was around noon or so, judging from the way the shadow was disappearing under the telephone-pole-sized saguaro that stood over the center of camp. Pete had already walked through camp about 10 minutes before and then trotted back down to where the grown-ups had huddled at the bottom of the hill. I guess he'd reported that we hadn't descended into Lord of the Flies mode and nobody had slung a noose over a tree limb.

The PTG walked about three steps ahead of the other two and was carrying a piece of wood from a dead cholla cactus. When it's dead and all the fleshy cactus parts rot away, cholla leaves behind these honeycomb-looking branches and the PTG had laced the honeycombs with little bits of yarn and stuff. It was the sort of thing my 2nd-grade teacher, who tried to be all modern artsy, would have had us make for Christmas presents for our parents and our parents would have had to smile and wonder how long they'd have to keep it before it could be quietly misplaced into the trash.

He carried it in front of him like he was transporting a holy relic and he was approaching the gates of the temple. "Friends," he said, but without his usual chirpy tone, "let us come to the circle."

I'm not sure which was worse: the perky PTG or the priestly PTG.

We walked toward where he stood with Ron and Pete, more out of curiosity than obligation. Ron's stunt had robbed the grown-ups of some part of their authority. I was spitting sand out of my teeth for 10 minutes, but I'd still "won," if winning were an actual option. "Come to the circle" was far less of a command than "Circle up!" It bordered on request. We convened almost out of habit.

"Friends," said the PTG, still holding his holy cactus as though he were about to present us with an offering, which it turned out to be, at least in his eyes. "I would like to see what happened this morning as a sign of growth, of how we have been able to look into our soul-selves and our actions and see where we might be able to evolve."

He paused and looked around the circle, as though expecting us to stroke our chins like college professors and say something like "indubitably." Ron hadn't looked at me yet. Everybody else was giving me the up-and-down semi-constantly. Everybody but Vera and Greg had gravitated away from my point on the circle.

"I bring this as an offering," said the PTG (I knew it!) "And I hope all of you can accept it as such." I was already picturing it on my mantel. "I propose that each of us hold this token of respect and feel its weight while shedding the weight of our guilt and misgivings about what the day has shown us."

I began to suspect that the PTG was seeing me apologizing to Ron by the end of all this. It was like a ceremony and I was going to rope myself to the cross with barbed wire and duct tape in gratitude for our collective enlightenment.

"What I hope we can share this day," he started.

He was droning. Even he didn't believe this shit, but I didn't see what choice he had besides looking for another preachable moment. His eyes flickered to Ron for a half second. "What I hope we can share is what each of us saw in this, this abyss of self-doubt. I will begin with myself."

He held the stick out in front of him again, as though he were presenting the baby Jesus to the wise men or maybe offering the sacred dagger to the high priest. He closed his eyes in exaggerated solemnity.

"I saw today, in myself, the capacity for fear," he said. "It was fear that held me back. Fear that kept my better angels lashed to the anchor of doubt."

In almost any other situation, such a comment would have inspired the finger-down-the-throat retching pantomime with appropriate sound effects, but there was enough tension to keep us glued to our spots. We watched as the PTG turned and took the two steps to Ron, presenting him with the sacred artifact. Ron accepted it as though the PTG had given him an elephant turd. Ron turned back to the group. He stared at the turd.

"I saw in myself today," he began, "the capacity for anger. Anger controlled my actions, not me." It sounded about as sincere as a kindergarten playground apology. The only thing Ron was really concerned about in that moment was keeping his job. So, he laid it thick, but predictably, in a way that made it sound a lot like it was all our fault. "Anger was a teacher today," he said. "It taught us about the consequences of *our* anger." See? It was my fault. That's the Ron we know and love!

He gave the cholla stick to Pete, holding it in one hand like it was a baton or a flashlight. I could see the PTG's shoulders tighten. Pete went from balancing it on one finger to smacking it in his palm billy club style. I imagined the PTG thinking *How doth he dare*? but Pete didn't have it long. He said something about the "capacity for distraction," which doesn't even make sense in retrospect, much less then. And then he handed it to Tony, who said at low volume, "I saw in myself the capacity for apathy. It wasn't my deal, no way Jose!" Normally the PTG would have dissected that with one of his truth wrenches but I think he was gun shy after hat-pocalypse and the morning scuffle. Ivan said something about "the denial of responsibility," which was obviously designed to give the PTG a spiritual hard-on. Sarah told us about "the capacity for silence," which, we already knew, she had plenty of. Troy started with something similar but then threw in, "I also learned my capacity for Swiss Miss because we killed the whole carton while you three were confabbing down the hill."

And then it came to Vera.

She held the stick up to her eyes and peered down it like it was a telescope, pointing it right at Ron. Then she flipped it as though she was twirling a baton and caught it without looking. "Fuck this shit," she said, and she handed it to Greg.

He gave the stick this casual glance, and brought his eyes up to Ron, who was still intensely interested in something far off in the distance, and said "Ditto" before handing it to me.

I had anticipated a few more minutes of bullshit speeches, but it's not like I hadn't been rehearsing my rant even before the PTG led the holy progression up the hill.

The stick was lighter than I thought it'd be. Cholla wood is more or less the skeleton of the cactus and you see it all over the desert, but it's not something you pick up because under everything in the desert is something else, usually a bug or a snake, waiting to hurt you.

"Today," I said, "I learned about the capacity for humility. But not mine." I looked at Ron. "What I really learned was that things can change pretty quick and you can't always duck the punch. You gotta learn to take it, wherever it lands. And sometimes the punch lands on the guy who threw it. That's when he loses. That's when you beat him."

Everybody was watching me, of course, because it was my turn with the stick. I held it in my right hand and tested its weight like I was chopping with a tomahawk. Then I leaned back onto my right foot and brought it back over my shoulder as though I were going to throw it right at Ron. I stared right at him, but he shifted his eyes to the ground. I turned and whipped it out into the desert, watching it tumble end-over-end through the air and land in a cluster of still-alive and still-sticky cactus 30 feet down the hill.

I bowed in this really dopey way to give close to the dopey ceremony, but Vera was snapping her fingers with her arms raised.

"One more thing," she announced.

She reached into the puffy front pocket on her jumpsuit and brought out three Swiss Miss packets, flicking them out like she was dealing cards to land at the feet of Pete, the PTG and Ron. "Don't forget these."

I didn't know whether to be mad or be in awe.

20

It wasn't a particularly bad dinner. It wasn't the "hobo'ta-toes" I'm loath to even describe, but it wasn't chili dogs either. My guess was that the PTG felt bad for us and decided that taco biscuits were a reasonable peace offering. He'd left us to ourselves for most of the day, though he had offered a half-hearted entreaty that there was "so much to capture in our journals." I spent most of the day sitting with my thoughts and writing none of them down.

Most nights, we had a campfire and it sort of reminded me of watching TV at home because everybody stared at the fire the same way and nobody said anything.

But Ron was the only one with a lighter and he didn't get near the fire pit that night. We were all too happy to avoid anything that included the possibility of additional "sharing." Even the PTG was quiet.

Greg, Vera and I had been casting glances at each other as the light fell. We had a vague idea of when the train was coming, but it's not like we were wearing watches. The first dozen stars were in the sky when people started moving to their tents. I didn't want to look especially eager or anything. I crawled on top of the sleeping bag, zipping up the zipper just for the sound effect. I kept my shoes on.

And then I waited.

There's something about waiting, in the dark, in the desert, that gives you superhuman powers of hearing. I swear I could hear bugs crawling on cactus 20 yards away. Every zipper, every shift and turn in the sleeping bag for the whole camp was amplified to echo level.

It was like I had bionic hearing and I was listening to the most boring shit ever.

But it gave me time to think, something I'd had no shortage of since I made my debut on "the trail."

The first thing I thought of, was something I'd been thinking about all day, was that we didn't really have a plan. I mean, we had a plan to get on the train, but it's not like we had an idea of where the train even went. The whole "get to a pay phone and call Morley" idea was sounding far-fetched a dozen hours later. I mean, to make the TV news I'd need to have lost a limb or an eye or been forced into a cult ritual involving nudity, snakes and body paint. The whole thing with Ron and a mouthful of dirt was starting to look like a playground scuffle.

So, I'm running through all this in my tent, which I'd left open so I didn't trigger an alarm with the noise of the zipper, and I'm up against the good sense of staying and maybe playing the guilt card to get home early or risking a longer stay in some possibly shittier troubled youth program after we inevitably got caught. It's not like Vera and I were going to flee the country and be expatriate artists, drinking wine and wearing berets in Parisian cafes. At some point, we'd be calling our parents from a pay phone outside a Kwik-E-Mart. And it'd be a collect call because it's not like we're walking around with wads of spending cash bulging from the pockets or our oh-so-fashionable-nobody's-going-to-bat-an-eye yellow jumpsuits as we sauntered into our triumphant return to society.

We hadn't thought it through and as I played through an increasingly improbable set of scenarios that included "living off the land," which you basically can't do in Arizona because, as I've already mentioned, everything is trying to kill you, I accomplished the almost equally improbable act of falling asleep.

It must have been around midnight when I felt somebody shoving my shoulder, almost gentle at first and then a little harder until I blinked awake and saw Greg kneeling over me. He held his finger to his lips and stepped back in a crouch, allowing only the slight crunch of sand and rock under his feet.

A few seconds later, I'm standing beside him and I see Vera also holding her finger to her lips. But that's not what I'm looking at. I'm looking at Troy, who is standing out at the edge of the tents in an almost crouch with his head pivoting back and forth like he's gone full commando and suddenly I'm thinking that maybe I should crawl into my sleeping bag for real.

Except I can't because, well, there's Vera. There's

that old saying that "Behind every great man is a great woman," but a lot of the time it's more like "Behind every stupid thing a man did, there was a woman he was sure would think it was cool." Because as soon as Vera said we were doing it, there was zero chance that I wouldn't be involved.

It's not like I'd left all my misgivings in the tent, but I pretended I did. They say dogs can smell fear and that's probably bullshit. But girls? They can smell fear from a mile away.

She nodded in Troy's direction which was more or less the way to where the train was going to be chugging by and Troy does this two-fingered, swirl-and-point motion that I recognized from "The Dirty Dozen" and a bunch of other war movies because that fucker was not letting the commando thing go. Suddenly we weren't making a run for it; we were on patrol. And Troy thought he was leading the mission, which was about the last thing I wanted out of the whole misadventure. I'd been out of the tent for less than a minute and things were already worse than I'd expected.

And I'd expected them to be pretty bad.

I returned Vera's nod and we began this slow-motion creep out of the camp. A few years before, there'd been a show called "Kung Fu" about some mostly white dude who'd been raised in a karate temple. He'd do this thing where he tried to walk across rice paper without tearing it and then he'd know he could walk in complete silence. If we'd been at kung fu school, we would have torn the shit out of that rice paper because we weren't quiet at all. If anybody had been listening, they would have guessed that either half the group was sneaking out of camp or that cattle were lumbering through.

But nobody was listening. Ron and the PTG were confident that their "you'll die if you try to get out of here on your own" orientation was not going to be questioned.

That's why all of us were surprised when we saw Pete 50 yards outside camp.

He was sitting on a flat rock, leaning back on his hands with his legs stretched out in front of him. There was about a half moon which can feel really bright in the desert because there are no trees to block the light and everything's bleached by the sun, which means at night the moon glow is reflected all over the place. And there was Pete, sitting there on a rock as if he were out enjoying the night air. He looked up at us and said: "Nice night for a stroll."

He didn't exactly whisper but he wasn't ringing the alarm bell either. The words sort of hung there and the quiet of the desert wrapped back around us. Nobody had a snappy comeback to "Nice night for a stroll," mainly because we were all trying to make sense of what was happening. This wasn't a "busted!" declaration. Pete knew about our peyote party and never said anything to Ron or the PTG. There'd been no winking or nodding. I kind of forgot that happened, but here he was again. He must have known what we were up to but he didn't look ready to slap on the cuffs and march us back to camp.

He did make sure we were all looking at him while he spoke, exchanging eye contact with each of us, but all he said was what he'd already said. "Nice night for a stroll," but this time he nodded at the four water bottles by his feet. Vera grabbed two and handed one to me. Greg and Troy took the other two.

Vera stood in front of Pete in this way that I can only describe as "formal." Then she bowed to him and he nodded to her.

"Nice night, indeed," she said. She turned and started walking and we followed. Just like that, it was over.

We walked for probably five minutes in silence. All of us had helped carry water from the tank by the train tracks. We knew the way and there was not a lot of need for interaction. And we were all trying to make sense of what Pete might be thinking.

I managed to put myself between Vera and Troy on the trail. She was in front, obviously, and I was close behind. The path weaved through chest-high boulders and we had to slow down. It seemed like the moment for me to make a studied and articulate observation. I'd had time to think about it, after all.

"That was weird," I said.

"What?" she said. "Pete? That's just who he is. Pete's the guy who's going to write the book; you know what I mean? He waits. He watches. The PTG comes up with his games and Pete's diagramming the play as it happens. He probably knew we were leaving before we knew we were leaving."

"So why didn't he stop us? Why didn't he tell Ron and the PTG before we even left?"

"Because he's thinking six moves ahead of everybody else," she said. She stopped and turned to me. "He's figured out we're going to learn a shit ton more out here than we were back there wearing the PTG's party hats."

We kept walking. I could accept that.

The thing about the desert at night is how clean it looks. During the day, it looks pretty drab, dirt, rocks, sticky things. And the stuff that's green is a dusty green. I guess it's beautiful in its way but at night, when there's a moon to light it up, the desert looks sculptural, monochromatic gray, almost like stone, and all the saguaros look like statues marching up the hills. The desert is still trying to hurt you, but it seems a whole lot less threatening at night. Weird though, plenty weird.

As we walked along through this dusty sculpture garden, we got higher up the slopes of the pass where the train cuts through and way the hell off in the distance, we could see the lights of a small town. But here and there, and a lot closer, we could see other lights that were probably houses or ranches and who knows what, but really not that far off. There were days at Quest Trail when it felt like we were really "in the wilderness," which was basically the promise of wilderness therapy, but it turns out we weren't more than a few miles from somebody's house, a few different houses and a few different somebodies.

"Check it out," Greg said. "We've got neighbors." I could tell that Commando Troy was annoyed because Greg was being loud on purpose, which I'm sure was interfering with Troy's Force 10 from Navarone fantasy. So I replied even louder.

"Yeah," I yelled back. "We should really have them over some time. I hope they like beans, and linguini." I had this idea I could turn it into a bit of a Troy standoff. I don't know who he thought we were sneaking up on. How do you sneak up on a train? But I could feel him fuming behind me.

And I knew Vera was listening.

"Maybe we could all go caroling together," I shouted. "It's a fantastic way to build community." Greg replied with "Indeed, my good man," and I dropped into "Deck the halls" for a moment before Vera stopped me with "Ok, Ok. We're getting close." I don't know what I was saying "Ok" to, but I answered in kind. I felt like I'd irked Troy a little and I was still seeing his crash and burn in the cactus patch as a point in my column. I let it go. The thing about a pissing match is that you can piss on your own shoes if you're not careful.

It was dark and I couldn't see if Vera was doing that impatient-girl head nod. But I could feel the situation slipping toward it.

We reached a point where the tracks cut through the rock and it was maybe 20 feet down to the chunky gravel that they pile under the rails. The cut-out blocked the moon, keeping it all in shadow. We'd been walking in bright moonlight until then and it wasn't obvious until we got there that we were going to be jumping onto a train in the dark.

I think we all had that same thought as soon as we got to the top of the cut out. Greg and Troy caught up with us and we all looked down together.

"I don't suppose any of you have ever jumped a train before," Vera said. It was one of the rare times when she didn't seem utterly confident. It was a bit jarring, like her pedestal had a wobble to it.

"I like to think my best freight-hopping days are still in front of me," Greg said. It would have been a good moment for some hobo/hillbilly twang, but instead, he played it droll.

"Anybody have an idea how slow it'll be when it gets here?" Troy asked.

"Anybody bring a flashlight and a grappling hook?" I said.

We stood there, the four of us staring down at the track, and then Vera pointed down the valley, which looked so bright by comparison to the shadowed tracks we were standing over. "Check it out," she said. "One of our neighbors is on the move."

Trains have headlights that sweep side to side as the train rolls down the track. You'd think trains would be easy to avoid. It's not like they make sudden turns or arrive unexpectedly, but I have since learned that a surprising number of people are hit by trains every year. So it makes sense that there'd be a bright-ass light on the front. But when you see a train coming, and you've got the idea you're going to jump onto it, that light flashing back and forth looks ominous and I found myself holding my breath even with train still a mile away. I felt a little bit of Shaggy from Scooby Doo coming on, but I only thought *Yikes!* instead of saying it out loud.

Nobody said, "Let's do this," though that would have been a cool thing to say. We could hear the train getting closer and when we scrambled up the embankment it got louder, the sound trapped by the rock walls where it narrowed next to the water tank at the top of the pass.

I suppose there is a moment in every adventure when the adventurer has to think *what have I gotten myself into*? I imagine Columbus sailing away from Spain and thinking *I could have stayed on the beach and I'd be drinking wine right now and instead I'm out here inventing scurvy.* We were standing there in the half dark getting ready to jump onto a train and I was mentally rehearsing various renditions of "You know, guys…" when it became clear that the train was not stopping for a water drop. Everybody was looking at each other but pretending not to look at each other, waiting for that "I was ready to do it and then you chickened out" opportunity. Then I saw Vera staring down the track to that back-and-forth light that was making the shadows jump from side to side. And she almost looked like she'd done this before.

"We're going to wait for a flat car. They're lower, easier to climb onto." She was shouting a bit because the train was getting louder. "Two of us at the front. Two of us at the back." She pointed at me and I swallow my last "yikes," stepping up next to her while Troy and Greg stood back a few feet.

And then it was there.

It wasn't stopping.

The engines come by, two of them, and the air is thick with sound and the smell of oil. We could hear the engines straining, but the cars were still moving at 10 mph or so, which sounds slow until you think about jumping onto one. Too loud for talk, I feel Vera's hand on my arm, below my elbow. Two tanker cars roll by, then a boxcar. The first flatcar comes by, but it's loaded with big metal boxes. Another three boxcars. The sound changes as the engines roll into the cut-out and it's mostly the clatter and roll of steel wheels on steel rails. Then we see it. A flat car with huge pipes on it. Big chains hold the pipes in place and give us something to grab. Vera squeezes my arm, and we start running before it gets there. She throws the water bottle onto the car first and then just goes for it. I can do nothing but follow her lead. Holding onto the chain, I feel my trailing foot drag the gravel for a few feet and then I'm dangling there for a moment. But I see Vera swing her knee onto the wooden deck. I stop thinking and heave myself up like I'm climbing the monkey bars in grade school. Suddenly, we're rolling along, and it feels amazingly stable.

Vera grabbed my hand. I could feel her shaking against the rumble of the wheels. As we passed out of the narrow spot between the rocks, the moonlight returned. I saw her eyes wide on mine. I should have been looking back to see if Greg and Troy made it, but I couldn't pull away from what felt like one of those moments. Our breaths slowed from big heaves and fell into a rhythm. I wanted to lean in to kiss her. I really did. But then I heard a stupid "whoop!" from behind me and the moment was gone.

"Dude!" Troy shouted.

It wasn't the kind of comment that anybody would describe as eloquent, though it was entirely accurate.

He wasn't really speaking to any of us but instead making a rhetorical statement to the universe. Some moments are "dude!" moments.

More remarkably, he was standing up. For the first minute or so all of us had been more or less clinging to the deck of the flatcar. If there'd been seatbelts, mine would have been cinched up tight. People walk around on trains all the time, but those people aren't standing outside with the air rushing past, in the dark, with their hearts climbing up their windpipes from the rush.

I have to admit I was a little impressed. And I hated him for it.

Vera's hand was still on mine but as she turned to look up at Troy, she drew it away.

"Dude is right!" she said. "We made it, all limbs and appendages accounted for."

My heartbeat was returning to near normal from the machine gun intensity it pounded out moments before. I looked up at the moon-silvered landscape rolling past and I felt the train picking up speed, subtly but persistently. Getting on the train had been a demarcation in my mind, the point where the "now what?" questions started to stack up in earnest. But for that moment, I sat, as the PTG would probably say "in the experience."

On a train, you can't really see where you're going. The rest of the train blocks the view forward. You only see where you are. And that view changes constantly. What we saw was cactus and rocks and the valley where we'd been living for the past few weeks, all of it rolling by as we dropped down the pass. After weeks of living at walking pace, actually a kind of grumbling reluctant shuffling pace, it felt like we were flying when we were really going probably 20 mph as we dropped into the descent.

Vera was still sitting next to me. Troy was off at the other end of the car. I kid you not; Greg was looking drowsy. I'm trying to taper off the adrenaline overload and the sleepy giant looks ready for a nap.

I turned to Vera. "I'm glad we got a window seat," I said.

"Hell, yeah," she said. "I wonder if the dining car is open. We could get a drink."

"I could use one," I said. "That was scary as fuck."

"Indeed," she said. "And nobody chickened out."

"You thought I was going to chicken out?" I asked. I probably looked more upset than I wanted to.

"Shit," she said. "I thought *I* was going to chicken out."

I tilted my head to the side a little bit and brought my hand to chin in mock astonishment. "The mighty Vera chickens out? Say it ain't so."

I should admit that it never really occurred to me that Vera was afraid of anything, like she knew everything and everybody in every situation before she even got there. I had this picture of her showing up in "Star Wars" and saying, "Oh, yeah, you shoot something down the trash chute and the whole thing blows up, easy peasy." I knew a little more about her than I used to. "Real shit" happens in the desert, she'd said, and she was right. But she was still a girl, a beautiful girl and she dripped cool. I was still having a tough time understanding that such creatures experienced fear.

"What?" she said. "I'm a girl, so I have superpow-ers? Or do you think California is a magical realm and I am the daughter of elves?"

For a second, I was tempted to say "actually, kind of, yeah, on both points," because at some level, I probably thought both of those things were almost true. Hell, I still think they're almost true.

"Well," I said, "I've always wanted to meet an elf."

"A Tolkien elf though, right?"

"Right. Not one of those little Keebler fuckers. And certainly not one of those North Pole Santa cultists. I mean, all Hermey wanted to be was a dentist, and a little gay, a gay dentist elf. And he gets thrown out into the polar wasteland with his mutant reindeer companion Rudolph?"

"Right," she said. It was a quick "right," one syl-lable, short, curt. I felt like looking at my shoe to see what I'd stepped in. It was that abrupt a change in the conversational rhythm. She let the pause stretch out against the clatter of the train wheels.

"We were talking about something, weren't we?" she said, scratching her head in this exaggerated way like she was miming somebody thinking and she was worried her audience wouldn't get it, so she mimed even harder.

"We were talking about being scared," I said.

"Yes! You're right!" she began, but then she dropped about 90 points on the 100-point sarcasm scale. "But there's the part we didn't talk about, which is that it's ok to be scared."

It's not like it can "get quiet" on a moving train,

but it got quieter, or at least it felt like I did. "What do you mean?" I asked.

"I mean you don't have to perform for me," she said. "I mean, this is a flatcar, not a stage. Troy's stomping around like it's the circus and you're doing standup."

"But that's how we talk," I said. "We joke around."

"We joke because we want to, though," she said. "Not because we need to. I told you before. Real shit happens out there and jumping on a moving train is about as real as shit can get."

"Pretty much," I said.

"So let's be real with that. Make it ok to say we're scared. Make it ok to just be here."

"Then it's OK to say that we're not sure this is OK, then?"

"Yeah," she said. "Sounds like a book the PTG would have. I'm OK. You're OK. But this shit is not OK."

"Who's doing standup now?"

"You caught me."

With the train going faster, we'd scooted closer together so we wouldn't have to shout over the wind. Our knees were touching and I never in my life thought I could be so aware of one square inch of skin. She'd held my hand a few minutes before, but that was almost a terror reflex. I was sitting there trying to interpret what it meant that she hadn't moved her knee when I scooted toward her.

I was also trying hard not to look over my shoulder to check if Troy was witnessing our knee embrace. It wasn't like I'd even approached first base, but I wanted to think I could see the exit sign for the baseball stadium somewhere in the distance.

I risked what felt, this time, to be a half moment.

"What's he doing here?" I asked, flicking my chin towards my shoulder, but not actually looking over my shoulder. "I didn't know he was on team great escape until I crawled out of the tent."

"Troy?" she said, like there was any chance I was talking about somebody else.

"Yeah, Troy."

"He's the crash-test dummy, the sacrificial lamb. If we get into a situation where we could get caught, we put him out there to take the risk."

I squinted, just a tad. "What makes you think he'd volunteer for the slaughter?"

"Because," she said and she looked right at me with her eyes wide and dropped her chin toward her shoulder. I wouldn't call it a wildly exaggerated seductive glance, but it wasn't subtle either.

It was the first time I'd seen Vera acknowledge that hotness has its privileges. She didn't say it. She didn't need to.

I didn't say anything for a few seconds either. It was like I'd stared into one of those spiraling hypnotism discs and gotten sucked in several feet. I felt it in my chest. A 3-second glance and I'd felt it in my chest.

I was a little shaken, but I managed to climb out of the hypno-vortex

"And who's next on the chopping block?"

"Greg," she said, not hesitating.

"And he's gonna step up for the same reason?" Somehow that did not seem obvious for Greg, or at least not as obvious as for Troy.

"He's going to go because he'll want you to get through." I wasn't sure exactly what she meant, but it made sense.

"You're saving me for last? The last sacrificial lamb on the altar."

"I'm saving you because I want you there for the whole trip."

I was pretty sure this was another moment. She reached her hand out. I took it.

In her other hand, she held the leather strap with the glass bead on the end. The train swayed a bit in patches when the track was uneven and there was a general rumble, but the bead seemed immune to that, isolated in space from the bumps and jolts. "What's the deal with the bead?" I asked. "What does it do for you?"

"It's predictable," she said. "I can swing it. I can twirl it. And it comes to rest exactly where I know it will." She held it up now and I could see her watching it as though it were gliding across the desert landscape. "It's solid," she said. "It always finds its center."

We were quiet for a while. She tugged my hand and we crawled to the end of the flat car's deck. I followed her when she ducked into one of the giant pipes. They looked like the size of those giant steel culverts that go under roads, but they were smooth, which made them comfortable enough to sit or even lie down in. It wasn't obvious what they were for but that night they were great for getting out of the wind. We could sit up in them, just barely.

We remained quiet and I watched Vera slide around in this way that made it obvious that she wanted to put her head in my lap. I leaned back with an instant twinge of anxiety. As a 15-year-old boy, I could become aroused if the wind blew too hard and now a girl I was starting to wonder if I was in love with was putting her head in my lap. I went for the old standby – imagining my parents having sex – but it wasn't necessary. There was a sweetness in the moment, like it was too romantic for a hard-on. But the truth is I was also a little scared.

All she'd done is tell me she wanted me around and held my hand. I felt pumped in a way, but not in a way that gave me enough confidence to make a move on her. I got the sense she appreciated that, and I had a little fantasy about her thinking I was "not like other guys." But I'm sure plenty of other guys had been too nervous to even talk to her, much less pull her close for a kiss.

After a while, she fell asleep, and with my back bending into the curve of the pipe, I followed her. It wasn't the best night of sleep I ever had. We were out of the wind, but we were still on a train car and mostly outside. The pipes added this weird hollow echo to everything too, like a cross between a low hum and the throb of a muffled drum. I had Vera's head in my lap. I'd been excited about her knee before and now her head was in my lap and I could have run my fingers through her hair if I hadn't been too nervous.

To be honest, I was surprised I slept at all.

21

We couldn't have been on the train for more than a few hours before the light came up, first behind the mountains and then in all its fiery late-June rage. By the time I woke up, the walls of the pipe were already getting warm. There was a change in the sound of the train too. We were on more level ground now and you could sense a difference in the vibration of the car against the rails. Vera was sitting up when I crawled to the end of the pipe and swung my head out for a look. I wasn't exactly sure where we were, but from the look of the scrubby desert, it felt like somewhere west of Phoenix. People from other states have this idea that desert is desert but it's really different from place to place, and around Phoenix is more desolate than a lot of places. If you were making one of those movies where nuclear war had destroyed civilization and everybody decided that savage warlords with bad haircuts were the perfect form of government for the situation, outside Phoenix would be a good place to film it.

Vera was rubbing her eyes when I looked back. "Good morning, Sunshine," I said.

She gave me a look that said "it's a bit early for that" but it felt playful.

"When does the dining car open?" she asked.

"I'll ask the conductor," I said.

She crawled to the end of the pipe with me and looked out. "Where the fuck are we?"

"Somewhere between Phoenix and the Apocalypse, I think."

We stood up. It was the first time I'd done anything but crawl since we jumped onto the train, but it felt safer in the light somehow. We could see a lot of nothing for miles, punctuated by the occasional sun-bleached mobile home.

Greg and Troy were seated with their backs to one of the giant pipes at the other end of the train. We walked toward them, using the cables holding the pipes to steady ourselves. Both of them looked awake, but barely.

"Good morning, hobo comrades," Greg said, looking up. "What say we jump off at the next stop and get involved in a comic misunderstanding that teaches the townsfolk the true meaning of community."

"I don't know," I said. "Will there be food? Vera and I are hungry." I felt something when I said the words "Vera and I" as if that were important somehow.

"I don't think I heard you right," Greg said, dropping some twang into his speech. "I think you mean you had a hankering for some vittles."

I looked at Vera and she nodded back before say-

ing, "I reckon so," which I took to be a signal that our
hobo sketch was over for the morning. Sometimes
Greg was best in small doses and in the morning
those doses were measured in teaspoons. I'd already
sensed the train slowing. It didn't look like we were
near anything, but I saw cars ahead turning onto a
side track parallel to the way we were going, sort of
like a freeway exit but for trains and we were moving
onto a frontage road. I'd always wondered how they
got trains to share one track going two different directions and it looked like it was our turn to pull off
and park while a train going the other way got the
main track. Our train rumbled to a stop.

We were in a dead flat stretch of desert, the kind
of place where a tumbleweed would stand out as lush
vegetation. I leaned out to look ahead to the engines
and saw a guy climbing down. He started walking
our way, stopping at each car to check what looked
like hoses or cables linking the whole train together.
"Hey guys," I said, and I whispered even though the
dude was still 15 cars ahead. "Somebody's coming."

We moved damn quick for teenagers at 5 a.m. and
scrambled to the other side of the car. We looked to
the front of the car and there was another guy doing
the same thing, walking down the train one car at a
time and checking the hoses and stuff.

We had two choices at that point. We could hide
in the pipes and assume that they weren't going to
climb onto the cars and check, or we could jump off
the train and hide in the ditch that ran along the track.
Hiding in the pipes was the smart choice, but apparently none of us thought of it because we waited until

the guy on our side of the train was leaning looking up underneath one of the tankers and we all jumped down and ran over behind a pile of railroad ties that looked like they'd been there since the last ice age.

I guess the plan, not that we really had one, was to wait till the two men went back up to the front of the train and then climb back on, but when I looked up at the car we'd ridden I saw the fatal flaw in that plan. Troy had left his water bottle sitting right by the edge of the car, not on its side as though it had been rumbling along with the train for the last hundred miles, but sitting perched like somebody had placed it there, carefully. A bright blue plastic bottle like a chrome hood ornament on a rusted VW Bug.

I grabbed Vera by the shoulder and pointed at the bottle with my other hand. She looked a little scared. She punched Troy in the arm and whispered. "We might need to make a run for it," she said, nodding toward the bottle. "Be ready."

There was still a chance he wouldn't see it, about as much chance as there was of somebody not noticing a squirrel family dicing onions on their kitchen counter, and as soon as the guy on our side of the train got to the car we'd been hiding on, that chance was over.

"Ted," he called out. "Come check this out." Somehow, I'd expected "Hank." I mean the guy was wearing overalls and one of those striped engineer hats that means you're either working on a train or hosting children's television. He was way more "Hank" than "Ted."

Not-Hank climbed over the big hook thing that

links two cars together and joined the other guy. They stood staring up at the water bottle like it was evidence in a crime scene or maybe an ancient artifact in a lost temple. The first guy even brought his hands up to his chin in this way that made me think he might begin his next sentence with "I presume" but instead he said, "What do you think? Kids or transients?"

"If it were transients that'd be a whiskey bottle, not a water bottle, George," Not-Hank said. He picked it up, again like he was examining a medical specimen. I almost expected him to put on lab gloves and whip out a magnifying glass. He turned the bottle around, and my heart sank.

I knew it was there, but somehow, I still imagined they wouldn't see it.

Stenciled down the length of the plastic bottle were the words "Quest Trail." It even had the phone number, which, at that moment, might as well have been 1-800-UR SCREWED.

All of a sudden we had three options: hope they don't look for us, turn ourselves in, or run out into the nothing-for-miles desert. George and Not-Hank looked from the train to the pile of railroad ties we were hiding behind. It was pretty goddamned obvious. Almost like a TV show. There might as well have been an ominous soundtrack. Everybody looked at Vera. Nobody had ever said, "Vera is in charge," but nobody ever questioned that either.

She didn't hesitate.

"Let's go," she said, and we were immediately sprinting into the desert, not toward anything but away from the tracks. About 150 yards into our run,

I took a half-glance over my shoulder and saw the two train guys standing there watching us. If you think about it, they didn't really have a reason to chase us. There were two of them and four of us anyway. Was one of them going to sit on three of us while the other guy wrangled the fourth? They didn't need to chase us. Like back at Quest Trail, the desert was a barrier between us and everything else, but more for real this time because we'd lost our only ride out.

"Hey guys!" I yelled. "They're not following us."

So we stopped and I think we were all disappointed because we'd grown up on all those stupid detective shows, half of which ended with a foot chase and we didn't even get to vault over a chain link fence and nail the dismount. But we looked back, and George and Not-Hank were just standing there. And then George gave us a sarcastic wave, which I translated as "Good luck kids, the buzzards will show us where to find your bodies."

Just like that, our little adventure had all of us thinking about how good a big bowl of beanie linguini and our own tent would be, but Troy feels the need to express his frustration with the situation and does so with his middle finger, which is kind of lame but kind of almost perfect enough that I notched up my hate by a couple of points and tried not to look at Vera to see her reaction.

But Not-Hank proceeded to turn the tables on Troy with an ironic "OK" sign and a big smile before the two of them walk back to the train like they couldn't be bothered to indulge our great escape caper.

There was little doubt what would happen next.

George and Not-hank would get back to their engines and get on a radio to talk about four grubby looking teenagers in yellow jumpsuits and "hey, here's the phone number for the losers who let them run off into the desert in the middle of the summer."

So, we stood there while we watched the train start moving again. It was completely gone before we saw that they'd left two-gallon jugs of water sitting next to the tracks and a paper bag of what turned out to be sandwiches. It was coming up on noon and wicked hot. We hadn't eaten since the night before. George and Not-Hank were my newest heroes.

"You know," Greg announced as the train receded into the distance, "I feel a great winnergy with those guys."

22

By our collective estimates, we figured we'd make it half-
way to sunset before the first helicopter squadron
would show up. The train dispatch office would get
the radio call and then they'd call the sheriff's office.
The deputy would already know we were gone from
Quest Trail and they'd suddenly figure out that they
were searching the wrong area because we'd gotten
a ride out of there. Then they'd have to shift the
whole search command 100 miles north. There'd
be some delay, but we didn't have time to hide in
the shade during the blast-furnace hours like smart
people would have done, waiting for it to get dark
before we snuck away somewhere into whatever
misadventure awaited.

We had to get to that next misadventure as soon
as possible.

So we started following the track, which seemed
smart because all tracks eventually lead to civilization and we hadn't seen much of that where we'd

come from.

The sandwiches were pretty much what you'd expect two train worker guys to pack: baloney and American cheese, made all the more gummy and gelatinous because we were trying to make the water last and we were really thirsty. We ate while we walked, and everybody was quiet because: A) we had baloney-and-bread paste clots in our mouths and B) we were less than enthusiastic about our situation.

We were maybe a mile and a half into our little trek when Troy did this really stupid thing which started with "Well, this sucks to the max" and ended there, because none of us had the patience to explain to him that a lot of our predicament had to do with him leaving a bright blue plastic water bottle sitting out on the train car like a monument to his stupidity. I looked at Vera, but she was already looking my way with a wide-eyed "Huh? Really?"

"Baaah," I said, in my whispered impersonation of a sacrificial lamb.

"Yep," she said. "I'm warming up the altar."

I was glad Troy and Greg weren't paying attention because I'm not sure how we'd be explaining that exchange. But they weren't paying attention to us because they'd seen something. Between a pair of notched hills, an adobe building sagged on one side with a metallic green dune buggy parked in front.

Troy waved us all over as if he were Columbus and had just discovered a whole continent when exactly nobody was going to walk down that stretch of middle-of-nowhere train track and not see a metallic green dune buggy parked 200 yards away.

"We need a plan," he said.

"Got one," Greg said. "We steal that clown car and go off-road'n."

"Gee," I said and layered the "gee" with a generous slathering of sarcasm. "I think we call that the beginnings of a plan. Don't you think four teenagers in yellow jumpsuits are going to look a wee bit conspicuous driving around in that green spaceship?"

"Duh," she said. "I thought of that, but I figure it's like shopping. This is the car store. The clothes store is the next stop and maybe we can trade in Speed Buggy for something a little more subtle, like a firetruck that's actually on fire."

"Sounds like quite the crime spree," Greg said. "Do we need outlaw names? Deadeye Daniel? Six-gun Troy?"

Vera stopped him with a quick "Not helpful" and then said the obvious: "Of, course, we're going to need the keys and unless the driver has a second car, he's in that crap-ass hacienda and probably not offering test rides."

"How do you know it's a him?" I asked.

"Did you see that car?" she said, adding in a smile.

Undaunted by his earlier screw up, Troy offered a very Troy solution. "I could hot wire that car, easy," he announced.

For a second I wanted to believe him, but it might have been less than a second because Vera cut him off. "Did you learn that in felon day camp? Was hot-wiring dune buggies an elective?"

"No, but a friend of my brothers explained the whole thing to me one time," Troy answered. He was acting incredulous that we wouldn't accept his badass car thievery skills. I didn't wait for Vera to cut him off.

"Bullshit," I said. "We don't have time for you to figure out that you don't know how to do it. We go in there. We tell whoever's in there that we're lost in the desert and we need a ride. Somebody distracts them and we grab the keys."

"Doesn't sound like much of a plan," Troy shot back.

I looked at him. It wasn't a full stare down, but maybe a half stare down. There was no background music, and I didn't think we had time for a full gunfight at cul-de-sac corral thing. "Well, we can't make a plan until we see what's in there," I said. "We're going to need to improvise."

There was no real way to get ready for what we were about to attempt because we didn't know what we were getting ready for, but I noticed everybody taking a deep breath. Troy even reached up to straighten his hair like it was a job interview. I surprised myself by stepping forward first. Vera looked worried, which worried me some.

Walking closer to the adobe shack, we saw a pair of plastic garbage cans bleached thin by the sun with evidence of a pack rat nest bulging from the back of one. A cinder block leaned up against a door on the side to keep it closed but another door was cracked open. I could imagine it getting blazing hot in the house and I took that to be the sole form of air conditioning. For a moment, I was tempted to push the door the rest of the way open, but I thought knocking was the safer move.

I didn't have anything better than, "Is anybody home?"

We didn't get an answer, not in the conventional sense. We got a grunt. Vera was right behind me. Greg was behind her, and still ahead of Troy by a dozen steps. I took the grunt as something of an invitation, which it probably wasn't, and I pushed the door open a bit. Dark in the shack and with the sun all blazing outside, I couldn't really see anything. But I heard the grunt evolve into something like a "who's there" and the only answer I had was, "We need help."

23

There's a kind of southwest decorator's wet dream nostal-
gia about adobe. I mean, most of the stuff built in
Arizona in the 70s was supposed to look like it was
built in the 1770s by Indians and Spanish missionar-
ies, even though it was just a bunch of stucco sprayed
over chicken wire and 2x4s. Real adobe architecture
was all over magazines like it was the manifestation
of all that is cool for rich people when 50 years ago
poor people couldn't wait to tear it all down. Let's
face it, adobe is bricks made out of mud and straw
and the shack we were standing outside had been
simultaneously melting into the ground and crumbling into the wind for decades.

And as I opened the door wider, we could see
it didn't look any better inside. A mattress on a dirt
floor was covered with one of those blankets they use
for moving furniture, and on that mattress, sitting in
front of a jug of water was a guy wearing what I first
thought was a loincloth, but turned out to be a very

dirty pair of too-big boxer shorts. He had long hair, but not the rock star-wannabe hair I was attempting. It was more like shipwrecked castaway hair, the Robinson Crusoe look. He sat cross-legged and looked up at us, squinting at the brightness. I got the idea that it might have been weeks since he'd opened the door. That idea was reinforced by the "Oh, there's that smell" bucket in the corner. I mean, this guy had access to the whole of the outdoor world, and he was using a bucket in the corner. I felt the bread-baloney lump suddenly less solid in my stomach.

"Greetings, travelers," the guy said. "What brings you to my desert dwelling place?"

That was not a question I had an answer for, but Greg leaned into the doorway and said, "We're lost," and that seemed to nudge Hippie Crusoe out of his bedraggled mystic pose. He stood up and started toward the door as though he'd suddenly realized he wasn't ready for company. I took a glance around the room and saw why.

Every wall and most of one corner of the room was stacked in ice chest-sized plastic-wrapped bales of what I instantly knew was marijuana, not because I was accustomed to buying marijuana by the bale but because every time the sheriff's department made a big bust, they always had their picture in the paper standing front of a huge pile of bales as if they were big game hunters and their latest trophy kill was giving them a hard-on. The room was dark because the piles covered the windows, and it would have smelled like a Scorpions concert if not for the stench bucket.

Hippie Crusoe was guarding a stash house and

had reached the pissing-in-a-bucket level of paranoia.

"Let's step outside," he said in this oddly formal voice. "And talk about what brings us here?"

I was all too happy to take the conversation into the sunlight. I'd seen a shotgun next to the dusty mattress and I could tell Vera saw it too. Any room with a shotgun and a bucket of piss was not a room for an enlightened conversation and this guy was not giving off an "enlightened conversation" vibe anyway. He was barefoot and stepped carefully on the gravel. His squint relaxed as his eyes adjusted. "Are you guys narcs?" he asked, which was a really stupid question because we were obviously too young to be cops. And what narcs would show up in the middle of the desert wearing yellow jumpsuits? It was a crazy idea, but a guy who'd been sitting on half a ton of pot in the middle of nowhere, maybe for weeks, probably had more than the average number of crazy ideas sifting through his head.

Greg seemed most at ease with this guy, which wasn't surprising because Greg seemed at ease with pretty much everybody. And the Sleepy Giant's brand of mellow appeared to resonate at a soothing pitch for the stash-house hermit. "We're on a field trip," he announced, which was about as implausible as being cops but not nearly as threatening to a guy guarding 50 bales of dope. "We got separated from our group."

The guy looked as though the light and had lifted some of the stash-house stupor. Greg kept going. "We are searching for the nesting grounds of Grayson's Fleck-winged hummingbird and we've heard tell of sightings in this area?"

If you were paying attention, you know that Grayson's fleck-winged hummingbird is found only in the desert near where we'd spent the last few weeks grooving with the PTG, but this guy did not look like the type to keep a nature guide next to his dirty mattress. Or Greg could have been full of shit about the hummingbird all along, which I wouldn't know because I'm not exactly poring over bird books either.

But something in the explanation seemed to wake up our host. "Fuck-winged?" he said. "Really?"

"No, fleck-winged," Greg said, continuing his super soothing forest-ranger rhythm, adding a little fatherly chuckle-smile. "A lot of people make that mistake."

It's not like it was just dawning on me that this was a weird little vignette we were posing through, but it was *really weird*. I hadn't envisioned talking bird sightings with a stash house hermit when I'd gotten up that morning, or any morning. But I was glad Greg was there because it was working.

"I seen some birds and stuff," the guy said, and you could see him reconnecting to a world beyond his bales-and-bucket universe. "But I don't know about fleck-winged. Who you guys out here with?"

"Our school," Greg said. "It's a summer nature program for at-risk youth."

"At risk of what?" he asked.

"Lots of things," Vera said, joining the conversation. She looked plainly impatient with the science lesson, but it had coaxed Stash House into something that resembled a conversation, maybe the first he'd had in weeks. Greg had warmed him up and after hanging back, she was coming in to close the deal. "Look, we need to get back to our group. Can we borrow your buggy?"

"Ain't mine," the guy said, quickly like he wanted nothing to do with the buggy. "A guy leaves it here."

"A business associate?" I asked, surprising myself by entering a conversation that seemed awfully free-form at that moment.

"Yeah," he said. "You could call it that."

Vera made it obvious she would be shepherding proceedings through the next steps. "Would your associate mind if we borrowed it then?"

Hermit guy looked suddenly a little suspicious in what I feared was a "wait a minute, I see what's going on here" way but was probably closer to "Quit asking me so many questions, man!" This was a guy who needed a day off.

Vera saw him teetering on his heels and took on a helpful tone. It was like watching a magician call a volunteer up from the audience, a choreography of distraction, misdirection and stage presence. "We could bring it to him, maybe, save him the trip out." Stash House looked like he was considering this offer, as though it made sense, which it certainly didn't. "We could bring you something back," she said. She might as well have been swinging a watch in front of his eyes and whispering, "you're getting very sleepy."

And then, just like that, the spell was broken by the sound of an airplane engine. We all stopped talking. It wasn't a big plane. It sounded a lot like a motorcycle, even a lawnmower, a ratty clatter-ing hum. My first thought was that the search was on. The train guys had radioed in and the sheriff's department put a plane in the air. I'd expected a helicopter, but helicopters were probably outside the budget of a county sheriff.

All that was going through my head, when I look over and see Stash House nodding with a weird little grin, as though he recognized the noise, and it was a good sign. But I was sticking with my search party theory.

"Maybe we should get inside," I said. It wasn't like four teenagers in yellow jumpsuits were going to be difficult to spot.

"Yeah, man," Stash House said. "You guys wait in there."

Vera shrugged. None of us were excited about spending any time in the piss-bucket palace, but Greg ducked under the doorway and Troy, who'd been silent this whole time, followed. I offered an "after you" nod to Vera and followed her inside.

There was not a lot of space, most of the room being packed in dope, and we were forced to stand on the mattress a few feet from the bucket and all its splendor. Stash House stayed outside, and we could see his shadow through a crack in the door. That was the only light coming in and it was easy to see how the accommodations could alter one's outlook.

It was starting to dawn on me, before my eyes even started adjusting to the lack of light, that this was not some sheriff's air patrol, sputtering overhead. It's not like I'm some aviation nerd who can name plane models by—"That was a Cessna P321, a '73, you can tell by the engine timing"—but as this one got closer, it became clear that no flight crew cleared whatever it was for takeoff. It was backfiring and basically coughing and spitting its way through the air and the fact that it was close enough for us to hear meant it was really low, which didn't seem to me like something that an air search party does. They don't buzz the treetops like hillbilly crop dusters. They get up real high and they try to see as much of the areas as they can. Whoever was flying this plane was coming in so low that peeking through the crack in the door we could see the shadow of the wings pass over the flat space outside the shack where our host was jumping up and down and waving his hands over his head like he was flagging in a rescue plane, which seemed appropriate to his whole castaway look.

And then the plane went silent like the motor just stopped and the stash house castaway whooped even louder.

I nudged the door open slightly and saw him gesturing at us, maybe less wild-eyed and a little more purposeful than he'd seemed before, as though he were starting to get the hang of this whole "interacting with humans" thing.

Troy said what we were all thinking *What the hell is going on?* And then he did what none of us had thought of at all. "I'm outta' here," he declared, and he shoved past us, pushing the door open so hard it banged off a tangle of cinder blocks and fence poles leaned up against the wall.

So he walked out, and the only thing I could think

to do is to follow him. I'd guessed that a guy leaping out of a desert shack in a yellow jumpsuit had more or less blown our cover. But at the instant the light flooded into the bucket and bales suite, I saw a bit of metal high in the door jamb. Hanging on a nail, right where the wood met the crumbling adobe, was a car key. I couldn't tell if it was the key to the buggy, but it's not like there was a parking lot full of other cars. I snatched it and shoved it in my pocket, making sure Greg and Vera saw me doing it.

I'd imagined Troy running off into the desert, but he'd stopped about 25 feet from the door and when we got outside, I could see why.

Out in the desert, there are no creeks and streams, only the left-behinds of creeks and streams. I mean, maybe four or five times a year, there's a huge rainstorm and these used-to-be-creeks will run all brown and muddy for an afternoon but the rest of the time it's just these strips of sand that we'd call a "wash" and down this particular wash, maybe 50 yards, was the plane. It wasn't crashed. It was sitting there, as though it was perfectly normal for airplanes to land in the middle of the desert.

This plane wouldn't actually look perfectly normal anywhere. It was the kind of plane you'd imagine was built in a junior high shop class, or at least fixed by the expert mechanics in a junior high shop class. I'm no aviation nerd, but I didn't think the FAA gives the thumbs up to duct tape on the windshield. The wire holding the engine compartment closed didn't look regulation either. And the oil dripping from the propeller wasn't saying anything good about the motor we'd heard clunking and spitting through the air a few seconds before. But the plane, settling into the sand and rocks on its bald balloon-ish tires, wasn't even the most interesting thing in the wash. Standing next to the plane, a step from the still-open-and-sagging-from-its-hinges cockpit door, was a guy in suede denim jeans matched by a suede denim vest and a shirt that could only be described as "pirate-y." The snakeskin belt even matched the snakeskin boots. Feathered hair and sideburns, he looked like he'd stepped off the stage at an Eagles concert, or maybe off an Eagles album cover.

I'd seen guys like him, but mainly in catalogs.

But there was one other place I'd expect to see a guy like that: he was basically the guy central casting sent to play the drug dealer on every stupid detective show my mom watched, like he'd come from the makeup trailer and somebody was about to yell "action."

And there he was talking to Stash House Crusoe. The contrast was the most surreal moment in a day that had included jumping onto a train in the dark

We caught up with Troy, who was just standing there, as though he were trying to figure out the coolest thing to say or the thing to say that would somehow get him on Slick 'n' Suede's good side. I imagined the sight of four teenagers in yellow jump-suits was requiring an explanation from the castaway. I could tell he wasn't buying the field trip story, fleck *or* fuck-winged.

But he didn't look like he was ready to get violent or anything. They walked toward us and the closer they came the more I got the idea that this guy's weapon of choice was a blow dryer. I kept waiting for Troy to say something. I'd been listening to him for the last few weeks talking about how he was "in the business" back on "the street," but I can't say I was surprised that he didn't know the secret drug dealer handshake.

Stash-House Crusoe and Slick 'n' Suede walked over, and he of the immaculate sideburns spoke first.

"Jimmy tells me you guys are lost from a field trip, something about a hummingbird, but it looks to me like you're lost from juvie. Tell me, junior jailbirds, what's the real deal?"

He slipped off his sunglasses—aviators because even cops and drug dealers can agree on some things—and he did it in this dramatic way, as though he were letting us know that he was serious, and that he had a stack of 8x10 glossies in the back of seat of his flying machine if we knew where he could get professional representation.

"You got us," I said, surprising myself by being the first one to speak. "We're fugitives from justice, or at least from our parents."

"Your parents dress you up like convicts?"

"Not directly," I said. "They sent us off into the desert to commune with the cactus and come back ready to live wholesome and productive lives."

Suede smiled as though he were trying to get a smile back from Vera in the exchange. He may have almost crashed his flying machine outside his secret drug hideaway, but a hot chick is still a hot chick. She was going to make him work for it.

"I heard of that shit," the castaway said. "They call it wilderness healing. Man, that's gotta suck."

Suede didn't even look at the castaway when he said: "shut up." But he looked right at us in a way that tinged his tough-guy-drug-dealer act with a sprinkling of panic when he said to us "Should we be looking for the kumbaya patrol to come marching over the mountain any minute now, because that could be darn inconvenient for my operation right now."

I loved how he said "operation" like we were all speaking in code, as though IRS agents, or his parents, were listening in.

"Actually," I said. "Camp Kumbayah is probably 200 miles south. We hopped a train. But it'd probably be a good idea to move your *distribution center*. The train crew spotted us, and I wouldn't be surprised if we got a flyover from a real plane.

"Or at least get that thing out of here," I said, pointing at his flying contraption.

For a second, it looked like he was hurt by the "real plane" comment, but he was obviously thinking, and he spoke very softly when he started talking again.

"Here's the thing," he said. He bit his lip and looked away from us. "The plane's out of gas."

Everybody got quiet for a second. The whole idea of running out of gas with a plane full of dope was so epically stupid that we were embarrassed just to know that it had happened. Vera broke the awkward quiet, with all the sensitivity she'd learned from Quest Trail. "You ran out of gas? In a fucking plane? In a plane full of dope on the way to a shack full of more dope?"

"Yeah," he said. Whatever sideburns-and-sunglasses dealer cool he'd managed to hold onto evaporated. "I guess I was lucky to make it to the stash house."

"You're lucky you've survived this long," Vera shouted. "You're lucky society doesn't allow us to feed the dumb kids to the coyotes. You sure the plane won't run on that High Karate cologne you're wearing. You look like the kind of guy who would travel with a few extra gallons. You smell like that kind of guy too."

Suede didn't say anything. He didn't even look up.

Greg, who'd had been silent through the whole exchange but not shrinking into the ground the way Troy was, stepped up even with Vera. He wasn't a lot taller than Suede, but he looked a lot taller right then. "Is there gas in the buggy?" he said. "Will it run on that?"

So now the guy who was embarrassed about running out of gas got the chance to be embarrassed about not realizing there was gas in a tank 20 feet away, except somehow, he took that as permission to suddenly take charge. He ran his hand back through his hair as he stood into this new take-charge posture. "That's what I was thinking," he said, even though it was completely clear to everybody there that he hadn't thought of that at all. "But we need to unload the plane to get the weight down before I can fly it out of here."

He looked around at us like we were all ready to get to work saving his ass. "If the cops see that plane, they're going to get really interested in this spot," he said. "And if you guys are here, you're going to be mixed up in the whole operation."

"He has a point," Vera said. She started marching toward the plane.

For a guy who said "operation" a lot, I was not entirely convinced of his criminal prowess. Obviously, he was flying it over from Mexico himself, which was fairly ballsy, but the stash house was already nearly full. Now he wanted to load in more dope and it's not like it was close to some place where he could sell it. Was the plan to load up a bunch of bales in the back of the dune buggy and drive it to the closest Aerosmith concert?

He waved us over to the plane and used a long screwdriver to pry open the door to the back of the plane which looked like the back of a station wagon with the seats folded down.

Only it was filled with bales of pot instead of groceries.

It was hot work and we'd been at it for 10 minutes, carrying bales of dope wrapped in Saran Wrap, which was a use the company had failed to showcase in their commercials, when we heard a banging metal sound coming from over by the tracks. I looked up and saw a red 4x4 truck popping over the track and then gunning it down the embankment, gravel spraying everywhere.

I looked over at Suede and the Crusoe and from the panic on their faces instantly made it out that this was not company they were expecting. The two of them ran for the stash house and slammed the door shut behind them.

All of a sudden, Vera, Greg and I are standing holding bales of drugs while what looks to be a rival dope gang comes skidding to a stop. They certainly weren't cops.

I looked over at Vera. She shrugged, but she looked scared. Greg looked oddly relaxed. We didn't know what to do but stand there and see what happened. Wandering into a drug deal gone bad had not been on my radar when I climbed onto the train the night before.

The two guys climbing down from the truck didn't look like mall drug dealers or Hawaii Five-0 drug dealers. They looked like normal guys, which I imagine is how actual drug dealers look. They also didn't look like guys you'd want to fuck with either, even without the guns.

That was the first thing I noticed. The second thing I noticed was that they had less of an idea what was going on or what to do than we did. In yellow jumpsuits, I surmised, we looked like a cargo crew at the airport and neither of them were certain what to do with that information.

The guy in front, who was wearing torn jeans and a gray Tee-shirt like he'd walked off a construction site walks up and says what just about anybody would say, I guess.

"What the hell's going on here?" and then followed that by something less likely: "Does Wesley have a cargo crew? Seems a little beyond his resources." I guessed instantly that Wesley was our finely coiffed pilot friend. Wesley, by the way, is basically the least macho drug dealer name of all time, though it seemed to go well with his sense of fashion.

Awkward silence ensued, as though nobody knew what to say. I was so accustomed to Vera taking charge that I half expected her to travel with a gavel and a podium, but she was shrinking behind me. It was clearly my job to speak. "We actually don't know Wesley," I said. "We're lost, long story, and we wandered into amateur hour here. He said he'd give us a ride to civilization if we'd help load his dope into his shack over there." I paused, as they were taking it in. My guess is their plan revolved around Wesley and his castaway sidekick being alone and now there were witnesses, one of whom was a frightened girl. "He a friend of yours?" I asked.

That got a chuckle out of gray Tee-shirt guy. "Not exactly," he said. All of a sudden the whole thing seemed remarkably casual, except for the guns, of course. "Where you lost from? The cleanup crew at the fairgrounds. What's with the jumpsuits?"

"We ditched a juvie program our parents sent us to," I said. "Thought it was time to see the world."

"Well," the guy said. "You've seen more than we'd really like, but if you forget what you saw, I guess it'd be ok if you let us take it from here."

This was the moment when Troy, who'd been smart enough to be quiet since the truck roared over the tracks, decided to be really stupid. I imagine guys like Troy get twitchy if they don't spill out a little bit of their tough guy act every 20 minutes or so and he decided it was his moment.

"Hold on here," he said. "What's in it for us?"

Gray Tee-shirt guy looked at his friend and shook

his head. Troy wasn't done. "Maybe we get some consideration," he said, because that was the perfect thing to say to some guy who's holding a gun.

"I can see that," the first guy said, his friend remaining silent. "I'll consider not blowing your head off, Johnny Jumpsuit."

Troy had obviously pissed them off. What he did next pissed them off even more. He takes off running. We'd been on the verge of maybe resolving this encounter with a "Nothing! We saw nothing!" agreement and all of a sudden Troy creates this loose end that they need to tie up.

The head guy rolled his eyes and shook his head. And then all of them went running after Troy, leaving the three of us standing there holding bales of dope. And I had the keys to a dune buggy.

I looked at Vera. She was staring blankly, still very not-Vera quiet. "Baah," I said.

She blinked like she was waking up and we started toward the buggy.

24

Ok, so my driving history consisted of driving around an empty parking lot with my dad and 30-40 minutes of driver's ed in a lame-ass simulator thing they wheeled up to school in a trailer the semester before last. I knew to hit the brakes when I see a red light and that pedestrians have the right of way. But I also knew how to drive stick.

My dad did what all dads do when they get divorced: they buy a sports car, or, in my dad's case, an *almost* sports car, though the Chevy Vega could more accurately be called an almost-almost sports car. So I knew how to drive stick, sort of, and the buggy was stick.

If any of us ever felt bad about leaving Troy behind, we never spoke of it. And by any of us, I mean Greg, because Vera and I had already had the "Troy is the sacrificial lamb" conversation and I was ready to wave a bright orange flag that said "good riddance." We were driving away without even looking in the rearview mirror, which was handy because the buggy had no rearview mirror. Upon closer inspection, it wasn't in a whole lot better shape than Wesley's plane.

Vehicular integrity was not our concern at that particular moment, and we weren't driving very fast. It was the desert and there weren't really roads. So, my best idea was to ride on the gravel embankment next to the railroad tracks. That kept us going toward civilization in a straight line, which was a plus, but it meant we were driving at a tilted angle that had a certain "here we go!" sensation to it, as though we were going to tip over any second. I found myself unconsciously leaning to the uphill side of the car and toward the passenger seat where Vera was sitting.

Greg, miraculously but not surprisingly, was asleep in the backseat.

"Looks like we lost junior," Vera said, after a quick glance at the back seat.

"Yep," I said. "The boy could sleep through a gunfight."

"Well, I for one, am glad we didn't have to test that theory."

"Indeed," I said and then instantly felt stupid because nobody except maybe somebody's British grandfather replies with "indeed." But I went on anyway. "You think they're coming after us?"

"What? And leave Wesley and his stash-house shut-in with 50 bales of dope and a plane back there?"

"A plane that's out of gas."

"They don't know that. My guess is that they caught Troy and he cried like a baby, begging for his life and now they're in negotiations to get the blunder twins out of the bunker."

I nodded and answered with, "Sounds about right," before adding, "so what now? We're still three teenagers in yellow jumpsuits driving a sparkling green dune buggy right down the track where we were last seen by the train dudes. I think we need some less conspicuous clothing and a *way* less conspicuous ride to go with it."

"Maybe there's another train coming," Vera said and gave me this quick grin that I was able to half catch because I was still concentrating on my stunt driver exhibition. "Keep your eyes on the not-road," she said, and she laughed this time before adding, "We'll figure out something when we get closer to civilization."

Civilization turned out to be a freeway and about three miles later, a rest stop where Vera insisted we stop, exclaiming, "Indoor plumbing!"

25

The thing about rest stops is that they bring together all walks of life. It's the great equalizer. Whether it's the guy in the bombed-out Plymouth with rusted fenders and Tee-shirts stretched over the bucket seats or the lady in the Mercedes Benz who puts a towel down, so as to not harm the finely cured calfskin, everybody has seen the "rest stop" sign with some sense of physical relief and impending release. Here we find the crossroads of the world: serial killers and business tycoons alike using the same stinky toilet and cursing the same prison-grade toilet paper.

And we were never happier to see anything in our lives.

Nature is beautiful. It's serene. But it'd be a lot more beautiful and serene if it had a working bath-room. Half the quest on Quest Trail was timing your latrine visit so you had: A) a good shot at privacy, and B) a good chance of not being there right after Ron. Hugging the toilet may be slang for puking, but it's the sort of affection for porcelain we were feeling. The rest stop stalls were covered with graffiti and sculptural relief in wads of chewing gum globs, but they also had doors. And the miracle of running water. The other miracle was that nobody complained about the facilities to the three people in yellow jumpsuit who looked like they were a bucket and a mop away from a United Fellowship of Custodians union card.

We reconvened under a shaded picnic table. A charcoal grill, hot enough by this point in the afternoon's solar assault that charcoal was not required, jutted from the dried remains of what had once been a small grassy area.

I looked at Vera and Greg and shared a shrug that encapsulated the entirety of our plan at this point. We hadn't talked much in the miles that encompassed the transition from train embankment to Jeep trail to dirt road to actual road to freeway. We'd never had a plan to begin with and now we had a car and indoor plumbing 20 yards away. We felt like royalty.

"I don't know about you," Greg announced in reply to my shrug. "But I say we stop here and build a settlement."

He continued his pioneer conjecture with observations about access to water and a prime location on "a well-trod trade route," but Little Rest Stop on the Prairie ponderings aside, we did need to come up with a plan, preferably one that included a wardrobe change and maybe a new set of less conspicuous wheels, something that wasn't green with glitter streaks and a chrome roll bar. As much as we were enjoying the rest stop Shangri-la, "yellow jumpsuits" was already on every cop's radio and we didn't need to add "sighted in a green-apple circus tent with wheels" to the all-points bulletin.

"Let's put the settlement idea on hold for a while," I said. "What's in our immediate future?"

"I like the trading route idea," Vera said.

It seemed an unlikely observation from Vera this late into a long hot and uncomfortable day, but she said it in such a way that suggested she was leading up to revealing an actual plan that was more practical than Greg's manifest destiny dream. She stared past me into the parking lot. I turned to look.

If the buggy was a rolling exclamation point, the car that had caught her attention was a comma at best. Blotted in primer gray with clouded and clumsy spray paint, it was one of those cars that you had a hard time envisioning as new. This car had had a rough life. But it was also the kind of car that fades into the background. You could probably find an old magazine, read about the development and design of the Pontiac Valiant, and then walk through a whole parking lot of them without noticing.

The passengers, on the other hand, stood out. They didn't stand out in that yellow Quest Trail jumpsuits way, but more in "Who are these dirtbags?" way, as if Grapes of Wrath dust bowl refugees had taken a liking to the Grateful Dead. Listless in faded tie-dye, they had the look of people who'd been on the road and not eating a balanced diet, one that was too far balanced toward ramen and Cheetohs. You could call it "jam band scurvy."

And Vera took an interest.

"These people," she said, "look like people who might take an interest in a small bale of marijuana."

On our drive, Vera had discovered some of Wesley's drug empire under the seat in the buggy. "Bale" was something of an overstatement though. Whoever had been in charge of the baling operation, had made a lunchbox size "sample bale" that was maybe two or three pounds.

Vera did not need to explain her plan. That Plymouth Valiant looked like a two or three-pound car.

She smiled at me. "Hopefully, we wear the same size too," she said. "Let's go talk to them."

The pair of them, a man and a woman somewhere in their 20s, looked, let's say "approachable," quite possibly even amenable, and we had nothing to lose but a few pounds of what qualified as free dope. It was as close to a "plan" as we'd had since we crawled out of our tents what felt like several weeks ago but had been less than 24 hrs.

I was surprised but encouraged to see Greg lead the charge. Greg's so-relaxing vibe was tuned to their wavelength, definitely the guy's hair length. The fact that we were wearing yellow jumpsuits required a certain level of finesse, or at least familiarity. The sleepy giant was born for this role.

"Greetings, dudes," he said, using the collective conjugation of "dude" that could encompass both sexes. "We're on our way to a show."

The guy looked up. We would later learn that, ironically, his name was Hank. He and the girl were sitting in the scant shadow of the Valiant on one of those fake Navajo blankets that are issued to every-body who attends three or more Allman Brothers concerts. Shade was a precious resource, jealously guarded, but rare in parking lots. Like every car on the lot, the Valiant's interior was set to "simmer," but despite all that they seemed comfortable sticking close to their home on wheels

"What?" he said, in the slow-motion giggle of the constantly stoned. "You're the parking-lot cleanup crew? Where's your bag? Where's your grabber stick thing?"

"Yeah," said the girl, who sounded more bored than stoned. "Shouldn't you be pushing a trash barrel on wheels?"

Greg did this chuckling thing that sounded awfully dad-like before explaining. "Yeah, we get that a lot. We're actually part of a DEVO tribute band, you know DEVO, right? The egghead rockers?" He dropped into a little bit of robot for *Are We Not Men?*

I wouldn't call what spread across Stoner Hank's face as a "flash" of recognition. Nothing happened that quick for Hank, I imagined, but everybody had heard of DEVO, way more people than bought their album. They were some sort of geek-pop band that played a set on Saturday Night Live that had every-body simultaneously laughing and scratching their heads. And they wore these crazy yellow jumpsuits. I hadn't made the connection between our Quest Trail outfits and our DEVO-ness but leave it to Greg to connect the dots.

Vera stepped up as Greg's wingman on the ruse. "Yeah, man," she said, slowing her voice in a way that reminded me of large type books for old people. "We're a DEVO tribute band, DEVO Youth or DEVOY."

The girl had lost interest, but Hank was nodding along. "Cool," he said.

"But we have a little bit of a problem," Vera said. This was the point where I think we could have huddled before we made our play. But we'd honed our improv chops on fake peyote, so I let her run with it. She was down on her haunches now, at their level. It was an awkward stance to settle into and I hadn't even noticed her change position. I don't know whether I was impressed or mesmerized, but there was this ballet-polished feel to the way she moved. "We're trying to come into the show under the radar, you know what I mean?"

They both nodded this time. Vera had recaptured the girl's attention. "It's been part of our act to pull up in that dune buggy over there. You probably never saw it, but it was on our album cover."

They sat up some to see where Vera was pointing. More nodding commenced, but in a way that looked more intrigued than stoner passive. "But the promoter doesn't want that kind of...what did he call it?" she said looking up at me. "Spectacle?"

"Circus, I think he said," I replied.

"Yeah, circus. Anyway, we're wondering if you'd like to trade cars, you'd get the buggy, and we'd drive away in this under-the-radar vehicle."

The guy looked immediately suspicious, the way somebody might look if they were offered free Kool-Aid in an alley from a guy in an orange robe with devil horns. But Vera moved in for the kill.

"We can sweeten the deal with some ganja," she said. The guy suddenly looked a lot more interested. The girl was holding onto a suspicious squint, but she obviously wanted to know more.

"How much ganja are we talking about here?" she asked. "A joint, a two-finger lid? We're already packing some green, but you know how it is? You can always use more."

"Yeah," Hank said, "we burn through it pretty quick, you know? It goes up in smoke."

Hank and the girl were leaning into each other and laughing. I wanted to groan and tell them they needed better material, but I wanted the car too.

"How does a bale sound?" Greg said. He had his arms over the frame of the car door the way some neighbor might talk over a fence on a '50's sitcom.

"It sounds fucking fantastic," was Hank's no-hesitation reply. He hugged the girl with one arm. "A bale and a buggy baby! A bale and a buggy!" he exclaimed and then stood up quick to see if anybody was listening in on our negotiations. He tried on a cool reserve pose like he didn't want us to think he was some sucker. But it didn't last. "Can we see it? Better yet, can we smoke it?"

"You can do whatever you want with it. Wait here. I'll be right back."

That left me and Greg alone with the pair, who were exchanging these weird little smiles and wrinkled-nose squints in that way that squeezes an extra u into "cute" and made me a little queasy. Ordinarily, I'd leave it to Greg to make conversation, that being his superpower and all, but I decided to try my hand.

"How'd you all meet?" I said. I looked at Greg and he gave me a deadpan "Really? That's all you've got" look. It's not like I'd put "easy with people" on my college application, but it's not like I'd asked her why she hadn't checked the spelling on her "Strawberry Feelds" tattoo. Or when was the last time either of them had showered.

Neither of them seemed troubled by my lack of conversational skills.

"We're not actually all that sure," the girl said.

"Yeah," Hank said. "We kinda woke up in old Val here after a Doobie Brothers' show in Riverside. I looked over at her and said, 'Hi, I'm Hank.'"

"And I said, 'Nice to meet ya, Hank, I'm Alchemy.'"

I looked at Greg. He had nothing. This was beyond even his powers. I blundered on. "Is that a family name?" I asked. "Or are your parents wizards?"

She looked at me like she was getting ready to say something, but Hank cut her off. "Her parents aren't wizards," he said. "They're assholes."

Alchemy was ready to defend her parents and then shrugged as if she realized Hank had a point. Having recently escaped parentally-imposed desert exile, I'm not sure I'd have a great comeback either. I was having a tough time letting the silence hang the way it was, and I couldn't believe Greg wasn't stepping in with his amiability. It was almost like one of those scenes where a kid doesn't know how to swim, and his dad throws him off a dock. I could barely dog paddle, and Greg was standing there with the life ring behind his back. I looked around for conversation starters, anything that would keep them from doing the googly-eyes couple thing, like one of those "Luv Is…" ceramic figurines that everybody's grandmother has, except the figurines looked like they were about to make out.

Vera rescued us. She was carrying the lunchbox bale in a paper bag she'd dug out of somewhere. She had the key to the buggy hanging from her pinky as she set the prize down before them. Hank's eyes widened in wonder the way I imagine a missionary would approach a holy relic, and his face glowed in the presence of divinity. Alchemy had her head against his shoulder as he pulled the bag open and breathed deeply through his nose to soak up the holy essence.

"That's some solid shit," he said. "Some solid-ass shit."

He stretched out backward to pull the keys to "Val" out of his pocket. He was clearly not willing to stand up and leave the arms-reach proximity of the earthly manifestation of his most-treasured dreams. "She's all yours," he said. "We'll clean everything out. Give us a minute."

At that point, he stuck his whole head into the paper bag and spent like 5 seconds there, which is a long time if you're standing around watching a guy with his head in a paper bag taking big, exaggerated breaths.

Even Alchemy looked impatient and when he emerged, smiling like a cartoon monkey to offer her a sniff.

"We just have a couple of things," she said, as

though she was a little embarrassed. Hank used the key to open the trunk and we all stood back while they pulled out a half dozen garbage bags. Alchemy reached into one and pulled three blurry tie-dye Tee-shirts. "Take these," she said. "We couldn't sell 'em." I'm no hippie casual wear expert but once in a while, you see tie-dye gone wrong. It was a color thing mainly—brown and tie-dye don't mix, sorry. Still, they were a step closer to the no-yellow-jumpsuits incognito we needed to achieve.

"You got any pants?" Vera asked. "The promoter doesn't want us showing up in yellow jumpsuits either."

Alchemy gave Vera this look that I interpreted as girl code for "I know your story is bullshit, but you gave us dope" and reached into a different bag. "I got these," she said.

"These" turned out to be smiley-face pajama pants. She had a whole stack. "They were throwin' 'em away behind a Kmart," she said. "We thought we'd tie-dye 'em and sell 'em with the shirts but early experiments were not encouraging."

Smiley face PJs and brown tie-dye were not ideal for our triumphant return to society, but again, they seemed an improvement from our escaped-chain-gang look.

"Thanks," Vera said. They shared that look again. "Really, thanks."

We waited while Hank and Alchemy took three loads of bags over to the buggy, shoving their illicit treasure under the back seat in a compartment where the battery fits in old VW bugs, which were what most dune buggies were underneath all the preposterous fiberglass.

On the last trip, Hank turned and gave us this little ceremonial bow that he'd probably learned from karate movies. Alchemy looked like she was ready to do the same but stopped herself.

Because, you know, the whole awkward encounter needed an awkward postscript.

They were walking away, and Vera turned to me. "That," she said, "is what they should put in all the anti-drug movies they made us watch."

I thought I understood what she meant, but I asked, "What do you mean?"

"Well, look at them? Look how hard they're trying to be cool. Look at the big act he was putting on and then think about what the difference is between what we saw and a possum rooting through garbage," she said.

There was a bit of a pause here, in part because Greg and I were trying to interpret what she said but more because we weren't sure how to reply to it. In stoner circles, reverence for the weed goes unquestioned. But she talked about it like it was that sugar-rush hunger for candy when we were kids or the enthusiasm that we'd apparently have for garbage if we were possums. In this version of reality, which seemed pretty damn real coming from somebody like Vera and not the P.E. coach explaining how three bong hits were going to turn us into zombies.

The quest for hippie cool looks desperate if you stand back more than three or four feet. And weeks away from our old lives, with a few "real shit happens out here" moments on the trail, we were standing back three or four hundred feet, or at least I was.

"Everybody thinks dope makes them cool," she said. "When all it does is make them boring."

I tried to come up with a counterargument. I didn't have one.

Five minutes later, we still looked conspicuous, but we looked conspicuous in a completely different way than we had in the yellow jumpsuits. We could guess that the cops weren't looking for three teens dressed like they'd been rooting through the dumpster behind a clown rehab clinic. In the car, we didn't look conspicuous at all, but we still hunched down in the seats all the same.

There didn't seem to be a question whether Vera would drive. It was an automatic. She'd taken the keys from Hank and held on to them. There also didn't seem to be a question whether I'd sit up front. Greg was taller than me and a bit cramped in the backseat, but there was no vying for "shotgun." I liked that.

There was *some* question about where we were going, but it was a short conversation. Most of Arizona is empty. Something like 80 percent of the state is owned by the government, not because the government's got a big hard-on for owning land but because nobody wanted it. When pioneers were racing across the prairie to grab their free homestead plot, Arizona was sitting there with a blinking neon "OPEN" sign and no takers. If the homesteaders had been promised a pool and some AC with their 200 acres, it might have filled up quick. Instead, you have Tucson and Phoenix and a bunch of towns so small that three teenagers in smiley face jammies would have been front page news if we even stopped for gas.

Phoenix was obvious because: A) It was closer, and B) My parents and Greg's parents didn't live there. Phoenix isn't a big city, but we had a way better chance of slipping in unnoticed than we did anywhere in a 300-mile radius.

I'd taken a look at the big wall map at the rest stop and it looked like we'd be there in an hour, less if we'd be driving like normal people. But we weren't normal people. We spent 20 minutes arguing how much to speed since not speeding would have made us stand out like Val was a mechanical fire-breathing dragon, and speeding too much could get us pulled over to answer a series of questions with no good answers.

We settled on 4 mph over the 55-mph limit and it still felt like we were crawling down the highway on our way to bingo night at the senior center. The drive turned out to be among the five or six times I saw Vera looking nervous. None of us had drivers' licenses or even learners' permits. However pumped I'd been showing off my stick shift skills, I'd been jumpy driving on dirt roads with no traffic, and there was Vera driving on a freeway into an actual city. We didn't talk about it. I assumed L.A. kids were born behind the wheel, but I could sense her anxiety.

It didn't help that we didn't really know where we were going, and it was getting dark.

And we were running out of gas. In less than 24 hours, we'd scored a car and an interesting change of clothes, but we were full-on broke.

With the sun setting behind us in one of those lava apocalypse light shows, we pulled into a side street off Van Buren a mile or two short of downtown Phoenix and not too far from the state capitol and got to work rooting through Val for change.

We were quite a sight, I'm sure. Three teenagers in pajamas and tie-dye, scouring a junker car for pennies with the occasional triumph of a nickel (Greg found a quarter and held it up like he'd discovered a Spanish doubloon). All of this happening 20 yards off Van Buren, a street that had been a big deal in the 50s but had "fallen on hard times" in the 60s and then even harder times in the 70s. It was lined with old-fashion-y restaurants and motels with ridiculously unlikely names like the Redwoods (we were in the desert, remember?) and the Arabian Nights. It was also lined with, let's face it, whores.

Still, with the spectacle of the sunset slowly replaced with the gaudy but colorful array of neon, it looked less sad than it did during the day and $2.37 in mostly pennies felt like a triumph. I was actually surprised that Hank and Alchemy would allow such largess to slip into the seat cushions and floor mats of life but mumbling "spare change" on street corners results in a lot of, well, spare change. We put enough aside for a gallon of gas and bought three hot dogs and a tub of fries from a log cabin tucked between a plantation-themed motor court and a boarded-up Polynesian restaurant.

We sat on Val's trunk with our banquet, each of us quietly scheming the mathematics of the remaining

French fries and suffering the awkward silence that hovered around the obvious "what's next?" question.

Vera slid off the back of the trunk and landed on her feet with a little "ta-dah" flourish and spun on her heel to face us. "Daniel," she said, "let's go for a walk."

I fought a little bit of wide-faced "Who, me?" reaction and recovered quickly enough to let a French fry dangle from my lips while offering a half-ass Humphrey Bogart impression with, "Why I'd be delighted to take in the night air." A few seconds later we were around the corner, stepping around trash and the occasional vomit patch on Van Buren, the two of us, soaking up the neon.

I left the Bogart out of, "So, what brings you to these parts," but the comic intention was clear.

She turned around and walked backwards to say, "I came for the culture, the cosmopolitan sheen of big city sophistication." We were walking by a motel that looked to have been a Spanish Mission brought to life through the magic of stucco but had been turned into apartments that rented by the week. I appreciated her touch of absurd.

"I, myself, was lured here by the promise of fortune, a chance to strike it rich in the land of opportunity," I said.

She smiled at me. The walking backward thing wasn't as impressive as it had been on the desert trail the day we lagged behind the PTG and had our first actual conversation. But she still glided as she walked. She still looked, to me, like a magical being. But I knew her as something more than magical by that point.

She turned around to walk next to me and held my arm above the elbow. It was insufferably hot, even with the sun down, Phoenix hot, but her touch felt cool, comfortable.

"Got plans tonight?" she asked.

I honestly hoped that sleeping in a real bed could be among those plans. We'd slept a little on the train, but it felt like a week since we'd ducked out of our tents. The three of us sleeping in Val just off Van Buren seemed less than relaxing. I fought to keep the anxiety from seeping into my voice.

"I don't know," I said. I dropped the Bogart and any other pretensions. "I'm thinking one of us calls our parents." We'd passed several prostitutes and more than one walking mural of home-inked tattoos, the sort of tattoos that look really good in a police sketch.

"Doesn't your sister live somewhere around here," Vera asked. "She might make a good reintroduction to society."

I wouldn't say I hadn't thought of that. I'd actually been trying to not think of that. We walked half a block before I answered. "I don't know," I said. "Jackie presents certain obstacles of her own."

"Like what?"

"Like whoever her boyfriend is. I never actually met him, but he sounds, let's say, rough. That's a pattern with her, actually."

"Rougher than this?" Vera said, waving her arm across the sidewalk to frame Van Buren like she was a tour guide at the Grand Canyon.

"You have a point," I said.

Vera tugged my arm and we stopped. She pulled me around to face her. She took a half step toward me.

"I know it's complicated," she said. "Everybody's life is complicated. Out in the desert, things looked a little simpler. We could hate our parents and the PTG and how unfair everything is. But back here, we live our lives in the details, in the close-ups."

I didn't have anything better than "yeah, I know," but I stood there, looking into her eyes and the way they caught the neon for several seconds. I could hear the cars and sense people walking by. Across the street, two guys were yelling at each other outside a liquor store. But all I really remember of that moment was her hand still holding my arm and her eyes steady on mine.

Finally, she said, "Let's go check on Greg and figure out how we're going to find your sister. You know where she lives, right?"

"Sort of," I said.

We walked by a porno shop, which was embarrassing, and no words were spoken, and then a headshop, which looked desperate in a very-*Troy* kind of way: all glass tubes and water pipe contraptions. *It's weed, not chemistry,* I thought.

There was no reason to think the lights sweeping the expanse of Van Buren had anything to do with us as we approached the side street where we'd parked. Cops had a lot to look after in that part of Phoenix and that they found something that would interest them was no surprise.

It wasn't until we were 20 yards away that we discovered the focus of their interest was the Plymouth Valiant and Greg. Vera had been talking about how much she was going to appreciate a shower and asking whether she and Jackie wore the same size when I saw Greg standing at the back of the car talking to two cops.

I grabbed Vera by the shoulder to stop her and we ducked in behind a van parked on the corner. My first thought was that it didn't really matter why the cops had decided to check on Greg. I mean, you see a teenage boy in PJs and tie-dye within a half mile of Van Buren and it's going to ring up in the cop brain as a runaway. But that was before I saw Hank and Alchemy sitting in the back of a highway patrol car parked behind the police cruiser. Somebody at the rest stop probably recognized the "three teens in yellow jumpsuits" from the "missing teens" story that was surely all over the radio that day. And "green dune buggy" is a very specific vehicle description. The battery compartment had been a lousy place to hide three pounds of dope and Van Buren had been the likeliest of places to look for us.

All of that meant that the cops were looking for Vera and me too.

I didn't need to know the whole backstory to realize we had to get out of there. At the first break in traffic, we ran across the street and into the closest alley we could find.

We ran for three blocks before we stopped behind a store and ducked in between a dumpster and a chain link fence threaded thick in clear plastic shreds.

"Damnit," I said. "Now we're completely screwed."

"Completely?" Vera said.

"Yeah," I said. "Completely. Is there some part of this evening that's not screwed, some aspect that escaped my attention? I don't know if you've been keeping up with recent developments, but I'm not feeling a lot of winnergy going on."

As I caught my breath, the panic I'd felt when I saw Greg with the cops was replaced by a twinge of regret for speaking so harshly along with a dose of misplaced guilt as though I should be the one on my way to juvie while Greg and Vera caught a movie. It made no sense, but I had a lot going through my head. I also hoped that Vera had heard "winnergy" as sarcasm and not the unconscious slip into PTG-speak it had actually been.

I pulled at one of the tufts of shredded plastic and wondered at who had taken the time to weave it through the links. It didn't make the fact that I was avoiding looking at Vera less obvious, but it gave me something else to look at. "What do you mean?" I said.

"I mean what did you think was going to happen when we got out? A ticker tape parade? A key to the city?" She let me sit with that for a few seconds before continuing. "We needed to get out and we got out. What happens from here on out is only barely in our control. It's not like we were going to get a job, set down roots and sign Greg up for little league."

A couple of things stood out for me in that instant. One was that Greg was so not the little league type. He was tall, but he had the athletic ambition of a bean bag chair. There was a movie that came out a few years before called something like the Boy in the Bubble about a kid who had some disease that meant his parents had to keep him in basically an aquarium and he spent all this time longing to get out into the world. Greg would have been the guy figuring out a way *into* the bubble.

The second thing that I instantly pulled out of Vera's assessment was that if Greg was the kid in little league, we were the parents, which meant we were a couple. I know it took several titanic leaps of hypothetical gymnastics to get there, but the idea that Vera placed me anywhere near such status was added to the scant, but growing, collection of evidence that she saw me "that way."

Somebody that beautiful, interested in me? Obviously, there was something wrong with her.

I gave up on untangling the shred of plastic I was idly tugging on and turned to her. She was sitting on a bucket that somebody had flipped upside down. "Well," I said, "I guess I didn't expect a parade, but I thought we'd make it a little further without a law enforcement encounter. If we make it to Jackie's we can hang out a bit before we call our parents. They're not going to be exactly happy to hear from us, but they're going to be relieved."

She looked up at me. I was standing over her and she reached her hand out for me to help her up. As she stood, she brought her head to my shoulder and let it rest there. "It's possible," she said in an almost-whisper, "that they'll be happy too."

The obvious thing to do was to get to Jackie's

right then. The fact that we didn't have a car and we didn't have the precise whereabouts of Jackie's apartment made that plan more complicated than obvious. I'd been to Jackie's apartment twice. I knew it was in east Phoenix, not far from the university. She lived in one of a half million stucco apartment complexes sprawling across the "Valley of the Sun" as the metro area was called, but I could kind of remember where it was because of its proximity to a water park called "Big Surf," which was basically a giant swimming pool with waves so you could pretend you were at the beach and not the convection oven that is Phoenix. I was relatively confident that if we made it to Big Surf, I could find Jackie's apartment or at least the complex she lived in.

But it was 11 o'clock and bus service was barely a fringe concept during daylight hours. I'd unconsciously put my arms around Vera and was holding her against my chest. The sun had gone down two hours before and it was still pushing 100 degrees. I could feel her sweating through the tie-dye. "We need to find someplace to crash," I said. "We'll find Jackie's place in the morning."

Ordinarily, sleeping on the street would be a scary idea, something that would happen on a super-dark After-School Special or on some TV movie like the Linda Blair "Portrait of a Teenage Alcoholic" that would inspire so much housewife consternation that the PTA would bring in a speaker or at least send home a flyer with helpful tips.

But this was no after-school special. This was real life, though not anything close to the normal kinds of circumstances most people are describing when they talk about "real life." In the past 24 hours, we'd jumped a train, disrupted a drug rip-off and traded some of those drugs for a car. Somehow sleeping in a culvert sounded like the next logical run on the rap sheet ladder and I found myself thinking about how I could fit all this on my college entrance essay.

"Let's get a little further from the scene of the crime," I said. "They'll be sweeping the area for public enemies two and three before long and there's no way to hang low in these outfits."

"But you see," she said. "That's where our luck has changed or started to change." I saw her pull on one of the plastic shreds and stretch it out from the fence and for the first time, I could see what they were – the plastic that dry cleaning comes wrapped in. For a second, I wondered who frequents a dry cleaning establishment on Van Buren but then I decided that pimps have to get their pimp coats cleaned somewhere. I still didn't know what a dry cleaners meant for us, but Vera was quick to explain.

"Dry cleaning places throw out tons of clothes," she said. "People drop off grandma's shawl or uncle jack's tux and then decide that it wasn't worth $2.98 to clean so they *forget* to pick it up. We used to dig out some really funky garb from the dry cleaner dumpsters back in Venice. The sequined mini I wore to middle school prom came from Brighten Up on Brighton. There's probably a bin of old duds somewhere back here. They leave it for Goodwill to pick up."

I liked her logic. We wouldn't stand a good chance

of walking anywhere, much less standing around a bus stop dressed as the tie-dye twins. Greg could have told them we were midget Asians, but smiley PJs trumped anything he could have come up with. And I doubted Hank and Alchemy had any loyalty.

It turned out there was more garbage than clothes. We had to move some boxes around before we got to the good stuff, but 10 minutes into my first shopping expedition with a girl, I had a white button-down shirt with black slacks and Vera was sporting a blue halter dress. I stood on the other side of the fence while she changed behind the dumpster. I shrugged off the teenage-boy instinct to steal a peek through the shredded plastic—I wasn't going to be that guy. Not tonight. She spared me the same consideration and a few minutes later, we looked like the wait staff at Denny's After Hours.

"You look divine," I told her. "Divinely divine."

I flourished the compliment with my best movie star snob voice, but it was about as sincere a compliment as I'd ever voiced aloud, especially to a girl. I'd been sneaking glances at Vera in Quest Trail-issued yellow for weeks and now she was in a dress. Looking past the desert boots, it was a glimpse of Vera at full volume.

I mean, she hadn't showered in a week—and that only if you count a bucket behind a tarp a "shower." We'd slept on an open train car and tramped around the desert half the day. And now we were standing in the alley next to a dumpster under a fluorescent streetlight a half block off the skeeziest thoroughfare in Phoenix.

None of that made her any less dazzling in that moment.

I couldn't help but stare. She couldn't help but notice.

"Stop it, loser," she declared.

I dropped the movie star bit. "It's just," I said, "you look so beautiful."

I expected to hear protest, "whatever, loser!" or worse, but playful. It didn't come.

"You clean up pretty good yourself," she said. It was my turn to "aw shucks" and I'm still amazed I didn't. I smiled. She smiled back.

"Take this," she said, handing me the remaining quarters and dimes left over from our seat cushion scavenger hunt. "I don't have any pockets."

After hot dogs and fries, we had enough for a gallon of gas except now we didn't have a car. Figuring in bus fare, we had enough left over for two sodas. "Can I buy you a drink?" I asked. "Perhaps something from the Coca-Cola vineyards."

"You really know how to show a lady a good time, don't you?"

"Actually," I said, "I'm hoping I know how to help a lady avoid dehydration and heat stroke."

"Like I said, a good time."

I started tossing the clothes we didn't grab back in the plastic bags and held the smiley-face PJs to mime a wincing sniff test. "I'll miss these," I said.

"They weren't exactly flattering," Vera replied. "I mean. They were comfy but I wouldn't wear them to prom or anything."

"Did you go to prom? Back in California," I asked.

She'd already said something about middle school prom, but high school was "real prom," and something universally labeled "lame" by guys like me who didn't think they could get a date for prom. "You don't seem like the prom type."

"What does prom type mean?"

"You know, big hair, curls, curves and giggles."

"Well, I think I may be short on curls and giggles," she said, employing a conspicuous pause to make a point of leaving "curves" out of the discussion, "but I bet I could rock a tiara if I had to."

"I have no doubt," I said, and I bowed slightly.

I had an idea, and it was the kind of idea that might have stayed frozen in the idea stage not so many weeks before, like my idea that it would be wicked cool to sneak into the principal's office and play some Zeppelin over the school PA. I mean something possible, but cooler to think about than to do. But I did it anyway, said it anyway.

"What if tonight was prom, Quest Trail prom?"

She paused for a second. Her eyes softened in a way that gave me a jolt of, "Oh shit, I screwed up another magic moment." And then those softened eyes looked up to me.

"Are you asking me to prom?"

"Well," I said, "I know it's kind of last minute."

She tilted her head to one side. "I don't have any giggles or big hair," she said. "But I'd be delighted."

I raised my arm, offering her my elbow, and she took it as though we were walking on stage together at the Oscars. I found myself an inch and a half taller, approaching the posture my mother nagged me about for most of my life.

"I have reservations at the Circle K," I said.

"Remember to tip the maître d⬚ for a good table."

I expected her to drop my arm as soon as we got to the sidewalk, but she didn't. She actually walked a little closer to me. At the time, I wanted to think that it was affection, that she was ready to "take it to the next level" if "next level" meant as much as a hug. But thinking back now, it may have had more to do with the Van Buren street scene than anything. It's not a gleaming boulevard that's chock full of upstanding citizenry by day and turns into an avenue of evil at as soon as the streetlights come on. It's more of a seedy-by-day and sleazy-by-night place, but during the time we were hiding and clothes shopping in the alley it had slipped further toward sinister, with a dash of desperation.

Hookers in hot pants stood like statues at the curb. Drunks leaned up against the storefronts. I had this weird thought that they were the lawn ornaments of the bad neighborhoods. The drunks were the garden gnomes and the whores were the ridiculous Grecian statues that you see people put on their lawns as though somebody is going to mistake their tract home for an Italian villa. Every bar looked like it had the same three central casting ex-cons leaning over a pool table.

And all this witnessed by a parade of lowriders, too-loud motorcycles and the occasional cop car. I felt like we were going to wake up with tattoos just from walking through.

"Perhaps we should repair to more civilized environs," she said, attempting something similar to my movie star snob voice but this time tinged with a hint of fear.

"Yeah," I said. "I think it gets a little less scary a couple blocks up."

Those couple blocks took us away from the street lights and through a neighborhood that was less "past its prime" and more "ready for the bulldozer," the kind of neighborhood where even when the house has a fence, the dog is chained outside and the cars look like the leftovers from a demolition derby.

We got to a street that was more boring than desperate, a mix of used car lots and carpet outlets, a station wagon street, basically and we stopped at a Kwik-E-Mart for our soda. As stores go, it was a bit of a downgrade from the promised Circle K on a commerce-of-convenience spectrum of service that peaks at 7-11, but Vera managed to talk her way past the "no public restrooms" sign and I waited by the magazine rack between the windows and counter quadrant where the clerk looked like he was standing on a stool, which gave him this weird pulpit/judge's bench posture, the lord of all he surveyed.

He gave me an up and down look while I sipped my Bubble Up, which I'd chosen not because I liked it—Bubble Up was basically Sprite—but because it came in this long neck bottle that made it look like I was drinking beer. I actually felt kind of stupid because Vera had gotten a plain-old Coke and I was knocking back fizzy lemon-lime like I was chugging a Bud, pure poser if you think about it. But there I was, a man of the world in the Kwik-E-

Mart with my stunt beer, and this clerk, well into his "so this is all there is?" pre-mid-life crisis says to me, "You guys runaways?"

You know in movies when somebody's jaw drops and it's over obvious and you think *nobody really does that like that?* I did that, like that. I tried halfway through my jaw drop to turn it into an incredulous reaction. "Runaways" seemed so desperate, at least a lot more desperate than I felt. I didn't attempt "the devil you say!" because I'm not a dapper Englishman in the 1890s, but I implied it with my eyes, and I croaked out, "Why do you say that?"

"Dude, I work in a convenience store," he said. "I'm an observer of the human condition, a witness to life's grand parade, all walk of life comes walking through that door."

"We're not runaways," I said. "We just got off work."

The guy sighed. "A tip from the professor," he said. "Steal your girlfriend some shoes too. Those don't go with the dress."

I was a little crushed by the exchange. I guess I'd talked myself into the whole prom charade at some level, as though we were a bright young couple out for a night of festivities and not on the run from our parents, the PTG, and maybe some cops with questions about stolen dune buggies and bale-ettes of marijuana.

"It's that obvious?" I asked and tangled my eyebrows into this world-weary expression.

"Yep," he said. "Pretty much."

At that point, Vera emerged from the bathroom

at the back of the store to make an exaggerated entrance. "Darling,' she announced. "Has the limo arrived?"

The clerk and I exchanged a glance and he whispered so that Vera couldn't hear from the back of the store. "There's a park five blocks north that the cops more-or-less ignore. Might be a nice spot for an enchanted evening." He didn't wink. He didn't need to. He didn't need to give me one of the foil-wrapped chocolate roses sprouting from the vase by the cash register either, but he did.

"Right this way, dear," I called back to Vera. And then I saw her.

She looked amazing in the dress when we got there, but she'd done some extra magic in the bathroom that made her more amazing. She probably just washed her face—the miracle of indoor plumbing strikes again!—but she'd also done something with her hair that required five minutes and a sink and was outside the abilities and knowledge of teenage boys. Like I said, she'd already looked amazing, except now, she looked amazing-er.

She put her arm up for me and we both bowed to the clerk. She saw the foil rose and pretended not to. Not only that, but she also pretended to not see me see her pretending not to see it. I wasn't sure what that meant in the moment, but I was ready to convince myself that it meant something cooler than a foil-wrapped chocolate rose from a convenience store.

I looked over my shoulder, half expecting a blessing or nod from the sage of convenience, but he wasn't even looking up. He was watching Benny Hill on one of those tiny black-and-white TVs that people bring into football games so that they can watch other football games, which always makes me wonder if they'd be happier staying at home and, you know, watching football games.

It's not like I was expecting some final words of wisdom, but really, I was in dire need of some wisdom.

There was at least the playful pretense that I was on a date, and not just on a date, but on a date with the kind of girl I had long assumed was outside the parameters of my romantic destiny. She was the kind of girl that happened to other guys, all of whom had more money, or muscles or cool than I could summon even when I had such a girl on my arm in the middle of the biggest adventure of my life.

As we walked out of the fluorescent-white sensory assault of the convenience store, we entered the one good thing about summer in Arizona: the nights are endless, or at least they feel that way. There's something about the nocturnal nature of desert towns that gives the night a quality of infinite possibility, as though the sun's merciless onslaught has finally been turned back and it is time to exult in the reprieve that darkness provides. We walked into that boundless opportunity with the unspoken agreement that the magic would die at dawn.

It's not like we were going to wake up and choose a college that we could attend together and then start picking out names for the kids. The Kwik-E-clerk was right. We were runaways.

We could pretend otherwise only in these never-ending hours of night in a desert town.

"What time does the band start?" Vera said. I had thought she might let go of my arm after we'd crossed the parking lot, but again she held on.

"Actually. I think we may have missed most of prom. We're going to the after party now."

"Will all the cool kids be there?"

"Only two of them. The coolest two."

"Ah, an intimate affair."

Ok, I'll admit that I heard "intimate" and my mind went *there,* but I didn't let it linger. I didn't want to spend the night wondering, can I put my hand on her shoulder, what about her neck, should I kiss her now? What about now? Now? There'd been an innocence to the evening so far, as though we were 5-year-olds playing house. There was an undercurrent of "something more," but I didn't want to get trapped in that current and pulled away from the moment.

But she hadn't let go of my arm.

We walked for some time without talking. The neighborhood was mainly small workshops and garages. Streetlights were sparse and we scurried from one pool of light to the next. I could see the park coming up. You couldn't miss it, seriously. And I could see why the clerk had suggested it. It wasn't much of a park: two shaded picnic tables and a small playground, but it was right between two car lots, and car lots, everywhere, like it's a law, are lit like football stadiums. All those cars need to gleam like gems and jewelry at all hours in case some lottery winner comes driving by at 4 a.m.

So if you were some derelict or drunk, it would be a

really lousy place to hide out because it'd be like you were hiding out on the exam table in an operating room or blinking in the glare of a police lineup.

Well into the last hour before midnight, the park was blindingly bright and filled, incongruously, with music. I'd never thought of this before, and I guess I'd never seen it before either because I'm not out cruising car dealers in the middle of the night very often, but what we were seeing made sense. Whenever you see a car in a car lot, they look like they were washed like five minutes ago, but you never see anybody out there washing cars. That's because they're washing them at 1 a.m., and, at this particular lot, playing Mexican pop music on a boombox.

I turned to Vera. "I guess the band is playing an encore."

She threw her head back and laughed. "Perfect!" she squeaked. "You're not getting out of it!"

"Getting out of what?"

"Dancing!"

"Who said I wanted to get out of dancing?"

"*All* guys want to get out of dancing. Dancing means letting yourself go and that's the last thing teenage boys want to do. The risk that for a microsecond you're going to not look cool is too great."

She looked at me. I had nothing.

"Most guys would rather face a firing squad than dance," she said. "The only reason you do it is to get girls."

"Does it work?"

She stopped and turned to me. We were about 30 steps into the park and about halfway to a basketball court. She smiled when she said, "Maybe."

"Then can I have this dance?"

"Why, of course," she said.

Ok, she was right. I'd do anything to avoid dancing, but the way she'd put it was almost a dare. I offered her my hand. She took it and I drew her onto the court. I don't know anything about dancing. All I knew that night was that I wasn't letting go of her hand.

I don't know if it helped that the music was Mexican music, but I hoped it kept her from feeling super confident and we could sort of goof through the dance. That worked for the first two or three songs and it seemed like silly fun.

Then came a slow song.

Slow songs are a cross-cultural thing, I think. I imagine guys around the world love them for the same reasons: you don't have to know how to dance and you get to hold the girl, really close. All you have to do is be taller than the girl, hopefully, and not trip over her. I was barely eking out an advantage on the first and I was reasonably sure I could avoid the second.

That doesn't mean I felt all relaxed and smooth. I was already stiff as I drew her near and then I had to make the life-changing decision of where to put my hand on her back.

It was a halter dress and didn't cover the upper half of her back. If I put my hand too high, I'd be touching her bare skin. If I put it too low, I'd be approaching her ass. At least that's what I was thinking in that particular instant. But when I froze for a second, she took my hand and guided it to a safe position on her lower back, which was embarrassing, but the way she smiled made it seem really sweet.

And then we danced, slow. I held her close and she put her cheek to my shoulder. I suddenly wondered why I'd avoided dancing for so long. It felt so right. I wanted it to go on forever and when I heard the same song start over again, I was ready to just go with it. But I looked over and saw the three guys from the car wash crew standing there. One of them gave me a thumbs up and I wanted to steer Vera to keep her back to them, but it's not like she hadn't noticed that the song had started over again. She saw them and broke away from me with a big smile, pulling me into a bow and laughing.

She took my other hand and started leading me to the playground, which was a little farther from the car lot but still brilliantly lit in that unearthly fluorescent white. I saw where she was taking me. The playground was old and still had one of those merry-go-round spinning platform things that most parks and schools have gotten rid of for reasons having to do with safety and science. Kids, being the fiendish theoretical physicists they are, were unable to restrain themselves from performing experiments in centrifugal force that inevitably sent a kid flinging into some other steel contraption.

But Vera had other ideas. "I love merry-go-rounds," she said. She led me to step up onto the platform but stayed on the ground to give it a shove and get it spinning. I completed three revolutions, watching her watching me. I first thought she was content to observe the spin, she the astronomer and me the satellite, but on the fourth orbit she stepped on and pulled me to the center of the disc where you can watch the world pass by without the dizzy sensation you feel at the edge.

We sat cross-legged and she took my hands. "My dad used to take me to the merry-go-round on the Santa Monica Pier," she said. "This is better." She was so beautiful, framed by the blur behind her. We hadn't spoken since we'd stepped onto the court to dance. It was the longest silence of the evening and I found some contentment in that. When she finally did speak, her words came softly, without the edge the Vera of Quest Trail carried into every conversation.

She looked at me. "We made it," she said.

I wasn't sure what she meant. "Made it?" I asked. "Made it where?"

"We made it out, not very far, but far enough. You actually do know how to show a girl a good time. This is better than prom."

It seemed the right moment. I pulled the chocolate rose out of my pocket.

And presented her with a foil-wrapped lump of melted mess.

The stem made it fairly obvious that it had been a rose or a flower of some kind, but 40 minutes in my pocket on a summer night in Phoenix had deprived it of its shape. We looked at each other and started laughing, loudly. We were still laughing when the disc spun to a stop.

I jumped off and gave it a running shove. She was lying down when I climbed back on and I lay down next to her to look up into a spinning pan-orama of palm trees telescoping into the sky and the two or three stars bright enough to penetrate the glare of the car lot.

"Do you think we could eat that chocolate or drink it?" she asked, tugging a playful version of her edge back in.

"I don't know," I said. "Maybe there's something to eat at my sister's when we get there."

"Oh yes, the real world. You had to bring that up, didn't you?"

"Well, we danced part of the night away, just not the whole thing."

"I think it was just the right amount. And the choc-olate flower thing was sweet."

"It was supposed to be a rose," I said.

"A rose by another name would be a gooey mess," she said. She'd turned on her side and I rolled onto my side to face her. We were inches apart.

"What if I kissed you?" I asked.

"I'd probably kiss you back."

26

We kissed for a while, but we were still on stage under the
fluorescent lights. The car-wash crew was one row
of cars in, but they were still, basically an audience.
The kissing was great though. Eventually, we got
sleepy and climbed into one of those big concrete
culverts that some genius decided could qualify as
playground equipment on the cheap if you painted
them some bright primary color. Ours was blue.

We probably slept three or four hours before the
sun crept into the end of the culvert we'd folded
ourselves into. I was on my side with my right arm
draped over her shoulder and it felt really peaceful,
despite the intrusion of traffic noise. I think we were
both awake for 15 minutes and afraid to move because that would mean the day had actually started
and the night was over.

When paging announcements crackling from the
speakers at the car lot broke the dawn air, we couldn't
pretend anymore.

I sat up, but carefully to avoid knocking my head on the curved concrete. "What time is Circle-Up?" I asked.

"I don't know. But I'd actually kill for some cheap-ass generic peanut butter right now. Never thought I'd say that."

We'd filled our soda bottles from one of the drinking fountains the night before. So we had lukewarm water and enough money for two discount youth fares on the bus and that was it.

"There will probably be something to eat at my sister's place," I said.

"How long does it take to get there?"

"I don't know, 30 minutes."

"Is she awake at whatever god fuck-saken hour this is?"

"I don't know. Sometimes she's up this early, but she doesn't get *up* this early. If she's up, it's because she's been up all night."

We crawled out of the culvert. I don't know how I didn't realize it before, but it was the second night in a row, we'd slept in a big pipe.

"You know," I started, patting the top of the culvert with my palm. But she stopped me.

"Yeah," she said. "I know. Freud would have a field day with this."

We walked past the car lot, realizing we looked like we'd been out all night and thinking *if they only knew*. My theory that a Bubble-Up looked like a beer bottle was feeling like less of a good idea than it had the night before, but I was still hoping the cops were looking for two teenagers in smiley-face PJs and not the hungover party kids we looked to be.

Luckily, there was a bus stop, which I half thought the car dealer paid to have put there and would have put a sign on it that said, "Is this really how you want to spend your summer?" if the city had let them.

Transit in Phoenix, and probably anywhere in the Southwest is a "for those people" afterthought, which is to say we waited what felt like a long time, hiding in the sliver of shade and getting up every once in a while to stare down the street and see if a bus was coming. Luckily, we were one bus ride away from my sister's neighborhood which I only knew because she lived across the street and down a little bit from Big Surf.

Big Surf was somebody's genius idea to bring the beach to Arizona. It was fun – a giant swimming pool with a wave-making contraption at one end and sand that I assumed they trucked in every few days because half of it came home in your shorts. But it was also depressing. In the real world, the beach goes on for miles and isn't surrounded by skillet-hot parking lots. At some point, you leave Big Surf and you're back in Phoenix, and within 5 or 10 seconds you remember that the real beach is 400 miles to the west and you start hating your parents for raising you in the hellscape of the desert southwest.

But every time we saw my sister, the drama of the encounter was lessened somewhat by a trip to Big Surf.

I explained none of this to Vera, who grew up on a real beach, for fear it would make me seem more pathetic. I'd felt something a little different in her since we woke up, as though she was making a statement that whatever happened with us the night before had hit its expiration date at sunrise.

The bus finally came, and we deposited our 30-cent youth fare into the change counter thing. We only ended up paying about 20 cents apiece because the driver said they didn't take pennies. He seemed happy to see us though. Driving a bus in Phoenix, I imagine, gets lonely. There were only two other people onboard.

"Not exactly the limo home from prom you were expecting?" I asked Vera, who had slumped down in her seat, leaning her face to the window frame where a slight stream of AC made a vain attempt at climate control. "Prom?" she said, squinting with her left eye, as though I were talking about alien conspiracy and not something that had actually happened, because, you know, it hadn't. I took it as a "quiet, now" and sat next to her, conscious of allowing a steady inch or two between us.

Thirty minutes was a bad calculation. Traffic was slow and the driver made a point of stopping at every stop, despite the evidence that pedestrians, and particularly pedestrians riding the bus, were the Bigfoot and Loch Ness monster of Phoenix, long rumored but rarely documented. About 20 minutes into the trip, Vera apparently decided that quiet time was over and drew her head away from the window.

"What's it going to be like for you seeing your sister?" she asked.

"I'm not sure," I said, which was the truth. "I hadn't thought about it a lot," I added, which was a total lie and one that Vera immediately saw through.

"Really? Am I going to have to smack you up with a truth wrench? You've probably been rehearsing a 'See what you got me into!' speech since you climbed into the Quest Trail van."

The edge was back, and it was an edgier edge.

"Ok," I said, "you're right. Maybe I meant I don't know what I'm going to say. It's complicated."

"I can only imagine. I don't have siblings. It was me and my dad and whatever sitter or nanny he left me with while he was in court or at some jazz club. I know your sister wasn't easy and she even made it hard for you, but she has to have been there in some way, maybe some good way."

I was quiet for about a block and another stop in a series of deserted bus stops. "Maybe a few times. It feels like a long time ago. She used to take me to her friend's house. They had a pool."

Vera raised her eyebrows in an exaggerated expression of shock, like a cartoon character who'd seen a ghost. I'm surprised she didn't throw her head back in a wacky double take. She was laying it on thick. "So you're saying a big sister let her little brother come to a pool party at her friend's house?" She doubled down on her incredulous look. "She didn't need to do that. Dude, that's like Gandhi cool, Dalai Lama cool."

I'd never thought of it that way. So I said something really eloquent about gratitude: "I don't know. I guess."

Vera shook her head and looked out the window in this way that I think was supposed to be dismissive, like she needed to regroup after hearing this shocking confession from my childhood as a snot-nosed pool party crasher, except she could only look out the window for maybe a half a second before swinging around to face me again.

"Look," she said. "Maybe you lead with that. You make her feel like you are coming to her for help, for advice, for lessons in how to deal with your parents."

"Yeah," I said, "because she's obviously mastered that."

"Did she get away with shit?"

"Yeah."

"Did she test them, make them stretch a little bit on boundaries?"

"Yeah."

"Did they have her carted off to the desert by thugs?"

I hung my head level with my chest when I said, "No."

"Then she's got some stuff figured out. I'm not saying you need to start wearing tube tops and dating bikers, but you can probably get something out of this relationship that would help."

"We'll see," I said. "Wait till you meet her and you can tell me if she is the great teacher."

We were silent for a few miles. I still didn't know if I could put my arm around her or anything. We'd been making out on a spinning platform in the glare of the Chevy dealership's floodlights the night before, but it seemed awkward on the bus.

And then she took my hand and held it in her lap. I leaned into her slightly, so our shoulders touched.

Big Surf, like any place you went to when you were a kid, looked smaller than you remember it and I wasn't surprised by that. But it looked a little dingier too, and with the parking lot empty at 7 a.m., it looked sadder. In two hours, weary moms would be arguing with their kids about sunscreen and donning ridiculously floppy hats and oversized sunglasses for a day on the broiler rack of parenthood in Arizona. As we got off the bus though, it looked abandoned.

"What's this place?" Vera asked.

"You don't want to know," I said.

"Oh, c'mon!"

"It's a big swimming pool trying to be a beach."

All she said was, "Oh," and I was happy to leave it at that.

We crossed the huge parking lot at an angle to get to the huge apartment complex where my sister lived. Like all the other five million apartment sprawls in Phoenix, this one had a name, and it was a particularly stupid one: Quail Shadows. "Mountain Shadows" or even "Cactus Shadows" I get, but quail are like 6 inches tall and the kind that lives in the desert are scurrying around on the ground instead of flying, so their shadows are pretty diminutive. It's more or less like sitting around a conference table and deciding to call your new development "Rat Shadows."

Vera could see I was nervous as we stepped into the stucco expanse and breathed in the ubiquitous apartment complex smell of chlorine and whatever it is they put on grass to keep it day-glo green when it's 600 degrees and sunny all the time. She took my hand. I think she knew I was nervous. This wasn't jumping on a train in the dark, but it came with a similar level of trepidation, just in a different flavor. "Which way?" she asked.

"This way, I think."

The truth is I wasn't really sure what building she was in and it looked there were several dozen. I mean we walked by building W, if that gives you an idea. But I remember it being near a pool and I hoped there was only one pool. Some of these monstrosities have several.

We were walking maybe five minutes with me pretending I knew where I was going when I saw Jackie's car.

The Dodge Dart is one of those cars they keep making even though nobody is exactly excited about it. They could have a commercial that would be something like "It's a Dart. So what?" and that would be about as enthusiastic as anybody could get. But my sister's Dart screamed personal history.

It wasn't just the bumper stickers, though I never could tell if the "California Dreamin'" sticker on a car with Arizona plates was a token of aspiration or resignation. It was more the dents in the bumper and the duct tape holding the side mirror into the frame that personalized it. It was the kind of car you'd see in the background when the TV news was covering a drug bust, or a raid on some doomsday cult, certainly not a car you see parked outside a church or in the "Employee of the Month" spot.

So the car narrowed it down to building H, which left us snooping through windows until I saw the jar full of troll dolls on the window sill tucked between the pane and what was obviously a bed sheet thrown over the curtain rod and then taped to the window frame to block light. Jackie had gone through a 10-year troll doll thing when she was a kid, dozens of them arranged on the dresser next to her bed. Other girls constructed elaborate soap operas in Barbie's Dream House and Jackie was building a troll doll army. They were cheap, which means she could pull mom's sleeve at Walgreens and stand a good chance of getting one. And they were small, which meant she could throw a few in her backpack for school or in her pockets for everywhere else.

But the Phoenix sun had done nothing good for the troll platoon in the apartment window. The crazy hair in greens, blues and purples was fading toward white and the plastic was drying out. The whole thing looked post-apocalyptic, mummified.

I must have stood there for most of a minute, as though I were examining some ancient temple full of artifacts before Vera nudged me with her elbow and then put her arm over my shoulder, drawing me into a squeeze.

I reached out my hand and knocked. The door had the hollow resonance of a closet door and it sounded like a drum, even at a light knock. I couldn't take it back. We waited. We were still short of 7 a.m. and I couldn't imagine my sister getting up that early unless the house was on fire, but the door peeled open maybe 20 seconds later and my sister was standing right there in front of us.

"I called it!" she said. "I knew you'd show up

here!" It wasn't that she was gleeful, but she was much more animated than I thought she'd be at this point in the day. She looked awake and not in that mysteriously fueled up-all-night way I would have expected if somebody told me she'd be up at 6:50 am. She spent maybe a half second giving me the up and down before turning to Vera, who got the full inspection in the awkward silence. Then she said to me, still staring at Vera, "Who's she?"

I took my first breath since I'd knocked on the door. "This is Vera," I said, with a pause stretched across three words. "Can we come in?"

"Oh yeah!" she said. "But be quiet. Jack worked late."

It looked really dark when we walked in out of sunlight bright enough to bleach diamonds. She had the sheets taped around the window, which would give you the idea of some albino solarphobia thing, but the lights were actually on, providing enough light to put on display the full manifestation of my sister in her native habitat.

I'd been so dreading seeing Jackie and the emotional chaos that I'd forgotten about the physical chaos that surrounded her. We're not talking plain old clutter or the life's work of a crazy old lady hoarder who keeps stacks of Cat Fancy magazines and empty jam bottles full of buttons. This was pure Jackie.

There weren't just candles, there were candles melted into other candles and candle wax covering half of a magazine sitting on top of a coffee table so thick with wax that you could see lumps of cigarette butts encased in it like flies trapped in spider webs.

And, of course, dragons, dragons on posters, dragon silk-screened pillows, a dragon ashtray made out of ceramic so that the smoke would come up through its nostrils. Surprisingly, there was no dragon bong, but all of the dragons more or less matched the dragon tattoo, on her back below her shoulder, except that they were more artfully rendered.

I'd warned Vera that Jackie was a train wreck, but I hadn't thought about her apartment being a train wreck rolled into a landslide on top of a plane crash. I'm sure she could see the embarrassment in my cheeks, even in the dim light.

Jackie sat down on a burgundy velvet chair, shiny in spots where the fabric had worn from use. It was the first time I noticed the nametag, "Jackie" in white type on black plastic like you'd see in some chain restaurant. She grabbed a half-gone cigarette out of the dragon ashtray and let it hang off her lip without lighting up. It wasn't like there was an awkward silence. It would have been awkward at any volume. But I spoke first.

"I take it Mom called," I said. "What did she say?"

"She said you'd busted out of 'the program', but she had to explain what the program was first. She hadn't even told me she'd shipped you off. What was that like?"

"It's a long story," I answered, looking over at Vera who was uncharacteristically, but understandably, quiet. "It's also a pretty sucky story."

"Well, Mom told me to call her if you showed up. She said some railroad guys saw you out near Wintersburg and their theory was you were headed to California because you were with some L.A. chick."

Vera cocked her head slightly at that but didn't say anything.

"Sounds a little ambitious for the circumstances," I said. "It's not like we robbed a bank. We were lucky to get here. Did you know Suntrans doesn't take pennies?"

"Color me impressed," Jackie said. She still hadn't lit the cigarette. "You guys hungry?"

Vera showed a sudden interest in life, and the gift of speech returned. "Hell yeah," she said. "What you got?"

What Jackie had was a couple of those styrofoam to-go trays with chicken legs and congealed coleslaw. She said it was "from work" but wasn't offering a lot of detail on what "work" was. I later learned that she was the host at John Boy's, which was this Phoenix-only sit-down chain that was trying to capitalize on this show called "The Waltons" set in the 1930s because nothing says good eatin' like the Depression. They should have served half portions for historical accuracy. The employment explained the outfit too – a denim pioneer-ish skirt and a plaid blouse that was a contrast to the black lace and a tank-top gypsy-rock-groupie look she usually wore. She cleared off a little patio table that had been dragged into the kitchen. It matched the furniture we'd seen around the pool. Jackie was nothing if not resourceful.

"Look," Jackie said, "I go in at 9. So, you can eat and then you're calling Mom. Jack could be up any minute and he's going to want to hear a plan for your departure. He'll say, 'We're not running a hotel,' which is true, but he's not going to say it in some happy way." Her 5-word Jack impersonation made it clear that "happy way" was not a common theme.

"You lovebirds goin' through a rough patch?" I asked.

She looked at me in a way that was part hard stare down and part the face of somebody weary at the edges. "You wouldn't understand, Danny," she said.

That was enough for Vera. Her hands gripped the tabletop and she stared right at Jackie. "Daniel understands a lot more than you think," she said. "He's been through some shit. You need to drop your tough girl act and start acting like a big sister. He gets it. As far as I can tell, he's the only one here who does."

I drew back a little bit in my chair. It wasn't nostril-flaring fierce, but there was a layer of girl-fight ferocity to it. Jackie was silenced, shocked a little bit. Vera hadn't said two words since we'd walked into the apartment and then she let loose with that. She wasn't done. "Do you think he came here for fried chicken and a chat? We came here because we needed help."

Ok, so it would be easy, and normal for me, to sit back and watch the punches land. Vera had the mic and there would have been a time, maybe a few weeks ago, maybe a few days ago, when I would have been too busy melting into the couch cushions to even watch, much less participate. "Look, Jackie," I said, "if I wanted to call Mom, I could have called her from the first payphone we saw. We came here instead." I was thinking as I was talking. Why hadn't we called Mom? I was going to be back there at some point. I'd come to Jackie's for something else. I got the sense that Vera was watching me figure that out.

"We came here," I said, "because you need to hear something." Jackie was sitting on the counter. There were only two chairs in the kitchen. She slipped off onto the floor a little more forcefully than she really needed to.

"I don't have to listen to this shit," she said, now standing over me but not actually looking at me. "Your problems and my problems are two different things."

Vera looked at me in that "Well? Say something" kind of way. So I said something. "As a matter of fact, I think you've got that a little bit turned around. You make your problems everybody else's problems. You cause trouble and everybody else has to come up with a solution. Sometimes they even take the blame. You know why I got packed off into the desert?"

Jackie was not backing down. "Oh please," she said, "tell me what did St. Daniel do to be so unfairly maligned?"

"Because of you. Because Mom and Dad didn't want me to turn into you."

Ok, so I'll admit that was a little harsh, but I will also admit it felt good to say it. You see TV movies and after somebody's mom or dad dies, they do this whole thing about "I never got to tell him I loved him." And then the person sobs into somebody's shoulder and the sun shines through the trees and they all learn a lesson about impermanence and love. Well, you know what? Somebody probably dies every day without hearing what a shit they were.

So yeah, it felt good to say it, but from the looks of things, it didn't feel very good to hear. I'd seen Jackie cry probably a hundred times and I'd probably seen her fake cry 20,000 times. I was the leading expert on the Jackie-in-tears genre, and this was no fake cry. Even worse, it was the quiet cry. No sobbing, no sniffing, just the tears on the cheek. And she tried to hide it. That was the giveaway that it was real.

"Jackie?" I said. I went to stand up, but Vera caught my arm. I don't know where I learned that guys are supposed to comfort girls when they cry. It's a programmed response, I think, like laughing when you hear somebody fart. But Vera wasn't having it. As soon as she stopped me, I understood. If I comforted Jackie, I'd basically be apologizing, and we didn't jump off a train and flee drug dealers to deliver an apology to my sister.

Jackie looked a little frustrated and added a bit of obviously calculated volume to the tears. It started as a real cry and it was acquiring some staging as things progressed. I'd seen that rendition before too. She looked at me in that "See what you've made me do!" face I remember from every time she got in trouble for tormenting me in some way. Then she looked at Vera who returned the glance with an expression that said: "This Window Closed."

Then she bolted out of the room. We heard her go into the bedroom. She didn't slam the door, but she didn't gently close it either. "And the award for most acting goes to..." Vera half whispered.

"Welcome to the Jackie Show," I replied. "What now?"

"What do you mean 'what now'? It's just getting good." She offered me something between a smile and a grin and reached across the table to take my hand. I took a breath and closed my eyes. By my calculations, a few things were about to happen. First, we were going to meet Jack. It was barely possible that he'd slept through the initial family reunion, but Jackie charging into the bedroom was not an "I slept through it" event.

Second, Jackie was going to come out and tell me she'd called Mom. She'd be looking to land a punch and that was the easiest right-on-the-chin jab available.

The latter was obvious. Jack was a black box variable. I'd never met him. I'd heard Mom complain to a friend of hers about her daughter's "low-potential paramour" and I'd inserted a caricature of a biker-stoner-construction-worker guy who for some reason was always wearing a leather vest in my mind.

I squeezed Vera's hand. I got the idea that she was proud of me somehow. "Enter stage right, the boyfriend," I said, in mocking stage whisper.

"Oh, goodie," Vera replied. There was a nervous tension to the whole thing that had us fighting inappropriate but irrepressible giggles, like when you're in English class and the teacher says "intercourse" like it's 100 years ago and you're supposed to remember it can mean "conversation."

The sound of the door opening cut that short. It was Jackie, and not Jack, which was a bit of surprise. She had her purse with her and her car keys, which she kept on a keyring attached to, obviously, a troll doll.

"I have to go to work," she said. She hesitated,

which I'm sure the PTG would call a "growment" because it's not like hesitation had been a big part of Jackie's repertoire before, but then she said, "I called Mom."

I asked what anybody would have asked, "What did you tell her?"

"I said you were here, moron; the girl too."

"What did she say?"

"She's coming up here, with Dad."

"And we're just supposed to wait for them? Watch TV. Hang out by the pool?"

Jackie was rocking back and forth, shifting her weight from one foot to another. I was struck, very suddenly, how normal she looked. I mean, the Walton's Mountain country chic had something to do with it. I was still stuck on this Depression-era nostalgia theme. I had this idea of a ride at Disneyland where you wait for two hours and at the end, they tell you there are no jobs left. That normalcy was only skin deep, however, because then she said, "Earth to Daniel, I'm going to work, like a real person. Mom is coming here. You sit tight with your girlfriend and wait."

I could have said something appropriate to the situation like "When did Mom say she'd be here?" or "Where's your phone?" or, of more urgency, "Do you have cable?" Instead, I said something stupid and not the first time in my life I would say something similarly blunderous. I said, "She's not my girlfriend."

I wasn't looking at Vera when I said this, but I felt the reaction. The truth was she wasn't my girlfriend and if we'd been talking about it, the two of us, I think we both would have calmly agreed that such was the status. I'm not sure we'd even made it to "fling" yet, but I'd made this pronouncement that sounded like I was 10 years old and Jackie was teasing me about a crush.

And Vera took it the wrong way even though there was really no right way to take it. "Nice to know," she said.

This was Jackie's opening. I wouldn't say she "cackled," but her "Hah!" was triumphant in this sort of lesser-known-Disney-villain kind of way. "I shoulda' figured on that, Danny Boy," she said. She put her hand on the doorknob. "Out of your league doesn't even begin to describe it."

I could see her preparing another "Hah!" Maybe even louder this time. Jack didn't give her a chance.

It's not like I expected him to come strolling out in a smoking jacket with a commemorative Masterpiece Theater Tee-shirt, but he still managed to exceed my diminished expectations of what Jackie's boyfriend would be.

For starters, I nailed it on the leather vest. It was 8 in the morning and not just in the morning, but a summer-in-Phoenix morning and he'd barely left his bedroom, much less the house. The vest was covered in pins celebrating various vehicular makes, mostly of the loud and two-wheeled variety, mixed into a constellation of additional salutes to the distilled arts. I hadn't specifically predicted the elongated goatee, but I probably could have guessed it. And cowboy boots, of course, cowboy boots.

"What the hell is going on here?" he asked in a

combination of bellow and snarl. "Why am I not back in there sleeping? I got a swing shift today and I need my beauty sleep."

The "beauty sleep" was obviously an attempt at incongruous humor, but I felt like nodding and saying, "Indeed you do, sir," because it was full-on accurate.

"Babe," Jackie said, her voice suddenly soft and borderline pleading, "this is my brother and his, well, friend, and my mom and dad are coming up to get them. They need to be here for a few hours, that's all."

"That's all?" Jack said. He was halfway across the room and Jackie had tightened her grip on the doorknob. "There's no 'that's all'. It's my apartment and it ain't no fucking bus stop waiting room."

"Babe," she said, even softer this time.

"What?" he said. "Don't babe me unless you've got a better answer than I just heard out of you."

"Babe," she said, sounding even less confident this time, "I have to go to work. I asked for the extra shift like you said."

"And you're going to lift those tips from the register like I told you?" he growled.

Obviously, he knew we were there. We were the reason for the morning fight. But I was starting to guess Jack didn't have a lot of trouble coming up with reasons to fight. What made this different was not only that he had an audience, but that the audience in some way mattered to Jackie. Fighting in front of strangers is better than fighting alone for a guy like Jack, I was beginning to assume, but fighting in front of family was like opening for the Rolling Stones. Audience matters.

"Yes, Jack," Jackie said. She wouldn't look at him. This infuriated him.

There are moments in life when things become so obvious so fast that you'd think it would also be obvious how you understood it so clearly and so quickly; what signs and triggered memories led you to this complete and correct conclusion. But none of that mattered. I knew what was about to happen and I knew it without doubt.

This guy wasn't merely cranky in the morning. He was violent. He'd been violent before and he was about to be violent again. I didn't stop to think. If you'd traced a triangle between Jack, Jackie and me, it might have been an equilateral triangle, but geometry was a late-in-the-day class so I don't have a really strong memory of the terms. It's easier to say we were all pretty much evenly apart and as Jack started to move toward Jackie, I had some quick decisions to make. Anybody who watched my eyes darting around the room could have assumed I was taking some kind of dragon census, but I was really only looking for one dragon.

The dragon I sought was brass, about a foot long and more Chinese than medieval.

And it fit nicely up against Jack's jaw.

If I'd been a little quicker, he wouldn't have been able to get to Jackie and throw her crashing into the lamp table and dragons 12 and 18, both ceramic, would have been saved. But if I'd been a little slower, he might have seen me coming and blocked me. A half second here or there and he wouldn't be lying on used-to-be-beige carpet, snorting blood out his nose.

I stood over him in case he tried to get up, but he seemed to have lost such ambitions. He wasn't out cold, but he was out of commission at any level that mattered.

Jackie was crying and this time it really was my job to comfort her and get her out of there. I stepped over Jack, and Vera was at my side as I kneeled down to pull Jackie up into my arms. I didn't figure we had a lot of time for a hug, but a hug was required. Vera draped one arm over my shoulder as I held Jackie, sobbing into my chest.

A picture formed in my mind in that moment of a Jackie I always knew but never understood. My fearless sister, brash, confident, caution-to-the-wind, was scared shitless. She shook in my arms. Behind us, I could sense Jack had further emerged into consciousness. My guess was he wasn't itching for a repeat engagement at the moment, but it was his apartment and it's an easy guess that a guy who will wear a leather vest and cowboy boots at 8 a.m. has a thing for knives, maybe even guns. Masculinity is all about the accessories for some people.

I pulled Jackie into a standing position and nodded to Vera to grab the troll doll keys where Jackie had dropped them. By the time we had the door open, Jack had sat up part way and was leaning on his elbows as though he were at the beach watching girls walk by. There was a mix of snot and blood on his chin and some of it had landed on his Marlboro Tee-shirt. "Later, much," he said, but his jaw was swelling up; so it sounded more like, "Wafer mush," as if we'd been told off by a toddler.

27

Outside, the heat was coming on in that bright rush that makes you feel like you've been mugged by a blast furnace. Jackie was still crying. Vera was on one side of her and I was on the other. We guided her toward the car, which I'd pointed out to Vera when we were looking for the apartment. We didn't have a plan or a whole lot of options to build into a plan but moving had to be part of whatever we came up with.

The Dart was parked next to a motorcycle that had that "It's gonna' be super bitchin' when I'm done with it, man!" look. Tape on the seats, a hazy mix of two spray paints on the gas tank and a twisted coat hanger kept the muffler from dragging. I didn't have to ask Jackie whose bike it was. I thought about yanking some spark plug wires out, but then I remembered that the point was for him to leave. If Mom and Dad were driving up, that meant we had no way to call them and we had to be at or near the apartment when they got there. Jackie didn't argue about Vera driving. I sat in the backseat with my sister and we drove about two miles to one of the parking structures at the University so we could find a shady spot to park and a payphone that Jackie could use to call her job. Vera and I sat on a concrete bench under a palm tree that qualified as "almost shade" while Jackie used the phone 40 feet of sidewalk away.

"So," Vera said, turning to straddle the bench and face me, "what's your major?"

I didn't have a quick comeback, but we were dazed enough by the *everything* of recent events that she seemed patient with my lack of response. Finally, I said, "Women's studies."

"You signed up for the accelerated program on that one," she said, sparing a smile.

"And how are my grades?"

"You aced the test this morning. Your essay on kicking Jack's ass was superb."

"Really?" I said. "You really think so?"

"Hell, yeah! We came up here for you to tell your sister some shit she needed to hear, which you did a stellar job of, by the way, and then you saved her from Mr. Macho Mayhem back there. I'm putting you on the dean's list with extra points for integrity and badassery all on the same day."

She took my hands in hers, sharing a flash of mischief with her eyes. "Even if I'm *not* your girlfriend."

I could have wilted at that. I'm still surprised I didn't. Instead, I smiled at her, held her hands tighter, and said, "I'm feeling so much greatitude for that."

We spent another hour and a half on campus. Jackie and I sat on the same bench while Vera used the phone to call her dad and I heard more about Jack, how he "could be so sweet" but also how Jackie was outgrowing his bullshit and that was part of the problem. She apologized for lots of things and said that "living with somebody who screws things up has a way of teaching you stuff about yourself." She talked about coming back to Tucson and going to community college, but it sounded to me like she'd learned a lot of what she really needed to learn already.

"You know it was your weed that got me sent off to Quest Trail, right?"

"I kinda figured," she said. "I'm sorry. I was down there a couple of weeks before you got packed off and Mom wanted me to go through stuff in my closet with her. So I stashed some weed I scored off Carla's brother that I was going to bring back to Jack. But then I spaced out. I feel kinda bad."

"Kinda?" I said. We'd been sitting next to each other and staring across to where Vera was on the phone, but I turned to her to say it again, "Kinda?"

"OK," she said. "Really bad. I had no idea it was going to get you sent off into the desert like that. They never tried that shit with me."

I probably could have thought a little about what I said next, but it turned out to be close to the right thing to say. "Maybe they should have," I said.

I was expecting a reappearance of Rage Jackie, but she was quiet. I was still facing her. She brought her eyes in from the distance and said, very softly. "Maybe they should have."

She was facing me on the bench, but she kept her eyes on her hands as she ran the hem of her skirt through her fingers. She was quiet for a long time and I couldn't tell if she was trying to think of what to say or if she knew what to say and was rehearsing it. Finally, she told me, "All I know is they tried harder with you. They gave a shit. It's like if at first you don't succeed, maybe things will work out for the next kid. That was their whole approach. You were the one that mattered. I was their expendable first try." She dropped the fabric from her fingers and looked up at me. "Do you have any idea how that feels?" she asked.

"No," I said. "But maybe you could share some of that."

I wanted to wince when I said "share," like I was afraid I was turning into the PTG, but it was the right word at the right moment, and with the right *in*tention.

Vera was on the phone for maybe 30 or 40 minutes reaching her dad. Jackie and I had time for another cycle or two of the "small talk edges toward important shared discovery and emotional truth" game that is so common to every one-on-one personal conversation I have had since or will ever have. We talked about stupid stuff from our childhood—Those Disneyland hats!—and annoying stuff about our parents that only the two of us would understand. She said she was sorry a few times. I did too. I'm not saying it was a hug fest and it wouldn't have been, even if it weren't 500 degrees out, but there were more consecutive minutes of honesty than the two of us had maybe ever shared.

When she got back, Vera could tell something was different. Or I imagined she could. She looked relieved.

"I talked to my dad," she said. "He didn't sound very surprised."

"What do you mean?" Jackie asked. In the TV movie, Jackie and Vera were going to be lifelong friends now after what they'd been through. In real life, it at least felt like maybe Jackie could thank Vera for being there, which she eventually did.

"I mean my dad knows I can take care of myself. It's not like I jump trains and escape desert compounds every day, but he said, 'I raised you to take care of yourself and it sounds like you took care of yourself.'"

"He got that right," Jackie exclaimed. "You guys are legends of the west, pioneer shit and all."

We decided to take the compliment without asking her to explain it.

It turned out Vera's dad was already in Phoenix. He'd flown out when Quest Trail HQ had made their awkward "So, about your child..." calls. He was staying at the DoubleTree near the airport and his secretary had connected them. That meant he was on his way and it wouldn't be very long.

I felt that in my stomach, as though I'd swallowed a jawbreaker, maybe *two* jawbreakers. Vera saw my reaction and took my hand, leading me away from the bench where Jackie, in a sign of her increasing consciousness that the world was inhabited by other people with thoughts and emotions, remained seated.

A cluster of olive trees shaded a patch of gravel outside the science library. It was the biggest, closest building to the payphone and where Vera had told her dad to meet her. We got there and we both stood facing each other but doing everything we could not to look at each other. Finally, Vera stepped toward me and put her forehead against my chest, holding it there with her hands on my waist. I held her by her shoulders, my hands on her bare skin.

"So this is it?" I asked.

I heard her voice, small and muffled some by my shirt. "Is it not enough?"

"It's a lot," I said. "But not a lot of time." I felt her shoulders tremble, just slightly. "If I say I never met anyone like you it sounds corny or stupid, but the not corny or stupid part is that I never met anyone the way I met you."

"And I hope you never do."

"You mean you hope I stay out of trouble and don't get shipped off to PTG games in the desert again?"

"No," she said. I could feel tears soaking through my shirt. "I hope you don't forget the special parts. I don't think you're a candidate for a repeat performance on the trail."

I remembered something I'd put out of my mind. "But what about you? You told everybody you were there twice. I think you said, 'two-time loser'."

Vera stood very still for what felt like a really long time. I thought maybe I'd screwed up, said the wrong thing, spoiled another of those moments I was so good at spoiling. But then she lifted her head from my chest and looked up at me. "I sent myself to Quest

Trail," she said. "Both times."

I said the first thing that came into my mind, that would have come into anyone's mind. "Why?" I asked.

She looked right into my eyes. I could see, for the first time, the small spikes of green that drove through the blue. I felt like I could see right into her. "Do you remember when I said real shit happens out there?" she asked.

"Of course," I said.

"That's what I went looking for, real shit, real people with real emotions and real ideas and real experiences. I didn't have that at home. Mostly, I had myself."

"Did you find it?" I asked. "The real shit?"

"I did," she said. "I really did."

"What else did you find?"

"I found you."

It was hot, blazing hot, biblically hot. And the two of us stood there, holding each other in the scant shade of three olive trees, her head nestled into my neck, my hands on her back. We were seconds away from saying goodbye, hopefully not forever but maybe forever. She'd told me something crazy, epically crazy, mad dog crazy, and the thing that was craziest about it was that it made sense.

It made sense because it was real. Real shit had, indeed, happened.

And it never felt more real before or since or ever, than when she got in the rental car with her father and drove away across the half-empty campus, my eyes stinging with sweat, and with tears, her eyes disappearing behind the tinted windows.

28

For most kids, I guess, seeing both of your parents in the doorway would be a big "who cares?" At Jackie's apartment, where we'd been relieved to see the motorcycle gone when we returned, it was a big deal that involved a lot of hugs, some tears, and a long story about a brutish wilderness therapy guide with a penchant for body slams. All of this was followed by a number of phone calls, one to a sheriff in Southern Arizona, another to a lawyer my dad knew.

Jackie drove back to Tucson with me and Mom. Dad drove the Dart. She got a job at a 1950s-themed restaurant so she could enjoy some nostalgia that actually made sense and signed up for a half schedule at Kino Community College. I wondered if she'd encounter any of the pre-Ed students she'd burned through in Study Club. She was different after we got back, I think. I know I was. We *both* were.

Greg was already back when I got there. I guess the cops decided that Hank and Alchemy weren't going to be great witnesses or were generally charmed by the soft tones of the Sleepy Giant. They were more interested in Wes and his "associates" anyway. Greg's parents and my parents hired the same lawyer to deal with Quest Trail. Through all that, we heard that Troy made it out safe too. I can picture him telling everybody at his school about the time he faced down a dozen armed drug dealers.

I spent a lot of the summer thinking about what had happened on Quest Trail, getting it straight in my head. And hanging out with Greg, both of us appreciating air conditioning, and each other, in a whole new way.

Vera's package showed up three days after we got back to Tucson.

It came in a small box, like one that might hold a necklace or a bracelet. I opened it. Inside, I found, wrapped in red foil folded in the shape of a rose and strung on a leather cord, the green glass bead.

There was a note too, written on the back of a postcard of the merry-go-round at the Santa Monica Pier: It was short. She signed it "Vera' Much."

"Our circle up," she'd written. "The one that mattered."

ACKNOWLEDGEMENTS

Much appreciation goes to developmental editors Steve Adams and Rachel Weaver as well as the many beta readers who helped smooth off the rougher edges, especially Summer Runestad, Eli Silver, Bill Giebler, Janet Kornblum, Alan Lewis, Karen Howard, Mike Frank and Doug Brown.

ABOUT THE AUTHOR

As a career journalist and a former newspaper reporter, Rick Polito has covered everything from political scandals and natural disasters to taking his dog to a pet psychic seminar. He attended the University of Missouri School of Journalism. He has won multiple state and national feature and news writing awards. A father of two and a native of Arizona, Polito now lives in Denver. Off Trail is his first published novel.

9 781953 944528